The Man Who Won

by

Mrs. Baillie Reynolds

The Man Who Won
by Mrs. Baillie Reynolds

Copyright © 2024

All Rights reserved.

No part of this publication may be reproduced, stored in a retrieval system, or transmitted in any form or by any means, electronic, mechanical, photocopying or Otherwise, without the written permission of the publisher.
The author/editor asserts the moral right to be identified as the author/editor of this work.

ISBN: 978-93-63051-47-8

Published by

DOUBLE 9 BOOKS

2/13-B, Ansari Road
Daryaganj, New Delhi – 110002
info@double9books.com
www.double9books.com
Tel. 011-40042856

This book is under public domain

ABOUT THE AUTHOR

Gertrude Minnie Robins was an English author who wrote over fifty books, several of which she published under her married name, Mrs. Baillie Reynolds. Gertrude Minnie Robins, Julian's daughter, was born in Teddington. Her father was a barrister. She attended South Hampstead High School. Gertrude Minnie Robins married a stockbroker named Louis Baillie Reynolds in 1890. They had three sons: Eustace (1893-1948), Paul Kenneth (1896-1973), and Donald Hugh (1900-1991). In 1939, she died in St Albans. Robins was active in the women's suffrage movement and served as president of the Society of Women Journalists in 1913. Four of her books were turned into silent films: The Man Who Won (1918), Notorious Miss Lisle (1920), The Daughter Pays (1920), and Confessions (1925).

CONTENTS

CHAPTER I
    LUTWYCHE'S 9

CHAPTER II
    MILLIE 15

CHAPTER III
    THE RIVALS 19

CHAPTER IV
    THE GUARDIANSHIP OF CAROL MAYNE 25

CHAPTER V
    A BOER BURYING 30

CHAPTER VI
    THE FLINGING OF THE GAGE 37

CHAPTER VII
    IN THE GARRET 43

CHAPTER VIII
    THE RESCUE 47

CHAPTER IX
    THE SCANDALISING OF SLABBERT'S POORT 50

CHAPTER X
    FRANSDALE 58

CHAPTER XI
    MELICENT'S COUSINS 64

CHAPTER XII
    THE JARRING ELEMENT 74

CHAPTER XIII
 LANCE BURMESTER IS CONSCIOUS OF
 A PERSONALITY 80

CHAPTER XIV
 THE BREAKING-IN OF MELICENT...............................86

CHAPTER XV
 A CLEVESHIRE TEA-PARTY 94

CHAPTER XVI
 THE BREAKING OF BOUNDS 100

CHAPTER XVII
 A CRISIS AT THE VICARAGE..107

CHAPTER XVIII
 A NEW HOME 111

CHAPTER XIX
 AN UNMARKED FESTIVAL...118

CHAPTER XX
 CAPTAIN BROOKE...124

CHAPTER XXI
 MIRAGE..132

CHAPTER XXII
 RECOGNITION 136

CHAPTER XXIII
 REBELLION 143

CHAPTER XXIV
 UNREST...149

CHAPTER XXV
 THE WAY OUT 155

CHAPTER XXVI
 THE END OF THE FIRST ROUND...............................164

CHAPTER XXVII
 THREE MONTHS' TRUCE 171

CHAPTER XXVIII
    THE GATES OF SPRING ARE OPENED 176

CHAPTER XXIX
    THE FRIENDSHIP GROWS 179

CHAPTER XXX
    THE TREACHERY 185

CHAPTER XXXI
    THE REPUDIATION 193

CHAPTER XXXII
    THE FRANSDALE SPORTS 199

CHAPTER XXXIII
    CALUMNY 206

CHAPTER XXXIV
    THE DISCOMFITURE OF OTIS 212

CHAPTER XXXV
    CONFESSION 218

CHAPTER XXXVI
    WHAT CHANCED UPON THE MOORS 227

CHAPTER XXXVII
    THE HOUSE IS BUILT 241

CHAPTER I
LUTWYCHE'S

"Handsome, were you? 'Tis more than they held,
   More than they said. I was ware, and watched.
I was the scapegrace, this rat belled
   The cat, this fool got his whiskers scratched."

—ROBERT BROWNING.

The talk had waxed political, and the audience was frankly bored. The man who had been haranguing his mates was hurt at the somewhat too obvious lack of appreciation which his truly democratic sentiments received.

"Ef yer could quit twinin' yerself araound that thar' post a spell, an' listen to a bit o' horse-sense"—he broke off angrily.

"It's usually hoarse when you take the floor, Amurrica," was the surly reply; "but it's blasted little sense I've ever heard come outer your head."

"Ef you was to listen, it 'ud make a powerful deal o' difference to what you heard," snapped Amurrica, whose eloquence was his chief vanity.

"I ain't good at listening," indifferently replied the blond and bearded giant, who was "twinin' hisself araound the post," "onless a man's talkin'; an' that's a fact."

There was a giggle of appreciation among the half-dozen men and youths collected at the gate of the farm enclosure.

"No good, Amurrica; chuck it! Bert'll git there every time," said someone cheerfully.

Amurrica snorted.

"Talkin', indeed! Why, you low-downers in this all-fired continent of Africa, you don' know what talkin' means!"

"Usually means lyin' over in America, don't it?" said Bert casually.

His eyes were fixed on vacancy as he spoke; the chatter of the group around him was nothing but a weariness, like the buzzing of flies. His mind was fixed upon what was going on in the low frame house, with the corrugated iron roof, that stood within the enclosure. He was experiencing something more like anxiety than he had ever felt before in all his four-and-twenty years.

It was oppressively hot. For miles and miles, the pitiless sun lit up the endless veldt, which undulated all around the little township: wild, yet with a dreadful sameness in it.

"As it was in the beginning, is now and ever shall be," seemed written upon the face of the desert; yet here and there its dignity was scarred, its monotony interfered with, by the ugliness and meanness of human habitation. The beginnings of civilisation, without simplicity as they were without harmony, jarred every sense. The places seemed to be devoid of self-respect or privacy; to consist, in fact, entirely of back premises. Rows of dingy linen flapped upon lines, on ground where the grass was irregularly worn away here and there by the treading of feet. Collections of old meat tins, old kettles, old shoes, heaped upon kitchen refuse, burdened the stale air with miasma. A wretched-looking, lean-to building bore a huge board with the flaunting inscription:

MOUNT PLEASANT BOARDING-HOUSE FOR GENTLEMEN

The gentlemen who boarded there were mostly assembled to-night at the gate of "Lutwyche's."

A little farther away the Vierkleur Hotel fluttered its flag in the heavy air, and rang at night to the coarse laughter and oaths of a set of idlers, attracted to what had been a purely agricultural district by the finding of diamonds.

Lutwyche's lay silent, sweltering in the heat. Round the stoep of the farm-house hungry poultry were congregated; to-day they were being neglected, and they were wisely determined not to suffer in silence.

It was a critical moment in history. All Europe was waiting to know what President Kruger was going to do. It was the period which preceded the sending of his historical ultimatum. The town for days had been buzzing with rumours of war, and Amurrica had spoken great things in the saloon of the Vierkleur. But local interests are strong, and it was not of British supremacy that the men were thinking now.

The sun was going down. They had all, as Amurrica said, quit work, and they were assembled by the barbed wire fence to gather news of the Englishman who lay dying under the corrugated iron roof of Lutwyche's.

Even the quarrelling was listless. It could be seen that Bert's heart was not in it. Where the heart of the huge young Boer was was matter of pretty common knowledge, though there was not a man in the settlement who would have dared to tell him so, except Amurrica, who had his own reasons for not indulging in the perilous amusement.

Presently the door of the silent house opened, and a Kaffir girl came out, with a dirty rug in her hand, from which she proceeded to shake clouds of stifling acrid dust.

"Here, Minnie, Topsy, Hattie, whoever you are, how's the boss—eh?" called one of the loungers.

The girl showed all her teeth in an apparently endless grin.

"You young gentlemen carled to inquire?" she cried, in high appreciation of the family importance. "You brought yo' visitin'-cards—eh?"

"Shut it," said Bert savagely. "How is Mr. Lutwyche?"

"He don' seem not just the right thing to-day, sir, with missus's compulments," grinned the girl, wildly elated by her momentary distinction.

To her intense delight, this last sally caused a giggle among the loafers. She edged nearer to the barbed wire fencing, to prolong this truly delightful conversation; and for a minute or two, idiotic questions and answers pattered across the farm boundary, while Bert's brow grew blacker and blacker.

Suddenly a silence, instant and deep, fell on the gathering. The Kaffir girl scuttled behind a shed with noiseless celerity. From the door of the farm issued two people—Tante Wilma, the Englishman's Boer wife, and striding beside her corpulent bulk, the slim, energetic figure of Carol Mayne, the English mission priest in charge of the station. Tante Wilma wore her most repulsive expression, her sandy eyebrows lowering over her cunning little eyes. Ten years ago she had been a handsome woman, in a redundant style; but six children and an invalid husband had reduced her form to shapelessness and her temper to rags and tatters.

She hated the English cleric, and could not bear that he should come and see her husband. The Boer Predikant would have sat and sympathised with her over his coffee for a couple of hours after his professional visit to the sick man. Carol Mayne never seemed to have an adequate idea of the importance of this woman, who owned half Slabbert's Poort, and had married her English overseer, a widower with a little girl of his own.

She was evidently accompanying the young man from the house much against her will. About half way across the yard, becoming perhaps aware of the audience at the gate, the clergyman halted, just out of earshot. He seemed earnestly recommending some particular course of conduct to Mrs. Lutwyche, who stood sullenly before him, hostility in every line of her coarse face.

The group of men at the gate dropped away silently, singly or in pairs, avoiding the parson; and Bert was left alone, his sullen scowl fixed upon the house, as though willing it to render up the face he had stood there for hours longing to see.

After a while, Mr. Mayne, having finished his colloquy with Tante Wilma, lifted his hat with that unconscious English University manner which had piqued her in her husband, but which now she hated as only the ignorant can hate the thing that they can never understand. The young Englishman's parting salutation, delivered so entirely as a matter of course, belonged to an order of things which, had she been able, Tante Wilma would have destroyed, ravaged, trampled under her gross feet.

She stood glowering upon him as he made straight for the gate by which Bert still lounged. And she was pleased to note that the young man made no effort to open it for his passage.

"Good evening, Mestaer!" said Mr. Mayne, as he reached the gate. "How's the world treating you?"

"I'm —— if I care how it treats me," was the engaging response.

The smile that passed over Mayne's face was particularly humorous and winning.

"Don't care came to a bad end," he said, "and that's what I particularly hope won't happen to you. Are you going my way?"

"No; I'm staying here, if you're so mighty curious to know my plans," was the answer, given with a discourtesy so studied that to notice it would be to allow the speaker to fancy that he had "scored."

The rudeness must, of course, have been obvious to the priest, but he disregarded it entirely. A smile again flickered over his face, as of one who holds a trump card. "Well, then, good-night!" he said briskly, opening the gate at once, and passing through it with an air of having no time to waste.

Bert cast another look at the silent house. Nobody was in sight but the big Boer woman slouching back to the doorway. He lowered the point of his rapier, so to speak.

"Say—how's he goin' on?" he asked.

Mr. Mayne at once dropped his appearance of hurry, and closed the gate slowly.

"Well," he said, "he's just lingering. It may last two or three weeks yet. God help him!"

Bert beat his clenched fist softly on the top bar of the gate.

"Look here!" he burst out, as if the words were torn from him, "they let you go in and out—you can tell—you oughter know. Is she givin' that girl hell?"

"I think things are going on much as they have done this last six months," said Mayne, speaking reluctantly.

"But what'll it be when he's gone? I ask you that? What kind of a life's she goin' to lead then?"

Mayne hesitated. "I don't know," he said at length, with a touch of reserve.

"You know how the she-devil hates her," hissed Bert. "She won't keep her, never fear. She'll chuck her out to any of these blanked scum around the town, and then say the girl's disgraced her, and she'll have no more to do with her! I know Tante Wilma!"

Mayne looked keenly and kindly at the excited speaker. He was sorry for him, from the bottom of his heart; but what to say he did not know, without betraying confidence.

"I think you see things in too black a light," he said at last. "Mrs. Lutwyche is not without a sense of duty, though we know she is not good-tempered. And Millie is not friendless, nor incapable of taking her own part."

Bert lifted his leonine head, and pointed with a gesture of his hand towards the house.

"He told me, with his blanky British pride, that he'd sooner see her in her coffin than married to a man with an ounce of Boer blood in him—him that let a Boer woman marry him," he growled. "He knows my mother was English; I told him. I'd take care of her."

Mr. Mayne was able to follow the trend of the jerky, disconnected sentences.

"Millie's young yet to think of marriage," he said.

"She'll have to think about something worse, before he's cold in his grave, or I'm much mistaken," said Bert, scowling.

The clergyman pondered.

"Do you want me to speak to her father for you?" he presently asked, point-blank.

Bert hesitated; he grew red, then pale.

"Don't like to be beholden to me, do you?" said Mayne cheerfully. "Well, I sympathise with you. But you and I are just walking round the question, you know, Mestaer. The whole point is, what does Millie say? Will she have you?"

The colour again rushed over the crestfallen face of Bert. "Gals like that don' know what they want," he grunted.

"Then it would be very wrong to push her into a life-long contract."

"She don' know what's good for her," repeated Bert. "She'd oughter be arranged for; that's the way to do it. She'd not repent it if she married me."

"Well, look here; I'll make a bargain. If Millie comes to me and says she's willing to marry you, I'll speak to Mr. Lutwyche; but you know quite as well as I do, he would never hear of it against her will."

Hereupon Bert damned first British pride, then his own Boer ancestry, then Tante Wilma, who had caused her husband to contemn all Boers for her sake.

"Swear-words won't help your cause, be sure of that," observed Mayne drily. "English girls aren't going to be won that way."

"Think I'd say words like that to her?"

"More than probably. Well, good-night! I'm due at the Mission; not coming, are you?"

"No," breathed Bert, and said no more; for his eyes were fixed upon a little shadowy figure, moving under the shadow of the stoep.

Mayne saw it too, and walked quietly away.

CHAPTER II
MILLIE

"The world was right when it called you thin."
—ROBERT BROWNING.

The sun had dropped, as the red billiard ball slips into the pocket, suddenly behind the heaving mass of veldt. Darkness was advancing with tropical, seven-leagued stride, and all things were grey.

The pale figure detached itself from the shadows, and resolved itself into the advancing form of a frail, undeveloped girl of fifteen or sixteen. A strange eye would have been lost in wonder, at the first glance, as to what Bert Mestaer could see here, on which to fix his turbulent affections.

His lady-love was skinny, hollow-chested, stooping and round-backed; her arms were almost like sticks.

She wore a soiled calico gown, too long behind for its length in front. Her pale-coloured hair was drawn off her white face, and plaited into an untidy pig tail which hung down her back. Certain small wisps of it escaped in front, and made what looked in the dim light like the rudiments of a nimbus about her head. She was drawn down on one side by the weight of the heavy, clanking, copper bucket which she carried.

The well was right across the yard, quite near the gate where Bert stood, and his large person was very visible; but the girl came on with no sign that she saw him; and, reaching the well, hooked her bucket on the chain, and let it down, with a stony, expressionless countenance.

Bert leaned over the gate; the expression of his face had altered completely.

"Millie," he said, below his breath, "Millie!"

She gave him a listless glance, from weary, heavy-lidded, dark-blue eyes.

"Oh, good evening!" she said curtly.

He unlatched the gate, came through, and took the windlass out of her hand.

"Thought you promised not to come inside," she remarked.

"Only jest ter wind up this"—perhaps the thought of Mayne and the swear-words flitted across his mind, for he pulled up short, and merely finished lamely with—"this 'ere bucket."

"What's an ear-bucket?" asked Miss Lutwyche, with cold contempt.

He winced like a child from a cane, but made no retort, merely setting all his finely developed muscles a-play, as he raised the gleaming bucket from the depths. When it was at the top, he paused.

"How's he to-night, Millie?"

"Mean my father?"

"Yes, Mr. Lutwyche."

"Oh, same's usual."

Bert's chest heaved with the burden of all he wished to say, and dare not. Some instinct, deep down in him, warned him not to speak to the girl of her father's fast-approaching end. And yet—he thought of all that Mayne had said! Now was his chance, if ever, to declare his passion. He wondered whether Mayne, or anybody else, knew how distant were the terms between him and Millie, what an impregnable barrier she stood behind, how far he was from being on such a footing as might be supposed to immediately precede a proposal of marriage. His tongue clave to the roof of his mouth, and he felt the sweat break out upon him.

The girl moved, leaned over to detach the bucket from the hook. He started, and reaching quickly forward, brought it down upon the side of the well where he stood.

"I'm goin' to carry it indoors for you," he said sheepishly.

She turned, without a word of thanks, and began to walk back to the house.

He strode beside her, in the gathering gloom, his whole being aching with the desire to comfort her.

"Millie," he said at last, "if—if she does anythin' to yer—if she gets too bad, or lays hands upon yer, you jest come to me, or send for me, won't yer?"

The girl let fall a laugh of such quiet scorn that he felt openly sneered at.

"D'you think I'm afraid of her, then?" she asked.

"No," he said warmly; "you've got the pluck of the—" he checked and almost choked—"the pluck of a dozen. But she's stronger than you."

"Is she?" said Millie drily.

He pondered on that answer.

There spoke the careless insolence of the Briton. He admired it, while he writhed under it; but he understood why it made Tante Wilma want to scratch her eyes out.

They had reached the stoep. Nobody was about. He set down the bucket and faced her squarely.

"Millie," he almost gasped, "look here! Give me a word! You know I'd——"

She broke in. "I got no time to talk. I must take this water inside. Goodnight!"

His choler rose. "A chap may do what he will for you, and you can't even throw him a word!"

Her languid expression changed; the dark blue eyes flashed wide awake in the twilight.

"I didn't understand you wanted to be paid for carrying the pail!"

"Oh, *damn* you!" cried Bert, hurt beyond endurance; and he flung away in rage that was not far from tears.

It seemed that the moment he was gone, the girl forgot him utterly. She turned away and went inside the *sitkamer* without a backward glance.

The *sitkamer* was full of her father's half-Boer children: two great boys of eight and nine years old, and three or four younger fry. They were rolling about on the floor, playing, fighting and cuffing. Millie took no more notice of them than if they had been mice or black-beetles. She filled the kettle from her pail, and set it to boil, and then, going to a cupboard, got a fresh egg, which she proceeded to whisk up in a tumbler, with delicate care.

Tante Wilma rolled into the room, sat down by the stove, took the coffee-pot off the rack, and poured herself out a cupful, which she proceeded liberally to "lace" with something stronger. She sat sipping it, looking furtively at her step-daughter as she moved, her small face grimly set, noiselessly to and fro. It is very rarely indeed that a Boer woman takes to drink. When she does, she becomes a creature to be avoided.

When her arrangements were complete, Millie took the tray and went out of the room, followed by malevolent glances.

"White rat!" growled Xante Wilma, in the Taal.

The children started a kind of chorus:

"White rat! White rat!
Ours is the corn that makes you fat!"

"Not much longer then," muttered the half-tipsy Vrouw. "Another week or two will see the end of it now; and then—out she goes! Aha! She'll wish before long that she had kept a civil tongue in her head. As sure as I'm a living woman, one thrashing I'll give her before she goes! Oh, there's a long account I've got against her—it wants paying, that it does! Much we've had to bear from him, but most from her that encouraged him from a baby to defy me. But I'll take it out on her, once he's gone, the little insolent, English devil!"

CHAPTER III
THE RIVALS

"But as if he loved you! No, not he.
Nor anyone else in the world, 'tis plain;
Who ever heard that another, free
As I, young, prosperous, sound and sane,
Poured life out, proffered it—'Half a glance
Of those eyes of yours, and I drop the glass!'"

—ROBERT BROWNING.

Bert Mestaer flung open the door of his farm kitchen, and strode in.

All was clean and quiet. His supper, covered up in a saucepan, had been left on the stove. Anna, his Boer housekeeper, had long since retired to her heavy slumbers.

The eye of the master roved round the kitchen that night, like one who saw it for the first time. He gazed upon the ceiling, and noted that it needed fresh lime-wash. He contemplated the shining rows of plates on the dresser, as though taking a new pride in his possessions; and then, moving forward, he pushed open a door at the opposite side of the room, and found himself in darkness and coolness. He struck a light, held it to a candle on the table, and his critical glance travelled round the parlour which had been his mother's pride.

There was a piano; he had a dim memory of her sitting there, playing to him, the hymns that had charmed her own English childhood—

"Once in Royal David's city—"

the sound of the tune floated across the brain which for so long had heard no such strains. He saw himself, a boy with yellow curls, in which she had delighted, lifting his piercing childish treble at her bidding. What would she not have given for the English Mission which had come to Slabbert's Poort since her death, and the ministrations of Carol Mayne! Bert had not entered a church now, for years. As he stood by her silent piano, he was invaded by a vague feeling that he could hardly expect a neglected God to take his part.

The room contained an old bureau and comfortable chairs. There were good engravings on the walls. The carpet was still serviceable, and there were clean curtains in the windows. From the wall before him smiled down his mother's frank, good-humoured face—the face of Alice Brooke—a brave girl, who had earned her living among strangers in a strange land, until the rich Boer farmer had persuaded her to be his wife. Beside her, the broad-bearded, benevolent face of her devoted husband, a Boer of the best type.

Bert folded his arms, and gazed at them both, with a heart full of curious longings, rebellions and regrets. Mrs. Mestaer had died when he was eight years old. Her death was the result of an accident—a runaway horse had cut short the happy life on that out-of-the-way farm; and people said that Mestaer had never rallied from the shock. He became an old man in a few short months. He turned a deaf ear to those who urged him to take some expansive Boer lady to look after him and his motherless boy, and he died of pneumonia when Bert was seventeen, seeming only too glad of the chance to be gone.

Bert did not remember feeling much grief when he was told of his father's death. He had been chiefly conscious of the excitement of leaving school and coming home to take possession of his property, and ruffle it in the streets of Slabbert's Poort.

Just at that time had come the diamond-finding craze, which changed the little rural hamlet into a haunt of needy adventurers, gamblers and sharpers, Slabbert's Poort was to be the new Kimberley. The usual influx of rabble followed; the usual mad period of wild speculation. To let off big portions of his land to speculators had seemed to young Mestaer far more "sporting" than to continue stolidly to farm the precious acres. He chummed in with the prospectors, who were only too ready to flatter a young fellow with money in his pockets. The result was that his proper business languished; and now it was universally allowed that the diamond-bearing capacities of the locality had been absurdly over estimated.

Bert had fallen into ways which would have wrung his mother's heart, when, for good or ill, the white face of Millie crossed his horizon, to remain as a fixed star in his heavens.

To-night he was beginning to realise all that it might have meant for him if his mother had lived. She was English; she would have understood and befriended Millie; she would have told him the things that English girls demand of their lovers, and have devised ways in which the acquaintance might be encouraged.

There was not, as it happened, a solitary English-woman in the place. Mayne, at the Mission, was a bachelor, so could not be used as a chaperon.

Millie had never seen the interior of Bert's house in her life. He felt sure that if she could see the rooms made comfortable by his English mother, it must to her seem preferable to her own miserable quarters. She only saw him slouching about the streets, in the unkempt condition affected by his pals; she took him, he felt sure, for other than he was, or than he felt himself capable of becoming for her sake.

Remorsefully he remembered that Millie had seen him drunk. He had not cared at the time—the thing was growing far too fashionable to be looked upon as a disgrace in the little place which had been so pastoral—but love was teaching him strange things, and now he felt as though he were looking upon the sordid episode of drunkenness through Millie's tired, contemptuous eyes.

What would he not have given to be able to make her understand that, if she would be kind to him, he would be what she chose—to be able to show her the clean, peaceful farm, known throughout the district as High Farm, owing to its being the only house for miles which was built English fashion on two floors—and tell her that, if she would be mistress there, he would use all his vast strength to work as never man worked before, and keep her like a lady?

But how to get at her? He felt that any written expression of his desires would be ludicrously inadequate. At one time he thought of begging Mayne to speak for him; but his pride jibbed too violently at the notion of having to confess that he lacked courage to speak. His heart was heavy as lead. Four times since his last strikingly unsatisfactory interview he had hung over the gate in vain. Each evening it was Kattie the Kaffir girl who had been sent to draw the water; and he was too proud to send a message by her.

But on the fourth night he had yielded to unbearable longing, and entrusted the grinning damsel with a note for Millie—a folded scrap of paper, on which he had written:

"Do let me have a word. I'm so blamed sorry I said that to you.   "BERT."

He had some self-questionings as to whether "blamed" might be looked upon as a swear-word; but he decided that it must be harmless.

"If you don't say that, dashed if I know what you could say," he reflected irritably.

His heart beat insufferably as he watched the girl stagger across the yard, the pail in one hand, the little note in the other.

Strange thrills crept through his nerves, his breath seemed to trouble him as he drew it If Millie herself should come in answer, what should he say to her? He was all unprepared.

A shadowy figure was stealing towards him stealthily in the gathering gloom. It was slim—it moved quietly. He grew crimson in the dark. An unmistakable Kaffir chuckle broke on his ear: it was only Kattie back again. She handed him a piece of paper and ran away in an instant He struck a match and looked eagerly at what he held: it was just his own message, crumpled up and returned without comment.

He had been enraged, but not daunted for long. It was highly possible that Tante Wilma had got hold of the message, and that Millie had never seen it. The thing now was to invent some new plan of campaign—some scheme by which the plenty and good plenishing of his home might burst upon the vision of the girl.

To-night he set down the kerosene lamp upon the table, which had a serge cover of a good shade of blue. He surveyed the well-upholstered sofa, with silk cushions of the same blue. He tried, with doubled fist, the springs of the deep easy-chair. He stared at the tall glass vases and glazed pots, and dimly recalled the fact that in his mother's lifetime these had been wont to hold flowers. A girl would like, perhaps, to see flowers in a room. He believed there were some in the yard; but he paid no attention to them, and never gathered any. A deep sigh escaped him at the thought of his inability to cope with the situation in general.

He strolled back with his lamp into the tiled kitchen.

Should he consult Amurrica? The Yankee was the only one of all the set for whom he entertained anything but a profound and steady contempt. And Amurrica was, he knew, untrustworthy. He had a secret fear—which brought the blood to his head when he considered it—that Amurrica himself was "on to Millie." It was possible that the Lutwyches might consider an American more akin to themselves than the son of a Boer. Even as he turned the delicate subject over and over in his thoughts, there came a tap at his door, and a long whistle, which told him that the man who occupied his thoughts stood upon his threshold.

He went and opened, standing aside as the visitor sauntered in, and manifesting no curiosity as to the reason of so late a call. Amurrica shut the door carefully behind him, and walked to the clean hearth. His face was of the hatchet variety, not handsome, but keen, with that eagle keenness which is the hall-mark of a certain type of American. The humour in his half-closed hazel eyes atoned for their lack of size; the composure of his manner hid his real thoughts from sight. Bert had never before considered him formidable, but to-night he was conscious of a foreboding as he mechanically produced the whisky-jar from a corner cupboard, and pushed it across the table. Amurrica sat down.

His eye roved around restless until it lighted upon the spittoon in the corner by the hearth. He made his shot with precision, and then, laying his pipe on the table, began to pour whisky into a tumbler.

"'S come at last," he observed.

"What?" asked Bert, slouching in his chair, his listless eyes on the fading red glimmer between the bars of the stove.

Amurrica shifted slightly in his seat, so as to face his host squarely. He took a pull at his whisky before replying casually:

"Lutwyche is cuttin' the stick."

There was silence. Bert knew he was being watched; felt instinctively that the time had come. With no other word spoken, he knew that they were rivals; that it would be perhaps a question of which man was prepared to give most to the Boer step-mother for the attainment of what he desired. He must feign indifference; for aught he knew, Amurrica might have his shooting-iron in his pocket.

He had no personal fear of him; his fears were all for Millie. His love was teaching him stratagem.

His eyelids did not flicker, he did not even remove his pipe from his mouth. Amurrica's eyes were boring him like gimlets, but he puffed calmly on, his thoughts racing each other over the well-known ground. What was he to do?

"Who told you?" he presently vouchsafed.

"Met Boka, galloping for the doctor like the very devil."

Boka was one of Lutwyche's Kaffirs.

Bert asked no question, manifested no curiosity; but the other was full of news, and intent upon imparting it.

"Said the gal had made him sleep in the kitchen nights, for a week past, 'n case she needed to call him up. To-night, down she come with a face like chalk, and told him to ride like hell: said he judged by the looks of her the ole man was gone already."

Again there was a silence, while both smoked. Bert presently spoke—two words:

"Mayne there?"

"Mayne? Not that I know of." A surprised inflection in the voice.

"Then I think," said Mestaer, slowly rising to his full height, and knocking his pipe against the chimney, to dislodge the dottle—"I think I'd better go an' send him."

"What's the blank good of that?" cried Amurrica, in a choice outburst of astonished profanity.

"Parson's the right man when it comes to dyin', ain't he?" said Bert tranquilly. "An' you done right to come an' tell me, Amurrica, for I'm the man who's concerned in this. I thank you. Put yourself outside o' that whisky, an' I'll make so free as to turn you out."

He was moving quietly about the room as he spoke, opening drawers, and Amurrica saw him slip a revolver into his pocket.

The Yankee sat for a minute with a frozen face, digesting his plans. Then he stood up, and his features relaxed towards a smile.

"Well, here's luck!" he said, draining his glass.

"Thanks!" said Bert

He approached the table, and took the empty glass, as though to carry it away; but as he moved, it slipped through his fingers, and fell in shivers upon the floor. Amurrica's nostrils twitched: was it an accident? Bert said "Damn!" quite naturally, and kicked the fragments with his foot. A second time his visitor decided, upon reflection, not to quarrel; and they left the house together.

CHAPTER IV
THE GUARDIANSHIP OF CAROL MAYNE

"These mothers are too dreadful!"
—ELIZABETH BARRETT BROWNING.

Millie sat before the cold hearth in the stale, stuffy *sitkamer*, which always smelt of dirty dish-cloths and unwashed humanity. Her lips were pressed tightly together, her face was white as wax. In its repose, one could see signs of the inner strength, the unnameable charm which had captivated Bert and Amurrica, beyond question the two cleverest men of the place. No young Boer would have looked twice at her.

Her father was dead. The doctor had come and gone, and told the orphan what she knew before. The death had been quiet and painless, only Millie there. But now, the Boer widow was beside the corpse, noisily weeping and wailing, and the girl was shut out.

It was perhaps a fortunate thing for Arnold Lutwyche that his inherent vacilation of character had been joined to a feebleness of constitution which released him, at the age of forty-two, from the burden of the flesh. He had passed beyond reach of the Boer woman's tongue, and of the complications presented by those lumpish Boer children who bore his name. His difficulties were over; but what of his child?

His first wife—his own love, and Millie's mother—had been the earthly stay of the weak soul. Everyone had always called him weak; but he had had the wisdom to love the strong, the fortune to be loved by her again. While she lived, his own lack of stamina had hardly been apparent to him. He had never quite lost his sense of having a grudge against God since her death.

What he had been through since! From the moment when the handsome, courteous Englishman, with the dark-blue eyes, presented himself in answer to an advertisement from the buxom Boer heiress for a competent man to manage her farm, his misery had increased, his bonds had tightened. But it was over at last. He had slipped through Tante Wilma's coarse fingers, and gone flying home to her, his love, his stronghold.

Their child was left behind.

She had apparently no tears for him. The look on her tense features was more triumphant than grieving.

A smart tap on the door aroused her. She looked up in languid surprise. The old Dutch clock pointed to three o'clock in the morning. With a resigned shrug, she lifted her aching limbs, dragged herself to the door, and opened it. Mr. Mayne stood outside, and stepped in without speaking, closely followed by Bert Mestaer. Millie drew back, a look of anything but welcome on her expressive face.

"Go back!" said she to the young farmer. "I don't want you round here, nor any of your lot."

"I—I came to see if I couldn't help, Millie." stammered he humbly.

In dialogue with the girl he seemed always to become a different creature. To-night there was some apparent difficulty in articulating, as his eyes rested on the untamed fire of the glance, and the droop of the small, exhausted frame.

"Let him come in and rest a minute, Miss Lutwyche," said Mr. Mayne gently. "He came all the way to the Mission to let me know."

"How'd he hear, I should like to know?" she demanded.

"Amurrica told me," stammered Bert, staring at the ground.

She gave a short laugh.

"Trust him to know other folks' business," she sneered. "He's the old woman's candidate, he is."

"Candidate? What for, Millie?" asked Mayne anxiously.

She had turned away, and Bert had fastened the door. She sank on a chair, leaning an arm on the table, the slenderness of her wrist, as it lay there, making a dumb appeal to all the manliness in Bert.

"For taking me off her hands," she said, with perfect calmness. "I'm on offer, didn't you know? Either o' you two in the running? Amurrica's given her ten quid on account; you'd better bet on his chances, unless you can go higher."

"That's not the way to talk," said Mayne sternly. "What do you mean by it? You are far too young to think of marriage."

"Who said I was thinkin' about marriage?" she flashed back. "Am I the old woman? Am I to answer for her dirty bargains?"

"Then tell us what you mean," said Mayne. "Is it true that Otis wants to marry you?"

Otis was Amurrica's patronymic.

"I don' know," said Millie casually. "I only know he's pretty thick with the old woman; an' she doesn't mean to let me go for nothing; all of you can bet on that."

"But why talk this nonsense?" urged Mayne reprovingly. "Mrs. Lutwyche couldn't dispose of you against your will, even if you were a Kaffir."

Milly laughed—one clear, liquid note.

"No, of course she can't," said she. "That's where the joke comes in. Think I'd go along o' that sort o' scum?"

She indicated poor Bert with a slight wave of that fragile wrist.

"Then what are you goin' to do, Millie?" burst out the young man in anguish. "If she turns you out, where're you goin'—eh?"

"What's it matter to you?" asked Millie sullenly.

"'S the only thing that does matter to me!" cried Bert desperately. "Look here!" He flung his hat on the table, and stepped in front of her with a sudden manliness which filled Mayne with admiration. "You don' know the sort of home I've got to offer you, Millie. I'm a rich man, as things go round here. I'd give yer pretty well anything you set your heart on. I'd take care of yer—yer shouldn't set them bits of hands to no rough work. I love you, Millie, and well you know it. Let the parson here marry us, an I'll—I'll do anything you want!"

He knelt down by the table as he concluded his appeal, and made a snatch for her hand; but it was sharply withdrawn. He laid his arms down on the rough wood, and hid his face in them, shaken through and through by the intensity of his feelings. Mayne turned away, and walked to the far end of the kitchen. But he heard the girl's short laugh of scorn.

"Tastes differ," she said icily. "I'm an English girl, and if the worst comes to the worst, there's the well in the courtyard. That's better than a drinkin' Boer."

"Millie," said Mayne, in wrath, "I am ashamed of you! Is that the way to answer an honest man, who offers you all he has to give? I am as English as you are, and I beg to say no Englishwoman I ever knew offered insult as a return for honour done her. If you can't feel affection for Bert, surely you could tell him so civilly."

The girl's fragile form quivered with dry sobs; she sprang to her feet.

"Mr. Mestaer, I can't and don't return your affection," she gasped. "I'm brought pretty low, but I've got my pride! I'm thinkin' just now more about funerals than about weddin's, though a black frock for me'll be as hard to fi-f-find as a white one would, I'm thinkin'!"

"There!" cried Bert to Mayne, in hot indignation. "You made her cry now. Millie, my dear, now don't you give it a thought. I didn't know it 'ud vex you! ... Millie!"

But she had staggered blindly down the room, not seeing her way for the streaming tears so long so unnaturally restrained; and as Bert stood hesitating, torn between his pity, his anger, his passion—the door of the kitchen opened slowly, and the new-made widow appeared on the threshold, truly awful in her *déshabille*.

"A clever girl, I'll warrant!" she cried, in high glee. "Her father not cold yet, and two young men in the kitchen at four o'clock in the morning! Well, what offers, gentlemen? Either of you ready to take her off my hands?"

"I am," burst in Bert at once, before Mayne could speak. "Fifty pounds down and a demi-john of the best whisky in Slabbert's Poort, and I'll make her my wife to-morrow."

"Millie!" screamed the virago to the girl, who had reached the ladder leading to her little room above. "Here's a husband for you, my girl! Get your bundle and pack! Off with you! Out of my house! We're all respectable here! Take your English lady-wife, Mr. Bert Mestaer."

Mr. Mayne stepped forwards.

"Perhaps you would be so kind as to listen to me for a moment, Mrs. Lutwyche," he said distinctly. "Your late husband made a will, and left it in my hands. In it I am appointed his daughter's sole guardian, until she reaches the age of twenty-one. The arrangements for her future rest with me, and have nothing whatever to do with you. If she remains with you for a week or two, until her affairs are settled, you will be paid a fixed sum daily, out of Mr. Lutwyche's small estate, as long as you keep her. But you have absolutely no control whatever over her marriage."

Vrouw Lutwyche gave a positive howl of fury. Her face grew purple—almost black; her eyes protruded, her rage was hideous and ungovernable. For so long had she waited for this moment—this coming time when she should have Millie helpless at her mercy—she simply could not realise that all was taken out of her hands.

Millie's tears had ceased. In surprise at what Mr. Mayne was saying, she had halted on her way up the ladder, the drops wet on her cheeks. Now she slowly came back to the ground, and stood with a set smile, showing her row of short, pearl-white teeth, as she gloated over the spectacle of the Boer woman's degradation. He had been weak, that father who had left her; he had disappointed her over and over again; but after all, there had been something in him which Vrouw Lutwyche could not reach. In death he had outwitted her.

Mayne's very soul sickened. He had seen much that revolted him in this wild land of beginnings—of that measure of civilisation which sometimes seems so strongly to plead the fact that utter savagery would be better. But he thought he had never seen anything more awful than the enmity of this girl's face—the hatred, the callous contempt, which showed how often the young eyes had looked upon like scenes.

"If she is left here, she will go mad," he thought; and again he earnestly wished that poor Lutwyche could have held on just another fortnight, until the arrival of certain letters from England. He was at his wits' end. There was not a house anywhere near to which he dare take Millie. He was in sole charge of the Mission, and in that evil place, to take her there, would be to blast her character. He thought of a good-natured old Boer widow woman who lived about a mile away, and stepping up to Millie, he suggested in an undertone, that she should go there.

"You cannot remain here," he urged.

Her refusal was prompt and resolute.

"Leave him alone in the house with her? Never!" she said doggedly. "You don't know what she might do. I'm not afraid of her. She daren't touch me, and she can't go up my ladder. She's roaring drunk now, but she'll be dead drunk presently, and then she's harmless. If you come round in the morning, I shall be able to talk to you; she'll take hours to sleep this off. I wish you'd go now, and take away that Bert. I've got no use for him."

CHAPTER V
A BOER BURYING

"—Within some glass, dimmed by our breath,
Our hearts discern wild images of Death,
Shadows and shoals that edge Eternity."

—DANTE GABRIEL ROSSETTI.

The sunrise flashed into their eyes, as the farm-house door closed upon the two men. They went together through the yard, and out at the gate where Bert had so often watched in vain for Millie. Their steps echoed with an unfamiliar ring upon the hard, caked earth at this unwonted hour of stark, raw dawn. The sight of the well gave Bert a twinge as he passed it.

"Even that 'ud be better than a drinkin' Boer," he muttered, under his breath.

Before they had gone much farther, he grappled with the new fear that was clutching at his heart.

"I say," he growled, stopping and planting himself before Mr. Mayne, who of necessity stopped also; "what did you mean by what you said up there about letters from England? She—she hasn't got friends in England, has she?"

"It is very doubtful," said Mayne hesitatingly. "Look here, Mestaer!" he added abruptly. "My hand was forced just now. You were not supposed to hear what I said. Can I trust you not to repeat it?"

"Repeat it! Who'd I repeat it to?"

"Otis; or any of your lot."

"My lot! That's her cry too. Has she learnt it from you? Do you lump me in with Amurrica's crew of thievin' idlers? — — them all for a set of — —"

Mayne's hand went up with the slight gesture which always stopped Bert's swearing.

"Mestaer," he said, "after what we have just seen, you will drop your fancy for Millie, won't you? There are girls who will play with a man's love to the very brink of the end; but if a girl has any sort of feeling for a man, she will turn to him in her trouble. Millie doesn't care for you—you must see that, don't you?"

Bert looked as though he had been suddenly turned into a graven image. Meeting the squareness of his jaw, the metallic glint of his hard grey eye, Mayne was conscious anew of the dreadful strength of undisciplined human nature, and the imperious quality of its desires. One is sometimes apt to wonder what twenty centuries of Christianity have done for Europe. The answer to the question stares you in the face the moment you step outside the circle in which Christianity has insensibly moulded public opinion.

"If she don't want me, she don't want no other man," said the giant doggedly; "and look how young she is. I've got patience; I can wait. But if she's going to be taken off to England—"

He broke off, and began to walk on.

"If she is going away to England?" repeated Mayne, trudging beside him.

"Why, then, I don't know as how I can."

Mayne thought rapidly for a minute.

"You're not reasonable," he said. "You own that Millie's too young to be married; but you wouldn't have her stay in Vrouw Lutwyche's clutches, would you?"

"The worse they treat her, the more likely she is to come to me," said Bert calmly.

"Or to Otis."

"Chuck it!" burst out Bert hoarsely. "Chuck it, I tell you." He shook with all the inward feelings which he could not explain. How could he say that it scorched him with sheer physical heat and shame, to hear Amurrica even suggested as a mate for Millie? "He'd poison her soul," he groaned; and Mayne felt an acute inward sympathy with him.

"Mestaer," he said kindly. "It seems very doubtful whether any of the English relations of Millie's mother will be willing—or if willing, able to receive her. Her father has left in my hands a little sum of money—very small, but enough to pay her passage home. It appears that the family of the first Mrs. Lutwyche all disapproved of her marriage. They are poor proud people, and as he has had no communication with them since her death, I do not even know whether his letter will reach them. If however they do write, and if they offer to have the girl home, on any terms, you have the sense to see that she most certainly ought to go."

"Perhaps she won't go. Who's goin' to make her?"

"I am her guardian," said Mayne, very quietly.

"If you try an' make her do anything she don't wanter, I'll choke you with my own hands," said Bert earnestly.

The priest was unable to help smiling.

"Mestaer, if you had lived in other days, you would have been a devout lover," he said. "As it is, you are a bit of a barbarian, are you not?"

"A drinkin' Boer; that's it, if you want to do any classifying," retorted the young man, with exceeding bitterness; and with no parting salutation, he flung off, turned the corner leading to the High Farm, and marched away, leaving Mayne to pursue the road to the Mission alone.

The news he had heard was working like some stimulating drug in the young farmer's brain. The fatal word "England" lit up the future in one long, awful glare, as of an endless avenue along which he seemed to see himself moving—alone. Surely there was something that a strong man could do to chain a girl's affections! What charm can lead a spirit captive? Bert knew well enough, though he never said so to himself in set terms, not being by way of analysing his emotions—he knew that it was Millie's self, her love, her soul, her inmost being, that he longed for. If he could make her long for him as he longed for her! He thought of the cold, white face and little delicate, sneering mouth till he was half mad.

The only plan of campaign which suggested itself was the simple one of being always on hand. He felt pretty sure, in his own mind, that the girl's stepmother would try to get even with her somehow. Her prey was to be snatched out of her hands; it would be odd if she made no attempt to revenge herself. The girl knew no fear; she had successfully cowed and defied the bullying woman for years. But Bert, with Boer intuitions in his blood, felt that she was less secure than she thought herself. It was truly British to despise an adversary; but it was a British mistake, sometimes. The kind of hate that Tante Wilma felt was hate that would improve with keeping.

Accordingly, Bert passed the next day or two in mounting guard in the immediate neighbourhood. There were various outbuildings which made it easy to hang about unseen, and he went to his post before Otis and the others were about.

On the first day, life at the farm went on much as usual. As Millie had foreseen, Tante Wilma was not visible. Various Boer ladies of her acquaintance came to condole, and discuss the purchase of widow's mourning. Mayne came and saw Millie, and gave her the money to supply her own black dress, which she sat up all night to make. There was no need for Bert to wait about when once he had seen the light of the candle in the little square patch of glass in the corrugated iron roof that lighted Millie's garret. In that fastness she was safe—safe among the coffins.[1]

> [1] In remote Boer districts, a coffin or two is frequently kept in the loft, ready for emergencies. Apples and fruit for winter use are sometimes stored in these weird receptacles.

Amurrica came not near the farm all that day. Perhaps it had leaked out that the Vrouw was not in a fit state for the conduct of negotiations.

The next day the vigilant lover patiently returned to his post, and waited until dark. Millie was all right, so far, for a Boer woman had been all day long plying her needle at the farm, and the pallid, unwholesome little man who fulfilled the profitable duties of undertaker to the community had been shuffling in and out all day. Moreover, the girl herself had appeared in the yard, and been occupied there for more than an hour in hanging out wet linen, unconscious that she was watched from behind the thick hedge of prickly pear which enclosed the orchard, with its haze of peach blossom. Bert made no sign of his presence. He had determined now upon his role, and adhered to it with characteristic persistency. His plan was to bide his time, and come on the scene when Millie needed a champion. Her extremity was to be his opportunity.

About nine o'clock, Amurrica stepped briskly up to the stoep, and was admitted by Millie herself. The sentinel, much excited, stood by, every muscle tense, in view of emergencies. At the end of about three minutes, the square of candle-light appeared in the roof, gladdening the lover's heart. Millie had retired to her stronghold, out of reach of importunity. He determined to stand his ground, however, until the departure of Otis. The sound of raised voices was soon heard. No doubt Amurrica was demanding the return of his "ten quid," and demanding it of course in vain. It must have come in very handy for the purchase of the funeral garb and bakemeats. He did not stay very long. The invisible Bert studied his countenance as he emerged, but as was usual with him, there was not much to be learnt from it. It was non-committal. Bert, as he strolled home, fell to imagining what his next move was likely to be.

During the whole of the third day, four women were ceaselessly at work upon the solid feast which was to conclude the obsequies of Arnold Lutwyche, in a manner befitting the importance and position of his widow. The kitchen was a scene of bustle, excitement, constant coming and going. Bert wondered how Millie stood it. Tante Wilma, the centre of attraction, kept meritoriously sober during all this exciting period, and Bert knew that the girl was safe, at least from physical violence, while all these people were about.

Next day, the funeral took place. It happened to be the first Boer funeral that Carol Mayne had ever seen; and he found himself unprepared for it. From early dawn the cape carts and slow waggons kept coming in from all the country-side. He did not at first divine that all these people were come solely to attend the funeral. The Pieters family, to which Tante Wilma belonged, was the leading clan of the district; and before noon at least two hundred were assembled, some of them having come distances of thirty or forty miles for the sake of being present.

When he arrived at Lutwyche's, the ceremony of viewing the corpse was in active process. Just to the left of the stoep, before you entered the *sitkamer*, was a small room, the function of which seemed indeterminate. Here, in one of the coffins which had for so long borne Millie company in her loft, lay the dead Englishman, his face still uncovered. By his side, as master of the ceremonies, stood the widow's senior male cousin, Cornells Pieters, a typical Boer, with a reputation for beating his wife. His fluent Taal was not very comprehensible to Mayne; but a sick disgust came over him at the way in which he was, as it were, acting showman — stroking back the dead man's hair, pushing or poking his hands or cheeks with great stumpy fingers, and encouraging the never-ending stream of gazers to handle the corpse and finger the linen. A great laugh would go up if some young woman or child made outcry at the unexpected coldness of contact. Mayne's thoughts flew to Millie, and he wondered how she would bear this. But he could not see her anywhere. The widow, surrounded by her children, and evidently deriving moral support from a black-bordered pocket-handkerchief, sat in the *sitkamer* receiving condolences. But Millie was invisible.

Mayne was on delicate ground here. The dead man had expressly stipulated that he should be laid to rest with the words of his own liturgy, and the services of the English priest; but the Boer Predikant was in evidence, and Carol, who was quick to learn, and was beginning to understand local etiquette, stepped up to him, and asked him to say a prayer, when — the ghoulish corpse-inspection over at last — the coffin was screwed down, borne in, and triumphantly placed upon the family dining-table.

The Predikant, gratified, though hardly placated, took full advantage of his opportunities. He talked to the Almighty about himself, the Pieters family and the Boer nation, for three quarters of an hour; while Tante Wilma's noisy, snuffling sobs filled the place.

After this Mayne stepped forward, and read the first part of the burial service. Then the coffin was raised and borne solemnly out, and down the fields beyond the Kaffir huts, to where a stone wall enclosed the little family burying-ground.

Melicent Lutwyche, standing by the open grave, saw the procession coming, and the sight of Mayne's figure, bareheaded and white-robed, shook her fortitude for the first time. Her eyes began to burn with unshed tears. All these days, all these sleepless nights, her heart had never ceased to repeat: "I am glad! I am glad! He is safe now—free! Out of her clutches for ever!" But now a new and desolating thought supervened—suggested somehow by the liturgy's majestic words—the thought of his immense distance from herself. Heaven had formed no part of her conception of his release from captivity; now the anthem of Resurrection smote her with inarticulate pain. What had she, with a heart full of black hatred, to do with Resurrection? The white flowers in her hands shook; she was shivering from head to foot on the verge of a breakdown.

Then, foremost among the great throng of following people, she saw Amurrica's hatchet profile, and her thoughts, just painfully striving to take wing, sank back to the black, bad earth she knew. Warfare was still her portion. Amurrica and Bert Mestaer should never see her weep. She turned, moved a little, and stood exactly at the grave's head. The light was behind her, and to Bert she seemed like an austere angel, waiting to bestow the dead in some still sanctuary, where vulgar hands and tongues could reach him no longer. As the earth and stones fell pattering on the coffin, her white blooms fluttered down with them. The set intensity of her small white face fairly terrified her new guardian.

The service over, people cheered up, and hurried back to the farm to eat and drink before setting out upon their long return journeys. Mayne made Bert a signal to wait behind.

"Mestaer," he said, "I have to ride to Leitersdorp and get this will proved. I can't get back inside three days. I am setting off at once, and I expect to find a letter from England waiting for me at Mr. Crick's office, so that, when I come back, I shall know better what to do with Millie. Can I trust you while I am gone?"

He looked searchingly at the young man's face.

Bert grinned. "To punch Amurrica's head? Oh, yes!"

"Exactly! Or your own, if you should feel that you deserve it."

Bert shrugged. He was in a hurry. He hardly paused to realise what the three days' absence of the guardian might mean. His memory was centred upon the strained expression of Millie's little face, and he knew, by the faculty of divination which possessed him where she was concerned, that she was near the end of her powers of endurance. He had premonition that before long she must collapse. It seemed like a duel between him and her. When she gave in he would be glad, but he must be there. This was just now all that mattered—that he should be near her when the steel springs of her will relaxed.

He hurried away with an abstracted air the moment Mayne had finished speaking; and Mayne, with a sigh, wondered whether he had done right to tell him of his departure—whether he did right to go. Until the will was proved, he felt uncertain of being able to maintain his authority against Vrouw Lutwyche and her ignorant kinsfolk; he felt that a weight would be off his mind when he was safely back again. There was an Anglican sisterhood at Leitersdorp, and he wished to inquire whether the girl might be placed there for a time should circumstances render it necessary. But his guardianship was a real puzzle, and it was seriously complicated by the passion of Bert Mestaer.

CHAPTER VI
THE FLINGING OF THE GAGE

"What god, then, bade those two stand forth and strive?"
—C. S. CALVERLEY.

All the world of Slabbert's Poort was enclosed within the walls of "Lutwyche's." The funeral feast waxed noisier and noisier; there were the elements of discord trembling in the cup. Boer *v.* Briton was soon to be the order of the day, and the present company was largely composed of disappointed men—those who had come to clutch diamonds, and had found none. Their sense that the times were out of joint had been growing by degrees, in proportion as their prospects waned; and the war rumours were fanning it into flame. Visions of plunder danced before their eyes. They would have torn treasure from the bowels of the earth; if this was denied them, there was many a rich homestead for the sacking, much plunder scattered here and there over the wide land. This was what war meant to most of them. A few were English, but the great majority were Africanders. Amurrica was the only man of ability among them. He meant to throw in his lot with the winning side, "anyway"; but he had for days past been making highly inflammatory speeches, from the Boer point of view, in the saloon of the Vierkleur.

The festivities were well begun when Bert Mestaer walked in. He was not popular now. Most of those present were jealous of his possessions, and of his great physical strength. They thought him reserved, and nobody ever forgot that his mother was English. It was not considered certain which side he would take in the forthcoming struggle.

He was greeted with a clamour of welcome which held an underlying sneer. He took no notice; he was not quarrelling to-day. His courage and strength were facts too universally accepted for him to care to prove them. His grey eyes went like lightning about the room, till he discerned Millie, a large apron pinned over her black dress, staggering under the pile of plates which she was carrying to the wash-house. He pressed forward at once, as if nobody else had been present, took the girl's burden from her; and they went out of the room together, followed by laughter and jeers.

They reached the sink, already piled with unwashed dishes. Bert deposited those which he carried, looked around, spied a broken-backed chair, and brought it to the girl.

"Sit down!" he said.

Millie began to roll up her sleeves. "I got to wash these," she said.

"Sit down, I tell you," said Bert, in a low voice. He stood between he and her work. "Can't I see that you're just fit to drop in your tracks? Sit down! If there's washing-up to be done, where's the nigger girl?"

Millie did not sit down. She stood her ground: but she did a thing she had never done before—lifted her heavy lids, and looked up right into her lover's eyes. A wash of delicate carmine dyed her thin cheek-bones. "It keeps me out of the room—away from those swine," she said, with a note almost of appeal in her voice.

Bert felt his inmost being surge up wildly, as his whole heart went forth to her, in answer to her first confidence: the only word she had ever spoken which seemed to distinguish between him and "those swine." All that was best in him arose, and strove to meet and honour the favour she had shown.

"That's all right," he said, in tones of easy friendship. "You sit down an' tell me what to do. I'm on to this job."

In a second his coat was off and his sleeves rolled up. He had flashed a look round, spied a boiling kettle on a vilely-smelling paraffin stove, and filled the greasy washbowl. Millie subsided upon the chair with a resignation which, had he known her better, would have alarmed him. As things were, it filled him with a wild enthusiasm. But he determined to walk warily. His face glowed with enjoyment as he proceeded with his menial task. He buckled down to work in good earnest, methodically scraping the broken food off the dishes into the dog-trough set by for the purpose, and handling the crockery with skill which surprised the girl, who, sunk back in the chair, watched him without a word.

But he was human. After a while, it seemed to him that his strenuous efforts merited encouragement. He ventured greatly.

"Millie, if these Britishers write and ask you to come to them, shall you go?"

The girl started, as if his voice had roused her from stupor.

"What business is it o' yours?" she asked.

"I told you that the night your father died," said Bert, quite simply.

"Well, if you want to know, I shall go, whether they want me or whether they don't, so it won't make any difference to you," she replied coldly.

He bit back the oath that leapt to his lips.

"You've made up your mind to that?" he said; his voice was audibly unsteady.

"Think I'd stay here, with all the world to choose from?" said she scornfully. "Not if Slabbert's Poort was paved with diamonds! No, indeed; I do know enough to know that all the world's not like this. I'm going to see what it is like."

Bert had completed the washing-up and rinsed his big hands in clean water. He stood wiping them on the roller-towel, looking down upon her, so sudden a dilation in his heart and throat that for a space he was unable to articulate. He had forgotten the party in the room beyond as though it never existed.

"Millie, let me take yer! Marry me, Millie, and let's cut an' run together. Oh ... you don' know how good I could be to yer! Millie, little woman!"

"Drop it, Bert Mestaer! I can't stand it," gasped the girl, dragging herself to her feet. "You're always the same, if ever I trust myself with you for a minute alone. Why can't you hold your tongue?"

"Hold my tongue, an' lose you? Why, what d'you s'pose I got ter live for?" he cried out, stung through and through by the idea of his own impotence, his utter failure to arouse one spark of feeling in the girl.

He was shaking from head to foot. It seemed so enraging, so absurd, that he, whose great strength could compel this frail creature to anything, absolutely dare not touch her—was reduced to stammering, humiliated silence, by her unconcealed disdain. It always came to this between them. He stood, fighting his feeling, facing the blank wall of her indifference, when there was a sudden increase of sound from the scene of the revels—a door opened, a furious voice bellowed: "Millie!"

It was enough; he was by her side again at once. Snatching the pile of spoons and forks, he put them into her apron, picking up a pyramid of plates himself, and they went back to the supper-room.

They were received with a babel of derisive remarks, the pith of which seemed to be that Millie had been away with one young man, when she was going to be married to another.

"Come along, Millie!" said the deep, guttural voice of Oom Pieters, rumbling in his hairy throat; "we're only waiting for you, to drink your health."

Since the irruption of diamond-seekers into the pastoral district, the temperate Boer habits had sadly altered. Peach brandy was on the table in generous quantity, and many of the more old-fashioned sort, following a bad fashion, had partaken, and not being used to such things, were not perfectly under their own control.

Amurrica was seated on Tante Wilma's right, leaning back in his tilted chair, and sending out smoke rings from a mouth which wore a gratified smile.

"Goin' to marry Otis," was bandied from lip to lip. "He's bought a share in the Vierkleur from Maarten Brandt, and he says, when Millie's a bit fatter she'll do fine in the bar. Goin' to sit up together to-night."

This in allusion to the old Boer custom which decrees that an engaged couple shall ratify their troth by sitting up all night together, and burning candles.

"Sh! Hold your tongue," said Millie, in a low voice to Bert, who was about to explode. "They're all drunk; what's the good of noticing?"

"They're all goin' to clear out o' this before I'm much older," growled Bert, shaking with fury.

He broke off; for, to his amazement, Amurrica had risen, and was calling for silence.

As the man stood up, his long, sinewy frame, with a subtle twist in the carriage, outlined against the dark, smoky background, swaying slightly on his feet, as a result of his potations—the humorous curve on his thin lips which fascinated women and made Bert hate him—he would have made a study for the brush of Franz Hals. One thing which the Boers admired about him, was his mastery of the Taal. The man was a born linguist; he chose that language now.

He said he had the happiness to announce that he was the accepted suitor of Miss Lutwyche, and the marriage was to take place the following day. "Their esteemed Predikant"—then present, and somewhat bleareyed—"had promised to unite them, in view of which festivity, he invited them all to a supper at the Vierkleur Hotel to-morrow. It had been suggested that the English minister, Mayne, had been left guardian of Miss Lutwyche. But this was to be set aside. If it were so, he had doubtless obtained such power by exerting undue influence over the dying man's conscience, and for his own sinister reasons. Vrouw Lutwyche was going to law about it. But in any case, possession was nine points of the law, and when he was the husband of Miss Millie he didn't quite know where the Britisher was coming in; not into his house, he was almighty sure about that."

There was a deep silence all the time he was speaking. Bert Mestaer stood up motionless, just opposite, behind the row of seated guests, and Millie stood quite near him. He was both hungry and thirsty, and he had, immediately upon entering, helped himself to coffee from a big pot on a side-table. He stood holding the untasted drink in his hand while he listened to the unfolding of Amurrica's plot. The moment he had finished, before he had time to sit down, Bert flung the hot contents of his cup full in the orator's face.

Amurrica was for the moment blinded by this unexpected shot. The coffee streamed down him, into the bosom of his shirt, and all over his clothes; and the words he used were not pretty.

There was a general stampede; but before the noise began—before the men took up the shout for a fight—even before Amurrica began to swear—Bert's ear had caught a sound that was to him like the bugle to a war-horse; the short, musical sound of Millie's applauding laugh.

He turned to her.

"Good-night!" he said. "We'll soon settle the question of his sitting up to-night or getting married to-morrow; and Mayne'll be back the day after. But listen to what I say; keep out of Tante Wilma's way to-night."

She gave her usual contemptuous answer: "I'm not afraid."

"No," he said; "but I am."

It was in his heart to plead for something to hearten him for the fray, if it were only a hand-shake; but he forebore. She should not be able to say again that he claimed a price for serving her.

He strode out radiantly to the battle. He was perfectly sober, and had a white heat of passion to inspire him. Amurrica, though usually a formidable adversary, had eaten heavily, and drunk too much. When they had taken away his revolver, he was an easy prey. Bert's object was to put him out of the running for the next few days, but not to injure him seriously. He went into the thing scientifically, and it was a sorry-looking object which was finally carried off the field by its backers; while the two great Lutwyche boys, who had been eager spectators of the fray, ran back home as fast as they could, to tell their mother what had chanced.

The victor was pleased, but gory. It was imperative that he should go to his own place and change. Amurrica was settled for the present, he had warned Millie, and felt that he might now give himself an hour or two off duty without anxiety. All the way home he was wondering to himself how Amurrica had known that Mayne was going away.

Anna, who had not been bidden to the revels at Lutwyche's, was in an evil temper, and said she had provided no supper. Hadn't he had his bellyful down there, where all the swine were swilling? Bert turned upon her, with the flame in his eye, the gall on his tongue, which everybody feared. She would wish, a week hence, he told her, when she found herself bundled out to get her own living, that she had kept a civil tongue in her head. Then he went and washed himself elaborately clean, and put on a clean shirt—an English superstition which he had inherited from his mother, with other vain observances which filled Anna with contempt. He had neither eaten nor drunk since morning, and he knew that, if he was to mount guard at Lutwyche's till late at night, he must fortify himself. As he sat at table, the door open, devouring cold meat and bread, he saw something move behind the fence. He watched steadfastly until the thing rose more fully into view, revealed itself as the tow head and flushed face of one of the small Lutwyches, beckoned him furtively, and disappeared again.

Bert got up and went out. He looked down over the fence, and said "Hullo!" His heart meanwhile misgave him.

The child, grinning up at him, said she had a message from sister Millie, and she was to give it to him his very own self. The message was: "Would he meet Millie at the sign-post corner at nine o'clock that evening?" She was to take back word.

"What's she want to do there?" asked Bert suspiciously.

"She wouldn't say; but I expect she wants to run away. Mother she's promised her a hiding."

"Then you'll go to your mother with the tale."

"No fear; I'm on Millie's side."

Bert thought a while carefully.

"All right!" he said, after a minute. "Tell her I'll be there."

"Certain sure?"

"That's me." The tow head nodded and disappeared.

CHAPTER VII
IN THE GARRET

"I met a lady in the meads,
 Full beautiful, a fairy's child;
Her hair was long, her foot was light,
 And her eyes were wild."

—JOHN KEATS.

Bert stood where he was, rooted in deep thought, watching the child as she ran away. He did not believe that what she said was true. Millie might very probably plot to escape, but she would never send him word to bear her company. Besides, he knew that she did not intend to run away until she heard the result of her father's message to her English relatives. He wondered that anybody should think such a device could impose upon him. It was a hoax, and its obvious object was to get him out of the way. What devilry was Tante Wilma plotting?

He laughed a little; they thought him easily deceived.

A moment's reflection convinced him that the child's message was part of a preconceived arrangement with Amurrica. But he felt sure that, after his handling of the subject, the prospective bridegroom would be unable to take his part in anything that night. He looked at the clock, which pointed to seven, and made up his mind that he would resume his sentry duty at Lutwyche's about eight. Anticipating a long wait, he thrust a sandwich into his pocket and a flask of spirits, and sallied forth to stroll down the town, and hear what was being said of the fight and the funeral.

The main street was thronged with people. For a minute it made him a little anxious. If the town meant to take up the feud, and back Otis, things might be a trifle strained, though there were some of the men on whom he thought he could rely as backers.

But he soon saw that there was a deeper preoccupation on the faces of the burghers. The fight, which in calmer times would have filled men's mouths for a week, was forgotten. The flag floating over the Post Office showed him that the weekly mail was in; and knowing the political tension, he guessed that there was news. He dashed into the Vierkleur. It was a babel of tongues. Men were fighting for possession of the newspapers; those who had letters or journals from Pretoria were being besieged in corners. For the moment, the remembrance of Millie faded from Bert's mind, as he mingled with the throng, and gathered first of all the main fact, that the British Government had ordered the immediate despatch of troops, both from England and India, to back up the demand for the Outland Franchise. Debate was keen as to whether the British Government would really fight.

The madness of conflict rose in Bert's blood as in that of all the men there. They shouted, argued, wrangled, drank, swore. At whatever cost, Bert felt he must get at the main facts of the position, and he listened while one of the men, perched on the bar, read aloud leading articles from English and Boer journals, and the talk hummed and buzzed more busily than ever.

He was recalled from his absorption by a touch on his shoulder. Cornelis Pieters, the field-cornet, stood by, regarding him with no friendly glance.

"Lucky for you the Commandos are to be called out; nobody will have time to set the law on you," he growled. "Otis is goin' to die."

"We're all going to die—some day," said Bert placidly.

"He's goin' on ahead," said Pieters surlily.

"I'm not taking any," returned Bert, unmoved. "I had the cooking of him, and I know what I done to him. He won't be gettin' married just yet a while; but he's all right."

"If Tante Wilma takes my advice, she'll give that girl a taste of the stick," rumbled Pieters. "A taller dip 'ud make as good a wife as her, to my way o' thinkin'; an' when a man that could stomach her comes along, you must needs knock him out o' time. It wasn't your affair. There'll be a reckoning, I can tell you."

"Hope so," retorted Bert. "Couldn't live in this township, if you didn't believe the right 'ud come up some day. So long!"

"Where are you off to?"

"To see as Tante Wilma don't lay a finger on the gal."

"From what I heard, before I came away, I shouldn't be surprised if you was too late," said Pieters, grinning in his face.

It was quite dark when he arrived at the gate of Lutwyche's.

He was panting with the speed he had used, and the sweat ran down him. He was blaming himself bitterly because in the excitement of the war news he had lost sight of his purpose; and it was more than half-past eight. To his untold joy and relief, the first thing he saw was the light glimmering through Millie's square of ground glass in the loft. His heart leapt, and the strain of his muscles relaxed. He halted outside the gate, wiped his brow, and listened with all his might. All was quiet. But there was one unusual thing. Lights were burning in the *sitkamer*, a most rare phenomenon in a pastoral Boer district, where everybody rises and goes to bed with the sun. This looked as though it were still planned that the sitting-up should take place that night. He carefully unfastened the hurdle gate and went into the yard. By degrees he drew nearer the house. Half-way across, a sound made itself audible—the thudding of a hammer against wood. It went on with monotonous regularity, but his fears sprang up anew at the sound. What were they doing?

He walked right up to the stoep, raised himself to a level with the window-sill, and through a gap between the edge of the blind and the window frame, could see right into the *sitkamer*. What were they doing?

Tante Wilma, like some unclean beast, stood balancing herself unsteadily against the table, her face purple, her eyes wild, a sjambok in her hand. The children were all clustered round the foot of the ladder leading to the loft, and the eldest boy was standing upon it, aiming clumsy, childish blows with a big hammer at the trapdoor above his head.

Ha! Then he was just in time, and only just! Lord! When the bolt gave way, they should find someone they did not look for, in the loft above!

The blood surged to Bert's head—he set his teeth. With stealthy tread he crept to the barn, found a ladder—his late vigils about the farm had taught him where most things were kept—and setting it against the low house wall, he lightly ascended to the roof.

The window was slightly open—secured by means of an iron bar with holes in it. It was not wide enough to enable him to see in. The blows continued upon the trap below, showing that the besiegers had not yet forced an entrance. The noise drowned the sound of his voice, and he ventured to call gently: "Millie! Millie!"

There was no answer. He called again, a little louder.

All was silent in the garret; he could not hear the least rustling. The idea that she was not there, after all, but hiding away somewhere in safety, made his heart dance. Suppose she really had run away, and was waiting for him at the cross-roads? It was most unlikely, but it was not impossible; one never could be sure of girls. Meantime, he must ascertain before that bolt gave. Putting in his hand, he lifted the window as high as it would go—high enough to enable him to put his head under it. The loft extended a good way, though only just in the centre, under the pitch of the roof, was it high enough to stand upright in. It was a pitiful sleeping-chamber for a girl.

The little camp bed was smooth and empty. He could not see Millie anywhere. A candle stood upon a deal chest, guttering in the draught, showing the void space and the neatness of the dreary lodging.

She was actually gone, then? He drew a deep breath....

Something had caught his eye—a red, wet mess on the bare boards, close to the trap-door. All round this was a series of smears, and another blotch, almost a pool ... and some big drops, dotted along the floor into the darkness, under the low part of the roof, where the coffins and the fruit were stored.

Bert became a tiger. One wrench of his iron wrists brought the skylight off its hinges, and without noise he swung himself down into the garret. Stooping, he assured himself that the iron bolt of the trap-door would stand a good deal more of such battering as it was now enduring before it gave way. Then he seized the candle, and crept along the trail of the blood-stains.

He soon found her; and at first he thought that she was dead. She was lying prone upon the ground, her head sunk sideways, all dabbled in blood. One arm lay so curiously twisted that he guessed it to be broken. Bending over her, he heard her breathe; and then, raising her as tenderly as he could, found with mingled fury and relief that all the bleeding came from her lacerated shoulders. She had been inhumanly thrashed. Her clothes were literally torn off her back.

With indomitable pride she had crept up here to die alone.

It did not take Bert an instant to consider what he should do. He snatched a sheet from the bed, wrapped it round and round the raw, bleeding back, then possessed himself of the dark woollen coverlet, and rolled the slight, unresisting form therein. Lifting her as easily as one might a child, he carried her to the skylight, managed, with the help of a broken chair, to get her and himself through it, and in a moment was descending the ladder, clasping all the happiness the world held for him in his arms, his whole heart one white flame of pity and indignation.

CHAPTER VIII
THE RESCUE

"She took me to her elfin grot,
  And there she gazed and sighéd deep,
And there I shut her sad, wild eyes—
  So kissed to sleep.
"... And I awoke, and found me here,
  On the cold hillside."

—JOHN KEATS.

Rapid transit through the night air, and the pain of her open wounds, brought back consciousness to Millie.

She was light and small, but for all that, she was some weight to carry far; and when she began to writhe and twist in his hold, Bert was obliged to call a halt. He sat down, after a few ineffectual attempts to soothe her, on a hummock of ground by the roadside, cradling her as easily as he could upon his knees.

"What's happened? What's happened?" she began to stammer, evidently not quite knowing what she said. "It's dark! it's dark! Light the candle, one of you! ... O-o-oh!"

It was a long-drawn wail of agony.

Bert was very white. His heart was hammering, but the heat and wild rage of the past half-hour had passed away, and now he was all gathered into himself like a coiled spring. Everything, he believed, hung upon his ability to make the most of this chance, this hour that he had snatched for himself. The awkward self-consciousness which held him, as a rule, tongue-tied before her, was clean gone; only the concentrated force of his will remained.

Drawing his flask from his pocket, he poured out some raw spirit shakily, his left arm supporting the girl's head in the crook of the elbow. He administered a mouthful. She gasped, and refused more; but she had swallowed it. He waited a moment, with outward composure, and then said quietly:

"Millie, d'you know me?"

She started, and began to struggle in his hold.

"It's Bert," he said steadily; and to his unfeigned and stupefying astonishment, her struggles ceased.

"I thought—'twas Otis," she whispered, so low that he could hardly hear.

"Well, it's not," he murmured, trembling; "it's me. Listen! You've been cruel knocked about—d'you hear?"

"Yes; the—old—woman—"

"I know, my girl, I know! I got up through the roof, an' fetched you away. You're safe now; there's only me. D'you understand?"

There came an almost incredible whisper: "They said you'd gone away ... to the cross-roads..."

One short laugh of triumph escaped him.

"No fear," he murmured consolingly. "I was on hand. I'm going to take you to my place, and get you fixed up, and fetch the doctor to you. But look here, Millie, it'll make folks talk. Jus' say you'll marry me, an' that'll set things right. That'll give a reason why I should be looking after you."

He paused, his ear almost at her lips, straining for her reply.

"I'm goin' to die," she whispered at last. He barely heard.

"Well, till you die, can't I look after you, Millie?"

"If you like," murmured Millie indifferently, as she lapsed again into stupor.

William the Conqueror, crowned king of England, after desperate and apparently foolhardy invasion, felt perhaps much the same emotions as coursed through Bert Mestaer, sitting there in the dark, by the wayside, the half-dead form of a half-grown girl upon his knees.

He raised his eyes to the star-gleam above them, and emotions hitherto unknown laid hands upon him, thrilling his nerve-centres with a triumph that was almost agony. A long minute elapsed before he could collect himself enough to rise and continue his journey. No amount of guardians, no letters from England, he told himself, could take her from him now.

Yesterday he had practically no hopes, only a dogged determination not to give in. To-night he was master of the world.

Anna was not a good-tempered woman, but neither was she an inhuman one. She was very angry at being aroused by Bert out of her first sleep; but she detected something unusual in his manner.

"I got something to show you downstairs in the parlour," he said, "an' when you've seen it, I don't much fancy you'll want to go to bed again."

So she lumbered down the stairs, and into the little parlour which had been Mrs. Mestaer's pride; and on the ample sofa, among the blood-stained linen, lay what she took to be the corpse of Millie Lutwyche.

"You got to help me make her swallow some brandy," he said, "and then you got to do what you can for her while I gallop for Dr. Fraser; but don't you meddle with that arm, because it's dislocated."

"Vrouw Lutwyche's carving?" asked Anna, with venom.

"That's it," returned Bert, pouring the brandy.

"Drunken sow! I hope you see now, Hubert, where it is the drink leads to."

"I see! I'm going to swear off drink for ever now."

"She's past brandy," said Anna, hanging over the prostrate girl.

"Nonsense!" said Bert shortly; and he managed to make her swallow a table-spoonful. "Anna," he said, "you shall have a silk gown on my wedding-day."

"If you're going to marry a willow-shaving, may the day never dawn," said Anna tartly.

But she handled the misused girl tenderly enough, for hers was a maternal heart, though soured by spinsterhood; and Bert, when he saw her set about it, turned away with haste to the stable.

Before setting out on his long ride, he came back to warn Anna not to admit anybody on any pretext while he was away; and arranged that when he returned with the doctor he would give a certain number of signal taps upon the window.

Then, springing to the saddle, he dashed away through the night, his wild heart drumming to the music of the flying hoofs, and his imaginings soaring to the purple velvet dome of heaven.

CHAPTER IX
THE SCANDALISING OF SLABBERT'S POORT

> "Priests
> Should study passion; how else cure mankind,
> Who come for help in passionate extremes?"
> —ROBERT BROWNING (Caponsacchi).

When Carol Mayne got back to the Mission on the afternoon of the second day after this, he was told that Oom Pieters and the Boer Predikant were waiting to see him.

The news they brought fairly staggered him.

Bert Mestaer had, during the night after the funeral, forced an entrance into Lutwyche's and abducted Millie. That he had done this by force was evident from the blood-stained floor of her garret and the evidences of a struggle, the bedding being torn and scattered about. He had taken her to his own house, and kept her there, in defiance of all Christian laws, to the crying scandal of the whole community. Oom Pieters had been insulted when he went to remonstrate; and the Predikant, who, at his urgent entreaty, had gone to warn the headstrong girl of the penalties of living in sin, had been literally, not metaphorically, kicked off the premises by the lawless ravisher. Putting things together, they would have been inclined to fear that the girl had actually been made away with, but for the assurance of Anna to the contrary. They thought that heavy drinking must be the cause of Bert's outrageous behaviour, since he had picked a quarrel with Otis earlier in the evening, and so mishandled him that he had been unable to appear in public since.

Horrible as the news was, Mayne, knowing the violence of Bert's passion, his fear that Millie was to be taken away, and his intemperate habits, felt it possible that a great part of what he heard might be true. His disappointment was keen. He had looked for better things from Mestaer, whom he liked better than anyone else in Slabbert's Poort; and the behaviour now attributed to him was that of a wild beast. He hurried off without rest or refreshment to the High Farm; and all the way he was trying to piece the story together—to think how the lover who had always been so tongue-tied and shamefaced, could possibly have proceeded to such lengths; and the more he reflected, the more he felt sure that he had heard a perverted version of what had really happened.

But when he neared the white house, with its pleasant green shutters, his fears became acute; for the owner was leaning over the little garden gate, and one glance at his face showed that he was inflamed with triumph. He had evidently been gathering flowers; his hands were full of them; the fact impressed the new-comer much as though he had seen a lion sitting down to tea in a lady's drawing-room.

Bert was dressed with scrupulous care; his linen was fresh. He looked ten years older; had graduated from boy to man in two days. There was a steady blaze in his eyes; his mouth wore a defiant curve. The exaltation and triumph of his aspect affected Mayne strongly. But no look of guilt or remorse crossed his handsome face at sight of the approaching guardian.

"Hallo!" he frankly cried; "come in! Things have hummed since you went away."

Mayne stiffened in fierce wrath.

"Mestaer," he said, keeping himself calm with difficulty, "tell me that this I have heard of you is a slander—tell me that Millie Lutwyche is not here!"

Bert's eyes flamed.

"Millie Lutwyche is here," he cried, "and what's more, she'll stay here. Didn't you leave it to me to see she wasn't murdered? Well, I managed it, but only just."

Mayne came in through the gate and walked into the house.

"I've heard one side of the story," he said. "It's only fair that I should hear yours."

Bert followed him in. His style was abrupt but convincing. He told how Amurrica and Tante Wilma had tried to steal a march on Mayne, and how the Predikant had been willing to aid and abet. He told how he had foiled this plan, how he had been sent a message to decoy him out of the way, how he had gone down to the farm, but too late to prevent violence. He told how he had brought Millie home, and at once called in Dr. Fraser, who could corroborate all he said. He spoke without eagerness, and with an underlying confidence in his voice which showed how sure he felt of his position.

"If ever a man earned a woman fair, I done it," he remarked simply. "She's better to-day; but Dr. Fraser was a bit afraid of collapse at first. Anna's nursed her. I've not been near, except just to pass the time of day. I done the square thing, as I told you all along I meant to; an' we'll come to church an' get married, soon as she's up and dressed."

Mayne slowly shook his head.

"Mestaer," he said, "I have done you an injustice, I freely own it. I believe all you tell me. You have done better than I thought you would; now it remains for you to do better than you yourself believe that you can. You must let Millie go."

Bert flung himself into a chair, and pulling out a tobacco-pouch, began to fill his pipe. He gave an insolent laugh.

"We're engaged; you can't alter that."

"Under the terms of her father's will, Millie cannot marry under the age of twenty-one without my consent She is going to England."

Bert looked earnestly at him.

"Look here! I've played the game so far," he said. "Don't you push me; you'd better not. Hands off Millie; she's going to marry me."

"Perhaps she may, when she is grown up, if you have the courage and constancy to wait for her; but not now."

"Now, by — —!" His oath made Carol wince.

He sat for a minute in complete silence and close thought; then he rose.

"I should like to see Millie, if she is awake," he said, very quietly.

Bert looked at him piercingly. Had there been one shade of arrogance in his tone, or had he seemed to suggest that he doubted Bert's assent, there might have been open war. But he gave no handle; and the master of the house, after a very brief hesitation, rose and tapped at the parlour door.

Anna peeped out, and admitted them, with an anxious glance from one face to the other. Mayne walked in, and Bert followed him, with his bunch of flowers in his hand.

The waxen-white Millie lay with her flaxen hair loose upon the pillows. Her eyes were wide open, and flashed restlessly. Her whole mien otherwise was so still that one would have hardly thought her living. A look of expectancy kindled for a moment upon her face when she saw Mayne, but it soon died down.

He went over and sat down by her, with the naturalness of manner which frequent visits to sick-chambers give to the priest. Bert felt a pang of envy; he himself was so completely a fish out of water.

"I am grieved indeed to hear of the way you have been treated," said Mayne gently. "Poor girl! I wish you had gone away to Leitersdorp as I suggested."

"So do I," said Millie, under her breath.

"You thought yourself so secure," he went on regretfully, looking at her bandaged arm.

"Well, I'm paying for it," said the girl distinctly, "and got to go on doing that all the rest of my life, so I hear."

"Oh, I hope not! You will be all right in a few weeks," he assured her hopefully.

"Ah!" said she, "but he's got to be paid, you see, for what he did." She raised her uninjured arm and pointed to Bert, who turned scarlet as he stood awkwardly dandling his flowers. "Men don't help you for nothing; I've found out that much," she said, with biting intention.

"I am sure you do Mestaer injustice," said Mayne quietly. "No Englishman could possibly ask anything in return for the privilege of helping a woman."

"He says," said Millie, "that I promised to marry him the night he brought me here. I don't remember; but if I did, I got to do it, I s'pose."

"Certainly not!" was the emphatic reply. "Get rid of that idea. No man worthy of the name could hold you to a promise made under such circumstances. Besides, you are not free to marry for the next five years. Don't you want to go to England?"

The living blood flooded the white face with lovely colour; the eyes flashed fire.

"May I? Could I?" she gasped, half raising herself among her pillows, her face transformed with an energy, a desire for life, most strikingly at variance with her lethargy of a few minutes before. "Have they written? Do they want me?"

He drew a letter from his coat-pocket. "They have written, and they do want you," he said.

She sat quite up, unsupported. "Read it! Read it!"

Bert stood still as a stone, while Mayne unfolded a sheet of paper, written in a small, niggling, but cultivated hand, and read:

"FRANSDALE VICARAGE, CLEVESHIRE.

"Dear Sir,—I am in receipt of your letter, and note that my brother-in-law, Arnold Lutwyche, is dying, and leaving my niece, Melicent, only daughter of my late sister, wholly unprovided for. I also note that you consider her Boer step-mother is not a fit person to have the charge of her, and is likely to treat her ill.

"Under these circumstances, my duty seems clear, and my wife and I have no hesitation in directing you to send my niece to England by the earliest available boat, and we will give her a home for the present.

"At the same time, I must acquaint you with the fact that our means are small, and we have seven children of our own, so that Melicent will be under the necessity of making herself useful.

"Please send her by the cheapest line of boats, and notify me of her arrival. I fear that I shall not be able to come to London to meet her, but if she is fifteen or sixteen years old, she should be able to make her way to us as far as the railway will bring her—that is to say, to Birdmore Junction, where she shall be met.

"I note that my brother's estate will be sufficient to meet her travelling expenses, so conclude that no advance from me is necessary.

"With thanks to you for the trouble you take in the matter, and remembrances to Mr. Lutwyche, should this letter find him still alive.—I am, very faithfully yours,

"EDMUND CHETWYND-COOPER."

This letter had chilled Mayne by its formal coldness. No love was sent to the orphan, no message of welcome. But the frigidity of the style made apparently no difference to Millie. The great fact was there. Her way to England lay open, her destination fixed. Of all safe shelters, a remote English vicarage should have satisfied her guardian. But somehow, to Carol, the idea of Miss Lutwyche in such a situation, was not convincing. He could not see her in the part, as actors say.

No such doubts troubled her. For the very first time since Mayne had known her, her face beamed and sparkled with joy.

"I can be ready to travel soon," she cried. "In a fortnight—in ten days—ask the doctor!"

Bert made three strides across the room, hurling with violence the flowers he carried into the English grate.

"So you'll break your word," he began, and choked

Melicent turned her head towards him languidly.

"Bert Mestaer," said she, "have I ever once, since you knew me, said one word to make you think I liked you?"

He fought with himself for composure to enable him to bring out the monosyllable, "No."

"Then what d'you wanter marry me for?" she asked calmly.

"You know," he cried, terribly, wildly, in his frantic emotion. "You know I love you—you know I don't care for anything else, but just to have you! Where'd you be now, if it wasn't for me? Tell me that! I wish to God I'd never seen you! I'll—I'll kill you with my own hands before I'll let you go now! I'll do worse—I'll..."

He stopped himself suddenly, meeting the steady contempt of Mayne's eyes.

There was a moment of awful silence, broken only by two dry, tearing sobs from the furious lover; then Millie, who had turned chalk-white once more, fell back among her pillows with an impatient motion of the hand.

"Oh, get away; you make me sick," she said.

Before Bert could speak or move, Mayne went up to him, took him by the arm, and led him out of the room. Then, handing him his hat, he drew him as passively out of the house.

Neither spoke till they had walked half a mile. Mayne was half in fear that Bert, in his rage, might set upon him bodily, and congratulated himself, not for the first time in his missionary career, upon the possession of thews and sinews. But no ebullition came. Bert's face had gone grey, and he looked worn and shrunken in the strong sunlight.

At last, smitten by the despair in his altered manner, the elder man ventured to speak.

"Mestaer, you must come and put up at my place till Miss Lutwyche is well enough to travel. You did the best you could for her—you did well; but the strain is too great, and it must cease. I shall wire for one of the Sisters from Leitersdorp to come and help Anna to nurse her. As to you, you have to fight and win a man's hardest battle; and I'll give you a bit of advice—"

"Go to h— with your advice!"

"I'm not far away now, to judge by the sulphur in the atmosphere," retorted Mayne drily, and said no more.

They walked on until they came to the little Mission, and turned in to the sparsely-furnished living-room, with its crucifix and Albrecht Dürer *facsimiles*, and the Da Vinci Virgin on the rude mantel.

Bert walked across the room, planted both elbows on the shelf, and stared with blank eyes at the ineffable smile of the pictured face. Suddenly he wheeled round.

"Well, what's your blasted advice?" he said rudely. "A black-coated prig that doesn't know what it means to be..."

"Tempted," suggested Mayne drily. But he pushed a chair for his discourteous guest, and got down the tobacco-jar. "No man can fight the flesh and win, if he's living in idleness," he said reflectively, standing before the hearth and filling his pipe. "But there's another consideration. Do you realise that we are on the brink of war?"

"Kruger, perhaps."

"Steyn, too. You heard the news the other day? All the men ordered out on commando. What does that mean? The Orange Free State is going in against England."

"Well, they can fight their own blank battles without my help."

"That's rubbish, Mestaer. You'll have to fight on one side or the other. Now is the time to show yourself an Englishman. England wants men. They think at home that this war is to be a walk over. You and I know better. Go and enlist. There's a career for you."

"I'll be d—d if I do."

"That's a condition that seems to me far more likely to supervene if you don't," was the temperate reply.

Bert laid down his miserable head upon his arms.

"You don't see, and I can't explain," he said haltingly, "that it's not a thing—not a question of what you call the flesh. If there's such a thing as spirit anywhere in me, I've put it all in my love for her. If you take her away, I shall go to the devil."

"If I take her away! My dear chap, you cannot seriously mean to pretend that you think Millie wants to marry you?"

Sulky silence.

"I know you better than to believe you would be cad enough to marry her against her will. Were you to do so, I fail to see in what respect you would be any better than Otis."

No reply.

Mayne stood up, searching his book-shelves for the "Divina Commedia."

"Bert, did you ever hear of Dante?"

"No. Nobody as lives hereabouts, is he?"

Mayne did not smile.

"I'll tell you something of him—how all his life he lived for the memory of a dead woman—a woman of whom he knew even less than you know of Millie, and lived in hope, and cleanly, for her sake. Now, Millie is not dead. You are but a boy, and she a girl. Five or six or seven years hence, if you make a career for yourself what is to prevent you from trying again? By that time she would at least realise the enduring nature of your love; whereas now, neither you nor I nor she could say that it will last. It is just a boy's hot flame."

Bert stamped.

"You don't believe me capable of it," he stormed. "You just think that if you can get her out of my way now, that'll be the end of it all. You don't think I've the manhood or the pluck to stick to the thing through years of absence—"

He broke off, staring at the kindled face of the priest, who had risen, and stood facing him.

"That's just where you make your mistake, Bert," said his friend earnestly. "I do believe you capable of the best. Listen! When I came first to Slabbert's Poort, I found you a loafer. You were idle and good-for-nothing and intemperate. Now you have shown me what you are capable of. Your love for Millie has made you a different man. You have fought for her, saved her, respected her! ... I rather wish you had heard tell of one Caponsacchi; but never mind. It's better to do knightly deeds than to read about 'em. Anyhow, you have set your foot on the road to become a true gentleman; why turn back now? Hubert Mestaer"—his voice took on the deep note it sometimes had in the pulpit—"by the memory of your mother, I ask you, why turn back now?"

CHAPTER X
FRANSDALE

"Ankle-deep in English grass I leaped,
And clapped my hands, and called all very fair."

—ELIZABETH BARRETT BROWNING.

It was mid-October. St. Luke's summer brooded over the solitary acres of heather, which crowned the hills that flung encradling arms about Fransdale.

The golden bracken was turning brown, but the heather still carried its glory of purple. The woodlands were forsaking their devotion to pure green, and rioted in every hue of red and yellow, and the light air sang and hummed about the uplands of the glorious land. All the summer had been fine; the becks had sunk to musical murmurings; one might walk from Tod's Trush to the Three Howes, across country, without getting bogged.

In a stable-yard surrounded by grey stone out-buildings stood the Reverend Edmund Chetwynd-Cooper, harnessing his horse to the dog-cart. Near him a big, loose-limbed, clumsy girl, who had evidently outgrown her strength, stood listlessly watching him through half-shut eyes.

"How old is Cousin Melicent?" she asked, in a voice which always sounded fretful.

"I have told you I believe her to be about sixteen."

"Nearly as old as I am. I wonder whether we shall like her?"

"I hope you understood what I said at dinner-time. There is to be no intimacy until we have decided that Melicent is a fit companion for you. No intimacy, mind."

His voice was even and quiet, low-pitched and cultivated. He was a handsome, dark man, with regular features, and a cold, blue eye; clean shaven but for a straight line of black whisker down each cheek, which made him look vaguely out of date.

His daughter looked at him with a sidelong glance.

"All right, father," she said, in a kind of formula, adding, in an injured tone: "I should have thought you might take one of us to meet her."

"I do not know what luggage there may be."

Mr. Cooper would not have said, "I don't know," for the world; and the fact was typical of his extreme correctness.

"Where is your mother?" he asked, when the last strap was adjusted. "I promised her a lift as far as the Mill. Go, Madeline, and tell her I am ready."

The girl slouched away, with a bored expression; and the parson, having fetched the dust-rug and whip, walked the mare out of the yard and up to the door of the square, uncompromising grey stone Vicarage.

Nothing could have been finer than the prospect. The church and Vicarage stood near the head of the Dale, close to the bolder, wilder, more heathery part, and looked down on the valleyland, the trout stream and rich meadows below. The minutes ticked on, while the vicar waited. Presently Madeline emerged.

"Mother says she won't be long."

"Will you tell her please, that I positively must start in five minutes."

The girl disappeared. The five minutes elapsed; three more passed. The vicar got into the trap. Madeline once more appeared.

"Mother thinks, before she starts, she had better give Bee a dose of her tonic."

"Then tell her I am off without her. The train will not wait, even for your mother."

He was just going out of the gate, when a window-sash was raised, and a voice cried:

"Aidmund! Aidmund!"

He checked the horse.

"Well? Come if you are ready," he said, quite temperately, his voice showing no annoyance.

"Oh, no, I can't do that; but I thought it would be so capital if you could get me one or two things in Birdmore? I shan't be very long writing them down."

"You should have thought of that before."

"My darling boy, think how busy I have been all this morning, preparing—"

The rest was lost, for the vicar had driven away. His cold eyes were quite gentle, but he did draw in his breath sharply once; at the thought, perhaps, of this helpmeet of his, in this remote village, where nothing ever interrupted her simple routine of duties—incapable of being ready for a drive at three o'clock in the afternoon.

The old mare had to step out. Mrs. Cooper had succeeded in making her husband ten minutes late; and nine miles of very bad road lay between him and the Junction. The train which was to bring his niece was just coming to a standstill in the little wayside station, as the old mare, conscious of having been hustled, trotted into the station-yard.

The vicar hastened through the booking-office, out upon the asphalte platform, whereon a small, slender girl in black stood lonely beside some solid-looking packing-cases and one modest trunk. She wore her left arm in a sling. He came slowly forward, with a resolute smile of greeting on his face.

"Are you Melicent?"

She raised her eyes searchingly to his face. "Yes, I am."

"You are not at all like your mother," he said, scanning the pale face.

"No; father did not think me like her."

"You have managed your journey well?"

"Oh, yes, thank you, it was all quite easy."

"How did you manage last night in London?"

"I went home with some people who were kind to me on the voyage; Mr. and Mrs. Helston."

"I expected a taller niece," he said kindly.

"I am small for my age, I know."

His anxious gaze was fixed upon the packing-cases. There were three of them, and their bulk suggested weight.

"Do those cases belong to you?" he asked.

"Yes; my father's books and valuables. He left them all to me, and my guardian insisted that Mrs. Lutwyche should give them up."

"Well, I don't quite know how they are going to be conveyed up the Dale," he said, in perplexity.

"Oh, that's all right," said Millie, with *sang-froid*. "Mr. Dow is going to take them in his waggon."

"Mr. Dow!" ejaculated the vicar, in a tone compounded of equal parts of astonishment and displeasure.

A big Cleveshire Dalesman, of the more prosperous type—handsome, well-dressed, a striking figure in his riding breeches and gaiters, now approached, lifting his cap from his fair hair, his eyes twinkling with a kind of enjoyment which he peculiarly relished.

"Your niece and me has been getting acquainted," he said, in his unrenderable soft-vowelled Dale speech. "Makin' friends, as you may say." It sounded more like: "Mäakin' freänds, as you mäay säa." But the phonetic rendering of dialect is a weariness, and will not here be attempted. "Fair enjoyin' werselves we've been, ever since leavin' York Station. I'm goin' to take her goods up t' Dale for her, since I expect you've only t' old mare an' t' cart with you, Mr. Cooper."

Mr. Cooper could barely acknowledge the kindness, for angry mortification. He was a Southerner, planted down among people whom he disliked, because he did not in the least understand them. His idea of the peasant's correct attitude was a servile obedience to the parson, and that kind of gratitude which is rightly said to consist of a lively sense of favours to come. The sturdy independence, and I'm-as-good-as-you indifference of the North Country, was a positive offence to him, his only armour against it being a crust of ever increasing cold dignity and aloofness, which the Dalesmen saw, and chuckled over. His wife, who had come among them, ready with the ministrations which she understood—with condescending smiles, ill-made soup, old clothes and patronage—found no market for these commodities. A premature exhibition of them had produced such a condition of feeling, that now, as she came down the road, full of amiable intentions, the village became a desert, everyone slipping within doors and disappearing, sooner than encounter her.

Moreover, the Dale was full of nonconformity; and the attitude of the vicar towards dissent was that of silent, rigid dislike—of his wife, that kind of shocked horror with which some people talk of "the heathen."

So the Chetwynd-Coopers dwelt as aliens in their Northern parish, attributing their failure solely to causes exterior to themselves, and resolutely setting the advantages of fine moorland air, and the low price of provisions, against the vague depression which their isolation naturally caused.

But, among all the thorns in the vicar's dignified flesh, Farmer Dow, of Crow Gate Farm, the leading Dissenter in the Dale, was the sharpest. Poor Millie could not have made a more unfortunate entry upon the scenes, than under his auspices. The ice in the vicar's voice, as he declined his kindness, was obvious to the bystanders. But Dow was not to be denied. He had promised Millie that her goods should be taken up, and taken up they should be, that very night. She had taught him more about South Africa in half-an-hour than the newspapers had taught him in half a year. She was coming to tea with his mother, at Crow Gate, and going to keep him posted in the war news. He owed it to her to see after her baggage, after such entertainment. He helped her into the trap with such *empressement* that the onlookers were deeply moved; and the vicar's heart was hot within him as he drove away. His niece was, as he had feared, hopelessly Colonial.

But it was not the vicar's habit to speak in anger. Experience had given him a power of self-control which would have kindled the admiration of his parishioners, had they guessed what manner of man lay hidden under the dry, precise manner.

He waited until he had himself well in hand, and then commenced conversation—not upon the burning topic.

"I am sorry to see that you have hurt your arm."

Millie, whose eyes were fixed in deep, increasing interest on the country they were passing through, looked up.

"It was the old woman," she said. "I thought Mr. Mayne might have told you. She sjambokked me pretty nearly to death, and threw me down and dislocated my arm."

The clear, soft voice, evenly cadenced, giving out this astonishing information, raised fresh tumult in the vicar's bosom.

"Do you mean your step-mother?" he asked, in horror.

"Yes. Mr. Mayne had to go to Leitersdorp to get the will proved. He was away three days, and she made up her mind to take it out on me."

"To take what out?"

"She was mad because father made him my guardian. She wanted to sell me to a Yankee; he'd given her ten pounds on account. So Mr. Mayne told her it was a case of hands off, because it was his show. So she got the children to catch and hold me, and they managed to tie me up; and she just went on until she was tired," said Millie unemotionally.

The vicar had no words. Uppermost in his mind was deep, abiding thankfulness that he had brought none of his daughters with him to meet this astounding young person. What would his wife say to this? Such people, they knew, existed in the pages of those sensational novels which cannot be too severely condemned by the well-regulated; but that his own sister's child should have been strung up and thrashed! ... The current of hot sympathy in him must have found vent in indignant words; but it was invaded by another thought. The carefully guarded propriety of his own children must suffer no contact with naked facts of life like this; and such was the feeling that spoke first.

"I must ask you not to mention this. I should say, I must order you not to tell your cousins, or Miss Lathom, their governess, how you came by your injuries. To your aunt, in private, it may be alluded to, but I cannot have so scandalous a thing generally known."

Millie looked up swiftly.

"I can keep a thing dark, if I am given the tip," she said, with amusement that sounded a little contemptuous.

He was conscious of great annoyance.

"I give no tips. I merely say that this must not be mentioned," he said frigidly. "We will refer to it later. And now to touch upon another matter. In England the—ah—fusion of classes to which you have probably been accustomed is not desirable. The vicar's niece cannot, with propriety, be on terms of equality with a farmer like Dow."

"Oh," said Millie, "why not?"

"We are socially Mr. Dow's superiors, and we must not let him forget his place, as these Dalesmen are most apt to do."

"I should have thought," said Millie reflectively, "that they would never be likely to forget their place, so long as we were sure of ours."

The vicar again felt uncomfortable. His wife and he were well-born—people of just enough consequence to be eager that nobody should forget it; undeniably belonging to the county set, but much ignored by that set, as being poor and desperately dull.

"You see, at home we shouldn't have been socially superior to Mr. Dow," said Millie.

"You have much to learn here," returned her uncle; and as he spoke, he was inly deciding that the girl was impossible.

CHAPTER XI
MELICENT'S COUSINS

"Girls' heads are not like jam-pots, which, if you do not fill them will remain empty; a filling there will be, of some kind." —JULIANA HORATIA EWING.

They had been crawling for some time slowly up a steep lane with hedges; now suddenly they emerged at the top, and a long sigh of wonder escaped Millie as she saw the moorland spread before her in all its untamed splendour. Great headlands, facing northwards, jutted forth into the heather, as into a purple sea; and on the brink of one of these the travellers found themselves, overlooking a vast stretch of wild country. The descent down which they must go was almost a precipice. Something in the keen racing air, the height, the freedom, the glory of it all, took Melicent by the throat England was like this—like this! Sunlight, colour, the adorable odour of peat and bracken, drawn out by the sun, the blue mysteries of distance ... it came about her like compelling arms. Solitude, silence, spacious calm—here were elements that appealed to the depth of her being. Reserved as she was, she had nearly cried aloud to her unknown uncle for sympathy in her sudden rush of feeling for the land of her forefathers. He had checked the mare to a walk, and was coaxing her downhill with caution and skill.

"Our roads are not much to boast of hereabouts," he said at last, as the cart slewed itself over a lump in the road, designed to prevent heavy rainfall from washing out the roadway on the violent slope. "But I daresay you are not much better off in Africa."

"Not much to boast of! They are glorious!" breathed Millie, insensible of jolting in her admiration. "We have nothing like this in Africa!"

"A few miles further on, I can show you a road, compared with which, this might be a billiard-table," he said cheerfully.

Millie became aware that he referred to surface and gradients, and not to landscape.

"Oh, I see," she replied lamely. "I was thinking of—of the heather."

"You will see plenty of that," was the composed answer. "It begins to grow all over the road, at no great distance from here."

Conversation did not seem easy. Millie was at no time talkative, and they fell silent, and so remained while they traversed several miles of open moor, crossed a desolate ridge, and presently found themselves dipping again into a lane with hedges, in all their autumn glory of ripe blackberries, fluffy travellers' joy, coral honeysuckle berries and wayfaring tree.

"Now we are in Fransdale," said Mr. Cooper.

They were labouring along, in narrow, sandy, toilsome windings, when the hoot of a motor, up somewhere over their heads, made Mr. Cooper start. He was leading the mare, and proceeded to drag her as far as he possibly could to the side of the lane—half-way up the hedge, in fact. The next moment the car came in sight, tearing downhill at a speed which was evidently calculated upon the certainty of clear roads. It began to bray loudly, as though, in response to the warning, the vicar could cause his dog-cart to vanish into thin air. Millie surveyed it with interest, and as it whizzed by, within an inch of their off-wheel, she caught sight of a young, handsome, bored face, and that of an older man beside it. They raised their hats as they swept by, having most narrowly missed smashing the cart to fragments: but the vicar seemed quite pleased, and not at all annoyed.

"Sir Joseph Burmester and his son—our big land-owners hereabouts," he explained.

"Oh!" said his niece; adding, after reflection: "Are they our social equals?"

For some reason, the question annoyed the vicar; he relapsed into silence.

Mrs. Cooper prided herself upon keeping all her Southern customs up here in the North. When Melicent came downstairs to tea, she saw none of that wonderful pastry without which no Cleveshire tea-table is complete. Her five girl-cousins and their governess were assembled to be introduced to their new relative. They stared at her with a passive and stony indifference. Madeline was seventeen, Gwendolen sixteen, Theodora fifteen, Barbara fourteen, and Beatrice twelve. Even Beatrice was quite as tall as Melicent; and the elder girls were vast, the two eldest nearing five-foot-ten, after the fashion of the modern girl, and not in the least as yet knowing how to manage their swelling proportions. In their outgrown, scanty frocks, and big, thick legs, they looked rather like men in a farce, dressed up to represent little girls. Two or three of them were handsome, but they all struck Millie as singularly expressionless. Their faces were like masks.

Mrs. Chetwynd-Cooper's hair was pale flaxen, and being brushed away very tightly from the face, gave the impression of her having no hair at all. The odd look of being out of date, achieved in her husband's case by side-whiskers, was bestowed upon her by long earrings. The couple looked like the Papa and Mamma of a virtuous family, in a very early Victorian story-book.

Mrs. Cooper sat down to table with a determined cheerfulness which Melicent soon learned was her characteristic. It somehow succeeded in producing deep depression in others. At least, nobody spoke; and the girl found herself with her attention fixed, with a fatal fascination, upon her aunt's smile and her aunt's earrings, and longing for something to divert her eye.

Her uncle's depression was a very real and well-defined thing that evening. There was something about his new niece which he found himself disliking with quite unchristian vehemence. He had confided to his wife that extreme care would be necessary, and that the new-comer must by no means be let loose among their own children. Mrs. Cooper could not share his depression. She had the boundless self-confidence of an entirely stupid woman. She had made her own girls models of all that girls should be. No slang was ever heard in the Vicarage; no loud voices; no unruly expression of opinion. Why should she not be equally successful with this raw material, doubtless sent by Providence to her good guidance?

Melicent sat watching her five munching cousins, and thought they were something like cows. Their eyes were vacant, their appetites steady. She was just wondering whether all talking at meals was forbidden, when Gwendolen, who sat next her, tossed back her long hair, and asked:

"How did you hurt your arm?"

Melicent's voice was soft, but singularly clear. It had a carrying quality.

"Uncle Edmund says I am not to tell you," she replied.

Mr. Cooper was all the more angry, because he felt sure that his niece could and would have skated ably over this thin ice had he not repudiated all wish to "keep things dark." She had done exactly what he told her to do, and he wanted to box her ears.

"Give us news of your Cochin China hen, Gwendolen," he broke in. "Has she been laying away again?"

"Yes, in the hedge," said his daughter, giving her reply in lifeless tone and fewest words; and silence fell again.

"Oh, by the way, I have a pleasant surprise for Melicent," said Mrs. Cooper suddenly, her countenance wreathed in smiles. She always spoke as though coaxing a very young child, who needed encouragement and reassurance; and her niece resented it as actively as did the villagers. "What do you think arrived for you this morning, Melicent? Theo, darling, if you look on mother's desk, you will find a letter for Cousin Melicent. I suppose the mail travels faster than the boat you came in, Melicent."

Theo brought a letter and handed it to her cousin, who took it with composure.

"I wonder whom that comes from?" said Mrs. Cooper archly.

"It's from Hubert Mestaer."

"And who is that?" pursued the lady, delighted that everybody's attention was so skilfully diverted from the broken arm.

"He is one of the men who wanted to marry me," said Millie clearly.

In the deadly pause that followed, she caught a glance, hastily passing under lowered lids, between Miss Lathom and her two elder pupils.

But the valiant Mrs. Cooper was equal even to this occasion.

"When dear Melicent has been with us a little longer, she will know that we do not talk of such things," she cooed, blushing as coyly as the heroine in a novel by Charles Reade.

The blush was not to be seen reflected on the stolid countenances of her daughters. They chewed on.

"What things?" asked Millie, bewildered.

"Our offers of—marriage," said her aunt, bringing out the bold word with a gulp. "You are a little young, darling, to be thinking of marriage for a great many years, are you not?"

"Yes; that is what I told them," replied Millie simply, fixing surprised eyes upon the lady's embarrassment.

The vicar cleared his throat.

"Perhaps you had better give that letter to your aunt, Melicent, and let her judge whether it is a fit one for you to receive."

Melicent removed her look of surprise from one end of the table to another.

"I think it would be playing it very low down on Bert to let anybody see his letter," she said, with decision.

"My girls show me all their letters," said her aunt, still smiling and coaxing.

"I beg your pardon if it sounds rude," replied her niece, "but I shall not show you mine."

The vicar rose from table with decision.

"We will discuss this at another time," he said. "Melicent will, of course, conform to the rules of the house while she is with us. For what we have received, etc. A word, Miss Lathom, please." Then, as the girls filed past, he said low in the governess's ear: "On no account is she to be left alone with her cousins for a moment."

The girls filed soberly out, led the way upstairs, through a swing-door, along a passage, into a shabby old room with deep window-seats, an aged rocking-horse, shelves of story books and disabled toys, an ink-stained, battered table, a high fire-guard, and all the usual accessories of the nursery turned schoolroom.

They fastened the swing-door behind them as they went through, carefully closing the door of the school-room also; and then all, as it were, exhaling a gasp of relief, turned to their cousin again with transfigured faces.

"Now we can talk! Now we can be ourselves! Now we can have some fun!" they cried, surrounding her.

The masks were dropped, the real girls appeared, tossing back their hair, stretching their limbs, assuming every possible attitude of comfort and inelegance. They all talked at once, crowding round; and the transition was so abrupt and so complete as to bewilder her.

"One moment," said Gwendolen, who was the handsomest, and seemed to take the lead, rather than the petulant and anæmic-looking Madeline. "Be cautious, girls! we may very likely be raided this evening; she's sure to poke her nose in after Melicent. Put out the things. Did you hoist the weight, Babs?"

"Yes, I did," said Barbara.

"That's all right. If you hear the weight fall in the passage, that's mother," said Madeline, explaining to Melicent: "You see, it gives us a minute to reform in."

They all went to a cupboard, pulled out work, thimbles, and so on, arranged them on the table, chairs in place; then threw themselves on the floor, in the various attitudes which their weak, overgrown spines demanded, with pillows wedged under them.

"Now for peace and happiness," said Gwen. "Oh, it was grand to hear you stand up to them, my dear! But it's no good, you know; you will have to knuckle under. They've got nothing else to do but bully us; and after all, it's not much they can do, you know. It's as easy as possible to circumvent them."

"Oh, hold your tongue, Gwen! don't chatter so," said Madeline crossly. "Give Melicent a chance. Go on, Melicent, tell us all about it. How was your arm hurt?"

Melicent looked surprised. "I told you I promised Uncle Edmund not to say," she replied.

"Oh, gammon! we absolve you from that," laughed Theo, slipping a warm arm about her cousin's neck.

"But I can't absolve myself, you see," said Millie soberly.

"Do you mean to say you won't tell us?"

"I never break my word."

Gwendolen laughed.

"We're five against one, and the youngest is as big as you," she said, half in fun, half menacing.

Millie smiled her own little smile of disdain.

"I'm more than a match for the lot of you," she said coolly. "I shall say just what I think to you, as I did to Aunt Minna. And it's this. I hate underhand ways."

Miss Lathom, who was seemingly poring over the correction of some exercises, grew uncomfortably red.

"We're not underhand," said Gwen hotly. "'Tommy'"—indicating her preceptress with a wave of the hand—"knows all about our goings on."

"Tommy" looked up nervously.

"When you have lived here a little while, Miss Lutwyche," she said, "you will see that the poor girls must have some indulgences. Their mother expects impossibilities."

"Well, why do they stand it?" asked Millie.

"We don't stand it," returned Maddie. "But you had better all shut up, girls; perhaps Melicent's a tell-tale."

"If you had any sense, you'd see that I've just proved that I'm not," remarked Melicent.

"How have you proved it?"

"If I keep my word to Uncle Edmund, of course I shall keep my word to you. I promise not to tell tales; and, when I promise, you can go away and bet on it."

The universal squeal of merriment at her funny phrase restored harmony.

"Of course," said Gwen, "I see that it's best to be straightforward; but we're not allowed to be. We simply have to make our own pleasures, unknown to them. We should never read a book, nor get a letter, nor meet a soul, nor do anything but get up, have meals, do lessons, go to bed. Mother won't let us read a book she hasn't read first; and as she never opens a book herself from year's end to year's end, there is an end of that. We mustn't have a letter unless she sees it; so of course we have to have our letters sent, addressed to Tommy, to Bensdale Post Office; and then there's the adventure of walking over to fetch them. You mayn't go out without saying where you've been, nor spend a halfpenny without telling her what you bought. She must really expect us to cheat, you know; and so we do."

"Maddie's going on for eighteen, and Gwen only a year younger," chimed in Theo, "and they're not supposed even to know what a young man is, let alone think about one. Gwen's awfully gone on Freshfield, who is Sir Joseph Burmester's agent. Well, if it was guessed, I don't know what would happen, for you see Freshfield is not our social equal—"

"My dears," broke in Miss Lathom, who was on thorns, "I think all this is very imprudent. Let your cousin wait a while, and see how she likes her aunt's system."

"I shall dislike it very much," said Melicent; "but I shall say so. Why don't you speak out?"

"Because we're dead sick of rows," said Maddie sulkily. "There were nothing but rows till Tommy came. No governess would stay; they simply couldn't stand mother. Then at last Tommy turned up, and we saw what a decent old sort she was, so we thought out our plans, and now we do get our fun somehow, and as long as we hold our tongues at meals, it's all right."

"Well, I'm very sorry for you," said Millie, "but I think it would be much simpler to say what you mean. The strongest always wins. If you stuck together, they would have to give in."

The girls laughed sardonically. "You don't know mother," they said.

"Well, we shall soon see," said Barbie, who was the silent one of the five. "Let Millie try her way, and see what happens."

Millie laughed. "I certainly shan't try yours," she said.

"But you won't side against us with mother?" suddenly said Gwen.

"Rather not. That isn't my way."

"Are you never afraid of anybody?" asked Theo earnestly.

"Of course not; what can people do?" contemptuously asked the girl who had been sjambokked.

Theo cuddled up against this new champion as if the sense of strength were pleasant to her.

"Show us your love-letter, won't you, darling?" she said persuasively.

"Certainly not," replied Millie at once.

"Then I won't show you my notes from Freshfield," said Gwen.

"Of course not. It's mean to show men's letters."

"We shouldn't do such a thing, except just among ourselves," replied Maddie indignantly; "and we hoped you'd be one of us, though goodness knows there's more than enough of us already."

"Look here," said Gwen eagerly, "we know you must be the real kind of natural girl—not the sort like mother believes in, Ethel May in the Daisy Chain, you know—we know you are not that sort, or you would not be having lovers to write to you all the way from Africa. You do like pretty clothes, and dancing, and young men—"

"No, I don't," said Millie, in her decided way. "I've had enough of young men to last me a good while. I want to see no more young men for years to come. I only want one thing really badly"—she looked almost pleadingly at Tommy's red, snub-nosed countenance, as if her sole hope lay there—"I want to learn!" cried out the girl who was to corrupt the Vicarage household.

"To learn!" The words were echoed in six different tones.

"Not *lessons*?" asked Babs incredulously.

"Everything," replied Millie, resting her pointed chin on her small hand. "I want to know things, and understand them, and find out how to earn my living; to do something ... or make something ... I don't know what, as yet. I want to get a grip on the world, and watch for my place there, and take it!"

There was complete silence for quite a long time. At last—

"You talk as if you were a boy," said Gwen. "What can girls do?"

"Everybody can do what they must do," quietly replied Millie. "I've got to earn my living, and so have you, I suppose."

"Earn our living! Mother would have a fit!" cried Maddie.

"But Uncle Edmund said in his letter that he was poor," said Millie, puzzled. "What should you do if he died?"

"Get married, if we could," laughed Theo. "Willie and Georgie say we're such frights, we never shall. But we think Gwen is good-looking, and you see she's got a lover already; and she says when she's married she'll see after all of us—take us out of this hateful old Dale, and go to live at Brighton or London or some place where we could make friends. Nobody will make friends here, because mother's such an old stick-in-the-mud—"

The filial sentiment died away, for there was the sound of a soft thud.

"The weight, girls! Mother!" whispered Bee; and in a moment, with a dexterity born of long practice, the whole flock of lounging girls had arisen, slipped into place, and were busily stitching when Mrs. Cooper, with her smile, her long neck, and her earrings, peeped archly round the door.

"Making friends?" said she, beaming.

"Yes, Mrs. Cooper," said Tommy, looking up.

The governess was feeling decidedly uncomfortable. She had repeatedly warned her pupils, during the preceding days, to hold aloof at first from the new-comer, until they had decided whether she could be taken into confidence. But Millie's love-letter, and still more, her calm refusal to show it, had sent the barriers down with a rush, and the girls had not been able to think of prudence with such a keen new interest in their blank lives. Tommy's heart was full of apprehension. She was afraid of this girl who wanted to learn. She knew that she had nothing to teach her.

Melicent had not moved a muscle when the general rush was made. She sat still in the window-seat, upright and solitary.

"Dear Melicent must join our happy little sewing circle," said Mrs. Cooper, beaming round. "No idle hands at the Vicarage, as you see, darling."

"I cannot use my arm very well yet," said Melicent.

"Oh, we give you one evening's grace," responded the lady playfully. "Have you been taught to work?"

"No."

"Oh, how sad! Why, Miss Lathom, we have a task before us! Can you not use a needle at all?"

"Oh, yes. I can make and mend my clothes, and so on. But I had to teach myself."

There was a silence. "You don't mean that you made the suit you have on?"

"Yes."

"Oh," said Mrs. Cooper. The wind was taken out of her sails. "Why, you are quite a *genius*! We shall have to take *lessons*. But now, I came to ask you to come with me, and I will show you your room, and we will have a little talk."

Millie rose obediently, and followed her aunt from the room; as they went, the masks dropped, the girls lifted their heads and looked at each other with intense interest.

"She's going to make her show the letter."

CHAPTER XII
THE JARRING ELEMENT

> "She was one of that numerous class of females, whose society can raise no other emotion than surprise at there being any men in the world who could like them well enough to marry them."—JANE AUSTEN.

The first idea suggested by Mrs. Cooper to the mind of the beholder was almost inevitably the above. How could any man ever have liked her well enough to marry her?

Mr. Chetwynd-Cooper was among those unfortunates who are sent into the world without a sense of humour. He thus fell a victim to the same error of judgment which poor well-meaning King George the Third had committed before him: that of mistaking a dull, pretentious prig for a really good woman. Perhaps no queen in history, of whatever moral character, ever made a greater fiasco as the bringer-up of a large family than did Charlotte of Mecklenburg-Strelitz. But in this respect Mrs. Cooper vied with her, and for the same reason. Each was so secure in her own belief in herself as possessed of all the domestic virtues, that to her the possibility of making a mistake never presented itself.

Such women are beyond the reach of argument. Mrs. Cooper had decided, quite early in life—on what grounds is not known—that to be such a woman as she was, ought to be the goal of all female endeavour. Hence, nothing could shake the complacency of her own content. She never tired of the pose of the perfect wife and mother, the parochial guardian angel; and this, although her nursery had been the epitome of untidiness and mismanagement, and her husband was obliged to keep her accounts, and in other ways to step into the breach continually to supply her glaring deficiencies. Neither was she discomposed by the fact that all her own children had found her out at an early age. If her husband ever broke through his habitual reserve, and remonstrated with her, she met him with the patient smile of the saint who is misunderstood.

Very soon after marriage he had found out the iron hand beneath her velvet glove. He had discovered that his own influence was nil, that argument could not move her, that opposition merely stiffened her smiling obstinacy. He had sunk into that life which is the most terrible form of solitude: complete isolation from those nearest to him. The worst of it was that, though he had no effect upon his wife, she had a gradual and insidious effect upon him. Continual contact with a dwarfed intelligence was causing inevitable deterioration, of which he was not aware.

Had the dalesmen known his daily martyrdom, he might have gained them; but his pride and his loyalty pushed him back behind barred doors. And what nobody yet had ever divined, this new niece of his knew before she had been twenty-four hours under his roof.

It made him hate her. The first time her grave, tranquil eyes rested upon her aunt, he felt that she understood and despised her. Then that same limpid gaze—direct, keen, pure—travelled to him, the man who was the life-companion of such a woman. He could feel her thought probing him, wondering at him, pitying him. He had not at first thought her like his sister, the dead Melicent to whom he had been sincerely attached. But when he encountered that wonderful glance, he saw the likeness so strongly that he afterwards never forgot it—was never able to look at the younger Melicent without thinking of her more beautiful, radiant mother, who had followed the man she loved into the wilderness.

But the very likeness embittered him. He had always nursed a grudge against his wilful sister—a half-contemptuous grudge, as against one who had stepped outside the pale of conventions held so sacred by his own wife. Was her young daughter to come from the wilds to sit in judgment upon this exemplary pair, who found the straitest paths of domestic dulness wide enough for them to walk in? He almost wished that Melicent would do something that should justify him in his dislike of her.

He was brooding over it alone in his study, where he wrote with much care his cold, dry, unreal sermons, when his wife's head appeared round the door, with her usual coy smile.

"*Quite* unsuccessful, my darling boy," she said. "She defies me openly; and yet I flatter myself I was *most* diplomatic."

Like many essentially cold-hearted people, Mrs. Cooper was prodigal of endearing epithets. Her husband, on principle, never used any.

"A direct command would, I imagine, have met the case better than diplomacy," he said, in his cold, collected tones. "What did she say? Was she rude?"

"Well, not exactly. She said it would be a breach of confidence to show her letter, but that she would see that the young man wrote no more. She also said that she insists upon her right to correspond with her guardian without the letters being overlooked. Rather a *shocking* way to talk to me, wasn't it? But we must be very forgiving at first, I see that, and make very big *allowances* for the poor darling! The guardian himself seems to be quite young, and unmarried. Why did not poor Arnold appoint you guardian? As it is, she evidently thinks we have no authority."

He sat, with a mind oddly divided between dislike for the girl who defied him, and a sneaking satisfaction that Minna had been routed for once—by his sister's child!

"However," said his wife, secure as ever in her own infallibility, "we shall manage her all right in the end. The example of our girls will be *invaluable*. It is best to put the matter aside for the present, and let her settle down."

"Will she settle down, do you think?" asked the vicar.

There was a tolerant, complacent smile. "My darling boy, I have trained five, and why not a sixth?"

The vicar did not contradict her; he merely asked:

"Did she tell you what her letter contained?"

"She said she had not opened it yet, which I fear must have been a—a—*tarradidle*"—Mrs. Cooper went, through certain evolutions of lips and eyes, intended as a mute apology for her use of a word so shocking—"but she said she felt sure it was only to say that, if she is not happy here, the writer had a home waiting for her."

"Preposterous nonsense! She is a child, and the man probably a savage," said the vicar, with some bitterness. "Picture Maddie or Gwen receiving a note of the kind!"

But when Millie did open Bert's letter, the contents were of a wholly different nature from what she had expected.

It merely contained a brief announcement of the fact that he had enlisted in that regiment of scouts which later was known to fame as Lacy's Lions.

In the schoolroom, the knowledge that Melicent had stood firm communicated an electrical excitement to the atmosphere. The idea of possible revolt opened prospects of which nobody had as yet dared to think. Unconsciously to themselves, her cousins already regarded her as a strike-leader—a Moses who should lead them out of the house of bondage.

And yet no creature could have been less anxious for revolt than this girl. Her one desire was to fall upon knowledge and devour it. She was ready to become the slave of anyone who would teach her.

But one day in the schoolroom was enough to quench hope from that quarter. The education bestowed on her by her father had been partial; but what she knew, she knew thoroughly. Her Latin and arithmetic and Euclid were all good; her knowledge of geography and English history made Tommy feel quite faint. Of French and German she was wholly ignorant, and could not pick out the notes on the piano.

But in all respects she knew enough to know that Tommy knew nothing. All the morning the governess was experiencing the annoyance which Mr. Cooper had known, feeling the clear eyes upon her full of judgment.

The leading point in the education of Mr. Cooper's girls was that they should have no judgment. They were always to be content to accept what they were told. When they came in contact with actual life, their only standard would be that such and such a thing was according to, or differed from, what they were used to.

"I am a great believer in the power of habit," the vicar was wont to say. Poor soul! Habit had moulded him with a vengeance; he might be excused for thinking highly of its powers over the human intelligence.

Melicent was a problem to her cousins. They were fascinated by her, as the weak must always be by the strong; but they resented her aloofness. And they were simply bewildered by her tastes.

Tommy was—*sub rosâ*, of course—reading aloud to them a thrilling serial from the *Daily Looking-glass*. It was called "Phyllis and the Duke," and was a story of the pure love of that gallant nobleman, the Duke of Mendip, for his sister's governess, the lovely Phyllis de Forester; of the machinations of his envious cousin, Captain the Honourable Percy Blagdon; and of how Phyllis turned out to be the unacknowledged daughter of an Earl, and the true owner of the Honourable Percy's estates. They had reached a thrilling chapter, in which the trembling young governess went to interview a clairvoyante, in a mystic kind of house in St. John's Wood, to ascertain what had become of her chivalrous lover. Tommy was uneasy when the story took this turn. She did not like the sound of a mysterious house in St. John's Wood, and began to reflect, with resentment, that nowadays you could not trust even the *feuilleton* of a halfpenny journal to be wholly inoffensive. But the writer was perfectly equal to the occasion, and knew his public to a nicety—or might we say, to a nastiness? The clairvoyante turned out to be Phyllis's deeply injured mamma, a young lady who would on no account have gone without the indispensable marriage ceremony; and the gentleman who exploited her, and "ran" the mysterious house, was her own brother, Phyllis's uncle, who long had sought his beloved niece in vain.

"I can't think why you don't like it," sighed Gwen, whose eyes were kindled, her cheeks aglow.

"It is so unreal and so silly," said her cousin calmly. "People don't go on like that. I like a story that makes you forget that it's not true."

"Such as what?" they asked her.

After reflection—"Such as 'Silas Marner,'" she said.

They had never heard of "Silas Marner."

The glorious autumn weather continued, and two or three days after Millie's arrival they took her for a long walk, out of the Dale, along Radlem Rigg, to look at the curious old prehistoric relic locally known as Tod's Trush.

The loveliness of her surroundings was again borne in upon Millie. The same up-soaring of spirit which she had experienced when her uncle drove her from the station once more exhilarated her. She could not analyse what it was that she found so different here from the land of her birth. She came from a country of clear air and vast spaces, of solitude and immeasurable distance. These dales were small in comparison with the endless rippling veldt she knew. But here there confronted her an element which she was quick to feel, though as yet too young to define—the element of mystery.

Strange it is that a few atmospheric effects should have power to lift the soul into new realms, into the brooding heart of a tender, tinted secret, which haunts the uplands and the valleys of Cleveshire, making a promised land of every peak that emerges, suggestive, from its golden, shimmering veil. The primal truth which underlay the power of the Veiled Isis was here; but in the North the magic is stronger, because to its mystery it adds the crowning note of austerity.

There is a loneliness which is the result, not of distance, but of inaccessibility. The dwellers in two valleys, perhaps five miles apart, divided by a high mountain, a dangerous pass, are separated far more thoroughly than those who dwell with fifty miles of plain between them, which the train will traverse in an hour. These dales give the impression of something remote, inviolable—something stern and shy, yet with a heart of glowing colour, of infinite tenderness, for those who can understand.

The Trush itself, when they reached it, was an old barrow, or tumulus, the earth covering of which had been entirely removed centuries ago. It was a square kist of stones, the top of which had fallen in. The coffin, or coffins, which it must once have contained, had vanished so long ago that a persistent local tradition maintained that there had never been any; but that the little house had been the abode of a being of supernatural origin, called Tod, concerning whom antiquarians cudgelled their brains in vain. Two upright slabs still stood like the jambs of a tiny doorway, with a lintel across; the whole surrounded by a circular wreath of large stones, which probably defined the original size of the mound.

To Melicent, who had never seen anything of the kind before, the vacant and lonely sepulchre was fraught with great pathos. Her thoughts took wing, and wandered to the times when human hands had erected this monument, and wondered whether it then stood in such unbroken solitude as it did now.

They had brought cakes with them, and a bottle of milk, and they all sat down among the heather and harebells, and refreshed themselves, while Tommy read a fresh instalment of "Phyllis and the Duke."

CHAPTER XIII
LANCE BURMESTER IS CONSCIOUS OF A PERSONALITY

"Our acts our angels are, or good or ill,
Our fatal shadows that walk by us still."

—FLETCHER.

Nothing compelled Melicent to listen, so she sat on Tod's Trush, just over his pathetic little doorway, her arms round her knees, her eyes fixed, full of the forward-reaching, time-devouring dreams of youth, upon the lovely lines of the land, ridge beyond ridge, dying into grape-bloom haze upon the faint horizon.

She was not unhappy. Her isolation hardly distressed her; she was accustomed to being an alien among unsympathetic people. She was, however, considering what she should do. She actively disliked her aunt, was repelled by her uncle, mentally herded her cousins and their governess together as so many silly triflers, not particularly honest. But all this she could bear, if only she might learn to fit herself for her future; and this, it appeared, was impossible.

If only it had not been so! For here she felt that she could live and work. Soul and body were being laved in pure air—renewed and vivified. The terrible sense of antagonism to all her surroundings which she had always felt in Africa was gone. There she had been craving, craving all the time for she knew not what; her cry had been that of Paracelsus—"I go to find my soul!" It seemed to her that she had found it, or would find it, in the stern keeping of this rugged land, where the only thing that was out of harmony was the attitude of her own kindred.

Just opposite to her, among the broken ground which rose from the main valley, forming a ridge parallel to that on which she sat, was a little house, embowered in fruit trees.

An ampylopsis creeper on the grey stone wall gave a touch of vivid scarlet; a great purple Jackmanii clematis smothered the porch.

"There," thought Melicent, "I could wish to be. There I could live and learn things, and the days would never seem too long."

She studied the little remote place, trying to see whether any road led to it, and admiring the way in which it stood, as if lifting its face to the kisses of the southern and western sun.

Lost in reverie, she had not heard the approach of anyone, and was surprised when a dog jumped through the heather near her, on the side of the Trush farthest from where her cousins were seated. A whirring of strong brown wings arose from their covert, and a grouse family shot up, with indignant "*Cock-cocks*," wheeling in the blue air. Three guns cracked, and in a moment the five Vicarage girls were on their feet.

As three sportsmen appeared, Gwen made one bound to where Millie sat, her face aflame.

"It's Freshfield," she gasped in her ear, "and young Mr. Burmester, and somebody I don't know. Oh, I wish he was alone! He won't dare to speak to us. Look at his nice curly dark hair! Isn't he scrumptious?"

The young agent, with an expression of acute discomfort, had raised his hat to the phalanx of great girls. Mr. Burmester was looking bewildered at the sudden appearance of what looked like a boarding-school out for a walk emerging from the heather. He also pulled off his cap, and said, in the deprecating tones of a very young man:

"Oh, I say! I'm afraid we startled you." With which he made as though to pass on.

Millie had not moved from her seat on the Trush; it was not her way to be startled. She had taken off her hat, and sat there bare-headed in the sunset, her heart full of quiet, like Wordsworth's nun—too steeped in Nature's calm to notice this intrusion.

The third member of the shooting party had paused to examine the lock of his gun. He was a short, rather thick-set man, with very blue, clear eyes, which redeemed his face from the common-place—which saw beauty in all Nature, and seemed to exact truth from men. When he raised these eyes from the gun, he saw Millie seated there on the Trush, and he gave a glad laugh, not at all surprised, but full of satisfaction.

"Hallo, Melicent! There you are!" he cried out heartily.

Melicent bounded up, looked around, pushed away Gwen, who stood before her, and leaping into the heather, flew to her friend. She gave a little cry of gladness.

"Mr. Helston! How did you get here? Is Mrs. Helston here too?"

"She's not actually here in sight, but she's not far off," he replied, putting his arm round her. "You'll see her very soon. You must present me to your cousins. Lance, I've found a friend."

Lancelot Burmester, in secret terror of what he called "flappers," came up awkwardly. He was a clever-looking fellow, fair, with an incisive profile, a pale face and pince-nez. He advanced from one side, as Tommy, anxious and heated, hurried up on the other.

"Miss Lutwyche and I are old friends," said Mr. Helston pleasantly. "We made the voyage from Africa together. Have I the pleasure of speaking to Mrs. Cooper?"

Tommy, blushing, disclaimed the honour, explained her identity, and shook hands with young Burmester. Freshfield, meanwhile, slipped round to Gwen behind the backs of the party.

"I know something of Mayne, Miss Lutwyche's guardian," said Mr. Helston in explanation; "and at his request my wife and I undertook the serious task of keeping this young person in order for the voyage." He did not add that he had himself paid the difference between first and second-class fare for her. "After her being so cruelly mishandled," he said, "you may imagine she needed care. She was not really fit to travel, but she was so eager to be off." He smiled down at her. "I think she looks a little different," he concluded quite fondly, "from what she did when we first took her in hand."

"But you have not said yet how you got here?" urged Millie, who was holding, in both hers, the hand that hung over her shoulder.

"Why, the very day you left us I ran up against Burmester in Pall Mall, and he said, 'Come down for a week's shooting,' and when we realised that Ilberston is, as it were, next door to Fransdale, you may imagine that we were doubly minded to come. Well, here we are! And how do you like England?"

"If by England you mean Fransdale," said Millie, "I like it in a way that can't be put in words."

"Oh, yes, it can be put in words; the thing's been done. You should read the works of one William Wordsworth," struck in Lance Burmester.

Millie raised her eyes to his face> and apparently liked what she found there.

"Should I? I will," she said thoughtfully.

"What have you done to your arm?" asked the young man kindly.

"My dear chap," said Harry Helston, "what this scrap of a child has been through would have broken the spirit of anybody else. Her brute of a Boer stepmother—"

Millie turned to him quickly.

"Please, Mr. Helston, my uncle does not wish it known," she said, with sedate dignity.

"What? Oh, very well, pussie!" replied her friend, gazing round at the eager faces of the governess and the girls; "I'll say no more, then. Mustn't get you into trouble. What are you up to with my gun? Want to shoot a bird—eh?"

"Oh, do let me," she begged; "I've not had a chance for so long! My arm is well enough for me to be able to take a sight. Do let me try!"

"Come this way. Freshfield says there are any amount of birds just over this ridge," said Burmester eagerly. "I should like to see you shoot."

Melicent possessed herself of the gun, and went forward, laughing and sparkling. The others followed as if spellbound. Nobody had an eye for Freshfield and Gwen, who came slowly behind, making the most of their moment. Very soon, up went the whir of brown wings again. Millie stopped, took aim with what seemed to be great deliberation; there was a breathless pause; a bird fell; everyone was laughing and congratulating the sportswoman. Lance Burmester presented her with her prize, and added another to make a brace. She was urged to come on, and repeat her exploit, but Tommy was growing nervous, and interfered.

"The vicar might not like it—they must be getting home."

Melicent went, quite happily, having received the assurance that her friends were at hand, and would look her up before long. She was unprepared for the torrent of reproaches and abuse which streamed forth upon her head as soon as they were out of sight of the shooting party.

"You mean little cat!" "You're a regular sneak!" "We know now, it's you yourself that want to keep it dark!" "Why couldn't you hold your tongue!" "Father said *you* were not to mention it, he never said a word about other people."

Their meaning began to dawn upon her at last.

"You mean my not allowing Mr. Helston to tell how I broke my arm? Well, of all the people I ever met, you have the most low-down notions of honour!" she cried indignantly. "You are just like my half-brothers and sisters! I always thought English people were straight, that it was only Boers that were such skunks!"

Tommy interfered, and reproved Millie for using bad language; and a more congenial topic was soon found, in the delights of having met and spoken to, not only Freshfield, but Mr. Burmester himself.

"Maddie wants him for her young man," explained Theo; "only we didn't see how the thing was to be begun, because, you see, we never get any chance to speak to him. Father and mother did go to dine with Sir Joseph once, but mother doesn't like Lady Burmester. She is dreadfully High Church, she thinks everybody ought to go to the Communion service every Sunday, and we only have it once a month, so on the other Sundays Lady Burmester drives all the way to Ilberston. Mother thinks it so impertinent of Lady Burmester to think she can possibly know better than a clergyman's wife. She said she wouldn't go there again; but I don't think they've been asked. You know really, mother doesn't know anything at all about it. I asked her why it was wrong to have that service every week, because we are supposed to believe in the Catholic Church, and all other Catholics seem to; so she said it was most improper for a young girl to argue about such things, as her father was sure to know best I said: 'If he knows, won't he explain to me?' and she said: 'You must wait till you are a great deal older.'"

"To-morrow is the first Sunday in the month," chimed in Maddie, "so they will all be there. What did you think of Lancelot Burmester's looks? Do tell us all about the Helstons. You were lucky to make friends with them, I daresay they will ask you to stay. Mother doesn't like us to go and stay away, for fear of our hearing naughty words. She doesn't think anybody is so well brought up as we are! If she could only hear some of the stories Willie and Georgie bring home from school!"

They all laughed at this.

"The real reason is, we have no clothes to go in, and she can't afford to buy us any," grumbled Theo, who was perhaps the handsomest of the girls, and the cleverest too.

"I daresay you could make your own if you tried," said Melicent. "I'd help. I think you ought to make your own clothes."

In the interest suddenly created by this new idea, nobody noticed that during the whole of the walk home Gwen, the talkative, never said a word.

"George, what an epidemic of girls!" groaned Lance, as soon as Tommy and her brood were out of sight. "Those poor Coopers! As if their own great, ugly five were not enough, but they must take on another to make the half-dozen!"

"It is an act of true kindness," replied Helston. "For a man with five daughters of his own to make room for another, shows him to be extremely conscientious."

"The little cousin," critically said Lance, "has something fetching about her. Nothing to look at, but one is conscious of a personality."

"I never look at her," said Millie's friend, "but those lines occur to my mind—

"The good stars met in your horoscope
Made you of spirit, fire and dew."

"I don't know about the dew; she's a skinny little wisp," was the uncivil comment.

"Wait till she grows up," said Millie's champion. "You would wonder there was anything left of her if you knew what she has come through. But I gave her my word, so I mustn't tell you; and after all," he added, musing, "I don't wonder that the vicar doesn't want the tale to get about; it's not a pretty story, and I daresay would do the child no good in a narrow-minded, provincial circle."

"I can't think how she will get on with those Coopers," remarked Burmester. "Did you ever see such raw material? And you heard what my mater said at lunch? They are such hide-bound, pragmatical—no doing anything with them. The vicar quietly goes his way, listening to nobody's wishes—thinks himself infallible. The pater has given him up as a bad job; says you might as well have a cabbage at the Vicarage! Hall, of Ilberston, is such a good chap! He might give this Southerner many a hint. But the Coopers won't have a word to say to him, because he has a weekly Eucharist, and makes the schoolchildren attend."

Helston listened with sinkings of the heart. This did not sound like a household in which Melicent would be happy. But report is often one-sided. He determined to judge for himself.

CHAPTER XIV
THE BREAKING-IN OF MELICENT

> "I could not hide
> My quickening inner life from those at watch.
> They saw a light at a window now and then,
> They had not set there: who had set it there?
> My father's sister started when she caught
> My soul agaze in my eyes. She could not say
> I had no business with a sort of soul,
> But plainly she objected."
>
> —ELIZABETH BARRETT BROWNING.

The following day Sir Joseph and Lady Burmester, with their guests, duly attended the ugly little church in Fransdale.

There had been a church there since the dawnings of English history. But, as the Reformed Church lost her grip upon the strong, narrow minds of the Dalesmen, it had been allowed to fall in ruins. Then had come the disastrous "churchwarden" restoration, which had abolished all landmarks. A stumpy little box-like structure now stood among the ancient graves, in a velvet-smooth meadow overshadowed by the frowning hills which closed round the head of the Dale.

Mrs. Cooper had been duly informed by Tommy of the meeting with the gentlemen from the Grange, and of the fact that one of them seemed to be a great friend of Melicent's. There was no valid reason why this news should displease her; but it did. She was vexed that her insignificant niece should have so many friends. The passion of jealousy was smouldering deep down in her heart, among other dormant forces of which she was unaware. Like many parents, while constantly assuring herself and her children that looks were nothing, she nevertheless expected the girls to be admired and sought out. When first she saw Millie, she had experienced relief at the thought that such a thin, pale shrimp of a girl could never prove a rival to her own. That she should be thrust forth to the notice of the Burmesters, so early in her sojourn at Fransdale, was most displeasing; she told herself that it must give the poor child a totally false idea of her own importance.

However, forewarned is forearmed. She was ready after service with the sweetest smiles of the amiable aunt, to be presented to the Helstons, and thank them suitably for their care of "poor darling Melicent."

Mrs. Helston was a picturesque woman, a brunette, with hair prematurely grey, which set off the tints of her bright complexion. She wore a wide hat with strings, and her smile captivated the hearts of the five staring Miss Coopers.

Lady Burmester was not a tactful person. She did not like the Coopers, whom she thought pompous and prosy. She proceeded to ask Mrs. Cooper to come to lunch the following day, and to bring her niece with her. She did not include any of the vicar's daughters in her invitation.

Mrs. Cooper smiled, and gushed, and seemed so delighted with the invitation, that her ladyship was conscious of a slight shock when she found that she was refusing it. It was early days yet, and would be unsettling for dear Melicent, who must get a little more used to English ways before she could bring her out. She knew dear Lady Burmester would understand. She suggested instead, that the two ladies from the Grange should come to tea at the Vicarage one afternoon; suppose they were to say Wednesday?

In a bewildered way Lady Burmester submitted to this unlooked-for dictation, and, taken by surprise, obediently said Wednesday; but as they were driving home, she suddenly turned to her friend and asked:

"Why wouldn't that perverse woman lunch with me, I wonder?"

Brenda Helston laughed her good, sincere laugh.

"My dear! You invited her niece, not her daughter!"

"O-o-oh! So that was where the shoe pinched," said her ladyship, surprised.

"You should always make allowances for human nature," commented Brenda. "It would not be human for a woman with all those daughters not to be touchy at seeing them passed over. We must propitiate her on Wednesday. I want to get Melicent to myself—to find out what she is thinking and feeling. I shall not be able to say half that I wish to, at the Vicarage."

"I daresay that supplies a second reason for her aunt's refusal!" said her friend, amused. "You and Mr. Helston have a very high opinion of that funny little white-faced girl, have you not?"

"Very!" said Brenda emphatically. "I never saw any creature so famished for the little tendernesses of life, so responsive to kindness, so eager to improve herself. Had you seen her when she first came on board—sullen, *farouche,* always on the defensive ... and how she melted and sweetened, and blossomed forth! Harry and I positively love her. We always, as you know, longed for a daughter. We have written to Carol Mayne, telling him that we will give her a home if she is not happy with her own people. He was doubtful; he thought the uncle's letter cold-blooded. But really, as I asked him, how could you expect enthusiasm on the part of a man with all those daughters, at the prospect of having another thrust upon him? I told Carol at the time, I liked the writer for being guarded; he could not know what she was."

"Does he strike you," asked Lady Burmester, "as being the kind of man to find out?"

Mrs. Helston hesitated.

"I fear not; he struck me as a dense kind of man. I heard Harry ask him, after service, whether this church were on the site of the old one—whether any of the old material had been built in; and he replied that he did not know, and had never inquired. I am afraid that will settle him, in Harry's estimation!" They both laughed gaily. "Harry looked," said his wife, "much as he might have done, had the vicar said that he did not know who his mother was, and had never inquired."

"There is a difference between him and Mr. Hall," observed Lady Burmester.

"Yes; was he not interesting yesterday? I shall not soon forget that wonderful church on the verge of the precipice. One feels that one knows the true meaning of sermons in stones when you have heard him talk of Ilberston. He knows every stone in his church, and every heart in his parish."

It was on Monday that Alfred Dow, riding down the Dale, came, as he passed the inn, upon Millie as she stood in the road with her cousins, waiting for Tommy, who had gone into the Post Office.

He promptly dismounted, and Melicent, her face brightening, proceeded to shake hands cordially, the girls looking on, divided between horror and interest. This was in the sight of the sun; for the inn, and the cluster of cottages known as Church Houses, composed the only nucleus the village could be said to possess; and everyone was looking on.

Upon this scene the vicar came, emerging from a vexatious interview with a stiff-necked churchwarden; and he was not pleased.

His manner, as he greeted his nonconforming parishioner, was congealed. His voice, with its inward stillness, frightened his daughters.

"Now, Mr. Cooper, I want you to let all your young ladies come up to tea with my mother at Crow Gate." He called it, in local speech, Crow Yat. "Let 'em come an' see t' ponies an' t' foal an' t' calves, an' taste mother's damson gin, for we've a drop left yet. Let this lady bring 'em, if she'll be so kind. Let's see"—he raised his cap and scratched his curly poll. "To-day's Monday. Suppose we said Thursday. An' we'll hear more o' they Boers," he added mischieviously, to Millie.

"If Mrs. Dow is kind enough to second your invitation, perhaps she would write direct to Mrs. Cooper," said the vicar, still more gelid. "I cannot say what her plans are for this week."

Dow turned slightly away, looked down at Millie, and deliberately shut one eye. Yet she could see that he was angry too.

"Oh—well; mother's not a grand letter-writer," he said cheerfully, "but I'll tell her your wishes. Good day, passon!"

"Good day, Mr. Dow!"

The vicar walked back with Miss Lathom and the six girls.

"You will, please," said he to the governess, "when you have occasion to enter a shop, take Melicent with you. I thought I had told you that she is never to be left with her cousins. She is wholly untrustworthy. After ten years in this parish I have more or less succeeded in showing these people that their free and easy ways are not for me; and now I am to come and find my niece and daughters unchaperoned in the public street, laughing and joking with a dissenting farmer! I will not have it!"

Tommy was abject. She trembled before him; but when he sent for Millie into the study, it was a different thing. He asked her what excuse she had for her behaviour. She asked in wonder:

"What behaviour?"

He explained the enormity of her conduct, adding that he was under the impression that he had told her, on the day of her arrival, that in England, social distinctions must be observed.

"Do you mean that you may not even speak to anyone who is not your social equal?"

"Certainly I mean it! When Mr. Dow greeted you to-day, you should have merely bowed, and turned to speak to one of your cousins; then he would have been obliged to pass on."

"In Africa," said his niece, "we should think that contemptible."

"As you know, that is just the point. We are not in Africa, but in England, where a social code exists."

"And as long as I am with you, must I behave so—pretending not to see people who have been kind to me?"

"As long as you live with me, you will do as I tell you."

"Whether I think it right or not?"

"Certainly; you have no right to set your judgment against mine."

"Thank you for explaining that to me. I am afraid I shall not be able to stay with you," she said simply.

"That is a foolish, as well as a rude speech, Melicent."

"I beg your pardon; I am sorry I am foolish, and I did not mean to be rude. Is that all you wanted to say to me?"

"Nonsensical impertinence!" said the vicar. "Where could you go, I wonder, if I declined to keep you?"

"To Mr. and Mrs. Helston," she replied unhesitatingly. "They have told Mr. Mayne that they would like to have me."

"Well, upon my word!" The vicar was well-nigh jolted out of his composure. He pulled himself together only by a strong effort. "Leave the room," he said. "Apologise, and leave the room."

"What am I to apologise for?"

"For gross impertinence."

After a minute's pause.

"I have not been impertinent," she said, "and I shall not apologise. I think you in the wrong."

She walked out of the room, leaving an angry man behind her.

The vicar's quiet insolence had aroused Alfred Dow, as it roused all his parishioners, to a feeling of active hostility. He felt a desire to get the better of him, if he could.

He sent a man next day with a note from Mrs. Dow to Mrs. Cooper—a note which the old lady had written with many protests, telling her son he was "nobbut a giddy fool" to be asking such a thing of her. Why should she make her best cheese-cakes for "them loompin' lasses o' passon's?"—when madam treated all dissenters as the dirt beneath her feet?

Mrs. Cooper was very undecided as to what answer she should return, when the unwelcome note arrived. On the one hand, she detested the Dows, and did not like to be indebted to them. They had never invited her girls before; she felt that this invitation was really on Melicent's account. Furthermore, Melicent was in disgrace, and did not deserve a treat. On the other hand, she knew that her five, who were never asked out, longed to go. It would be a sign to the whole village of a splendid condescension, did she allow it. Also, the fact of their being engaged to go to Crow Yat, would furnish an excuse, should Lady Burmester arrive on Wednesday, as seemed likely, with more invitations to Melicent. The vicar was for refusing; but he was disregarded. Melicent must be taught the difference between condescending to drink tea with one's inferiors and addressing them, when you met them, as equals.

The girls were wild with delight when they heard they were to go. They all walked to Bensdale Post Office that afternoon, and Gwen posted a letter.

Lady Burmester and Mrs. Helston duly came to tea at the Vicarage on Wednesday, and were received by Mrs. Cooper in the gaunt drawing-room—where she gave them what the girls were wont to call "pretence tea," as opposed to a solid, dining-room table arrangement—in elegant seclusion.

Her flow of amiable small-talk was so unceasing, that they had been there some twenty minutes before Lady Burmester, warned by recent error, could get in a request to see "your girls and Miss Lutwyche."

It was another quarter of an hour before Maddie, Gwen and Melicent appeared. Mrs. Cooper presented her girls to her ladyship, with the air of one showing off a promising baby; and Mrs. Helston drew Melicent to the window, to try and get a word unheard.

"Melicent, I have news for you," she said—"news which I think you will be glad to hear. We are not leaving Fransdale when we leave the Grange. Sir Joseph has let to us, furnished, for a month, the sweetest cottage you ever saw."

Melicent's eyes glowed

"Then I can come and see you," she began; but, checking herself, sighed. "That is, if Aunt Minna lets me. But she is so curious. She treats me like a prisoner. I am never allowed to go out alone. Are all English girls like that? Do you know, it does irritate me so."

"A lovely view from this window, isn't it?" said the suave voice of Aunt Minna, just behind. "Melicent, darling, go and fetch that curious photo of Slabbert's Poort to show Lady Burmester."

Melicent, with one glance at her friend, went off as desired. Mrs. Cooper beamed upon her visitor, and spoke confidentially.

"I am very hopeful of Melicent—very," she affirmed, as though someone had just expressed a contrary opinion. "Her faults may be turned into virtues, I feel sure. Her obstinacy will develop into firmness, when she has learned to obey."

Mindful of her desire to conciliate, Mrs. Helston smiled, as she said:

"I feel sure you realise how hard it must be for a girl who has been the mainstay of a delicate father for years, to bear restraint."

"We know, don't we," cooed Mrs. Cooper, with her little eyes almost shut, "that obedience is the foundation-stone of all training."

"Melicent's training seems to me to have risen far above the foundations of character," said Mrs. Helston, unable to help speaking with some warmth.

"Have you girls of your own, Mrs. Helston?" with an intonation of condescending pity. Then, playfully: "Ah, well; it makes all the difference, you know."

Melicent reappeared at this moment, and Mrs. Helston telegraphed to Lady Burmester: "Hopeless! Let's go."

Her ladyship rose and discharged the arrow in her quiver.

"I come with an invitation from Sir Joseph, which I must deliver," she said. "We are all going to Clairvaulx Priory Ruins on Monday, as Mr. and Mrs. Helston leave us the following day. Sir Joseph hopes to see yourself, the vicar, your three elder girls and Miss Lutwyche. We will send the waggonette and pair for you at half-past ten, unless it is wet."

Mrs. Cooper began to reply, with beaming smiles.

"What an enchanting idea! What a pity that Monday should be the beginning of the week, when it was specially important that nothing should interfere with lessons! Had it been another day, later on—a picnic was the most delightful of expeditions. But her girls were at an age when she must be very firm, and she was afraid—"

But at this point the vicar walked in, and on the invitation being conveyed to him, accepted it at once and unreservedly, for them all. He accompanied the ladies to their carriage, saw them drive away, and returned to the drawing-room where his wife awaited him by the tea-table.

"Really, Aidmund," she began; but he cut in.

"It is most short-sighted policy on your part, Minna, to affront Lady Burmester."

"But, my darling boy, the discipline of the schoolroom—"

"I believe to be excellent, but it must give way sometimes," replied her darling boy. "It is of primary importance that we should be on good terms with the Grange. You had your way about the Dow invitation. Let me have mine about this."

"Well, at any rate," said his wife, after a pause, "I have taught her ladyship not to invite my niece and exclude my daughters! A little firmness, dear Aidmund, as I often tell you, works wonders!"

CHAPTER XV
A CLEVESHIRE TEA-PARTY

> "And how came Miss Matilda not to marry him?" asked I.
> "Oh, I don't know. She was willing enough, I think; but you know, Cousin Thomas would not have been enough of a gentleman for the rector and Miss Jenkyns."
> "Well! But they were not to marry him," said I impatiently.
> "No; but they did not like Miss Matty to marry below her rank. You know, she was the rector's daughter, and somehow they are related to Sir Peter Arley; Miss Jenkyns thought a deal of that."
> "Poor Miss Mattie!" said I.
>
> —CRANFORD (Mrs. Gaskell).

The plentiful experiments, by various nations of late, in the difficult science of government by a democracy, have left some of us strongly of opinion that the ideal form of rule would be the despotism of the angel.

Failing the angel, however, one is reluctantly forced to the conclusion that despotism of any other kind is the very ... well, exactly the other thing.

The despotism of Mrs. Cooper was growing hard for Melicent to bear.

It was curious to watch the infatuated complacency with which she daily presided over that tableful of turbulent young lives, of whose springs of action she knew, and wished to know, nothing.

What she exacted was submission: nothing more. She did not desire to convince her children's understandings; only to hinder them from giving expression to their thoughts. As they sat in empty silence around her, while she prattled of trivialities, she congratulated herself on their docility. Like the Roman conquerors of old—"she made a solitude, and called it peace."

Miss Lathom had had the wit to see, within a week of her first arrival, the kind of service which was required of her. It was not asked that she should approve Mrs. Cooper's judgment; merely that she should not question it. So long as she kept the girls at lessons for the required number of hours, it did not matter how little they learned.

She had adapted herself to circumstances in order to find a *modus vivendi*; for she was poor and ignorant, and would have found it difficult to obtain another post. But sometimes she was frightened, of late, at the heat of the fires which she had kindled.

The animal side of these big, country-bred, well-fed girls was strongly developed, and cried for a vent. Their starved minds gave them no contrast, no resources. They were without the influences of dancing, drilling, tennis, cycling—without the stimulus of sheer hard brain-work, the thrilling interests of school-life and girl-friendships. There was nothing to stem the flood of their growing consciousness of sex. Gwen especially, vigorous and full-blooded, had arrived at a dangerous crisis.

Meanwhile, Melicent was beginning to find life empty and depressing.

From the moment of the arrival of Mrs. Dow's invitation, her cousins discussed Lance Burmester, Alfred Dow, and young Freshfield, from morning to night, except for those monosyllabic portions of time which they spent under their parents' eye. They talked of the way these young men walked, the colour of their eyes, the shape of their collars, the sound of their voices, their little manners and expressions. They meant no harm. They only needed an outlet for that natural craving for romance, which their mother thought proper to ignore.

Melicent laboured hard to find a field for her own superfluous energy. On the first morning after her arrival, she had risen early, made her bed, aired her room, borrowed the housemaid's brush, swept and dusted.

Her aunt did not, for two or three days, discover what she was doing. But when she did, she was scandalised. What would the servants think? Millie showed herself inclined to esteem but lightly the possible amazement of the two clumsy girls who formed the Vicarage staff. But her domestic efforts were straitly forbidden.

On the following morning, awake as usual, and roaming into the schoolroom while the household slumbered, she marked her uncle in the kitchen garden at work, patient and lonely, filling up the hours that must elapse before he could get his breakfast. She went and offered her vacant moments. He replied that her aunt would not like it. She was urgent, and he, wavering, presently allowed her to help him dig potatoes. They did not talk, but she worked with nimble capacity; and when she appeared again next morning, he surprised in himself a sneaking feeling of gladness.

But that day, Mrs. Cooper discovered the new pursuit; and it was stopped.

Millie, however, was not to be defeated. She next turned her attention to her cousin's dress; and, finding some stuff which had been lying in the house for months, cut out and made up blouses for Maddie and Gwen. This last matutinal pursuit found more favour; and henceforth the girl's fingers were fully occupied, though her mind continued to crave.

It was in wild spirits that the party started for Crow Yat, which was a fine old house, standing much lower down the Dale, and for a wonder, built of red brick, and not grey stone. It had been the shooting-lodge and toy of a baronet of George II.'s time, who had tired of it, and sold it to Alfred Dow's ancestor.

There was a drawing-room with four fine doorways, the pediments enriched with Adam's mouldings; and here the stiff-necked, proud old dame received the Vicarage troop with evident desire to show that she considered herself fully as good as they, if not better.

Alfred, a really first-rate specimen of his class, in that riding dress which is the natural garb of the well-to-do Dalesman—who does not drive on his unspeakable roads unless obliged—atoned for his mother's lack of cordiality by the sincerity of his welcome.

He led them through the garden, gathering late roses and dahlias with a lavish hand; then in among the deep lush orchard grass, filling their hands with delicious apples. He sent a boy up the meadow to gather mushrooms for them to take home; but on Melicent's vehemently expressed wish, laughingly allowed them to do it for themselves.

Then, at the clanging of a great bell, they came back to the house, where, in the elegant, panelled dining-parlour, sat Mrs. Dow, presiding over a real Cleveshire tea—jam tarts, cheese-cakes, currant sandwiches, cartwheels, turnovers—pastry in all its forms; ham that must be tasted to be thoroughly appreciated, cut in wafer slices; heather honey in the comb; peaches, great, luscious, Victoria plums, black Hamburg grapes, the despair of Sir Joseph's head gardener, who every year saw "they Dows" take the prize over his head at the annual show.

Had Melicent been a little older, she would have been amused at the keenness of the old lady's scrutiny—her suspicious glances from one to the other in search of charms which should explain her son's sudden interest in the Vicarage lasses, an idea fully as repugnant to her as it could have been to the outraged Mrs. Cooper.

To look at the fine young man, with his good physique, excellent morals and clean ancestry, was to make one wonder what better fate would be likely to await one of these ordinary, ill-educated girls, samples of thousands of their kind scattered over the land. And, had the vicar's niece read "Cranford," she might have thought of the silent tragedy of Thomas Holbrook and little Miss Matty.

It was a satisfaction to Mrs. Dow that Alfred took more notice of Melicent than of any of the Miss Coopers. She took her for about the same age as the vicar's youngest; such a child could not be dangerous.

All tea-time young Dow was trying to draw her out, a task which was never easy; but every time he coaxed her out of a statement about Boers and their ways, he roared with appreciation of her crisp, incisive style.

Tea was half over when a horse was heard to clatter into the stable-yard. Melicent, who happened to be seated exactly opposite Gwen, saw her face suddenly suffused with an overwhelming, unbecoming blush. A minute later, a shadow darkened the window, and a voice called in greeting. It was Freshfield.

Of course he was invited in to tea, and he expressed himself greatly surprised at the company he found. Gwen had managed to seat herself near one end of the table, an empty chair beside her; to which the agent gravitated naturally.

The conversation flagged, somehow. The rules under which they lived made the girls tongue-tied when in company. Madeline, at nearly eighteen, had no glimmering of the necessity that is laid upon the well-bred to set others at their ease. They were all gauche and heavy, and ate largely.

Tea over, a move was made to the fold-yard to see the beasts; and this done, someone suggested hide-and-seek. Miss Lathom demurred at this; she was uneasy at Freshfield's coming, though she had been privy to his being apprised of their whereabouts. She said with some decision that she was quite sure the vicar would not like it.

"Well, then, look here, Tommy," said Mr. Freshfield, with engaging familiarity, "the vicar must jolly well not be told. See? I hear from all those girls what a trump you are."

Under this pressure, Tommy yielded. But to the surprise of all, Millie declined it altogether.

"If you are sure Uncle Edmund would not like it, I shall not do it," she said simply. "I am always doing what he doesn't like unintentionally, but I won't do it on purpose."

She quietly went indoors to old Mrs. Dow, whose dignity and good sense had attracted her. This was a nature she could understand, a woman who thought no household work beneath her. Mrs. Dow, flattered, offered to show her the dairy. She had made no doubt that so small and pale a thing was town-bred, and was soon filled with astonishment at the knowledge and capacity displayed by the girl. Alfred, coming in, found them discussing the rival methods of African and English farms with much vigour. He came to ask Millie to go and look at some new plantations which, just now, were his particular delight. But as soon as they were out of hearing, he turned to her as if seizing a chance, and said:

"Should you be angry if I ask whether there's anything between your cousin and young Freshfield?"

"I'm not angry," said Millie; "but I know nothing about it. I can't tell you anything."

He took off his cap to run his fingers through his curls, which was a habit Millie had seen her cousins mimic.

"I had a mind to ask you to warn her; think she'd take it?" he asked. "Warn her that he's not in earnest; he's just playing. She's raw and doesn't see over-many young men. But I know for a fact that he's engaged to a girl with a bit o' money."

"Then why does he flirt with Gwen?"

"From something he let drop—something I heard him say—I think he has a bit of a grudge against the vicar. Thinks vicar looks down on him. Would like to put a spoke in his wheel."

Melicent made a small sound of dismay. "What a cad!" she said.

"That's what I think."

"It shows my uncle to have been right in holding a low opinion of him," was the contemptuous verdict.

"Eh, but you hit straight!" he returned, in admiration. "Only, if he'd been better treated the cur wouldn't bite."

They had no chance to say more, for two of the girls, all shyness now wholly cast aside, came charging down the path, and with shrieks warned them to make a dash for home.

Melicent was left in great discomfort. She had knowledge which she could not tell what to do with. She felt, rather than knew, that to warn Gwen would be worse than futile; especially now, when her refusal to play hide-and-seek had irritated all the girls against her, as well as Tommy, whose conscience was sore, and who consequently was for once downright ill-tempered.

Melicent had a dreary walk home. She would have been utterly discouraged but for the fact that she was to see the Helstons again on Monday; and some chance must be that day for her to tell her friends all that was in her heart.

Life at the Vicarage was too aimless. She had one hundred pounds of her very own, and she was determined somehow to make this yield her two years' good schooling.

CHAPTER XVI
THE BREAKING OF BOUNDS

> "And I, so young then, was not sullen. Soon
> I used to get up early, just to sit
> And watch the morning quicken in the grey,
> And hear the silence open like a flower,
> Leaf after leaf—and stroke with listless hand
> The woodbine through the window."
>
> —ELIZABETH BARRETT BROWNING.

Melicent's little bedroom was her sole refuge; and this her aunt, in her petty tyranny, denied her as often as she could. It was her theory that solitude was bad for girls. She liked them to be always herded together, under the eye of Tommy or one of their parents. Melicent must work, write, read, in the constant babble and racket of the schoolroom. The first time she found her niece curled up in the window-seat of her own room with a book, she swooped upon her with her sweetest smile, to see what the volume was. On discovering it to be "Alison's History of Europe," she shifted her attack from the reading to the spot where it took place. It was a draughty window; dear Melicent had better go into the warm schoolroom.

Melicent felt her tongue tingle to resent this aimless autocracy. The window of her little room was dear to her. It overlooked the grey stable-yard, with the glowing copper of autumn beeches, the dazzling gold of birches, peeping over the further wall, flanked by black Scotch firs, whose trunks seemed to glow red-hot when the sun was in the west; and behind them lay the long purple ridge—Weary Ridge—that fenced Fransdale away from the world on the eastern side.

The window was quite close to one inner corner of the quadrangle formed by the house and outbuildings. At right angles to it was the warm, dry, stone barn, on the upper floor of which the old mare's fodder was stored. There was a door, the upper half of which had a wooden shutter, on a level with Melicent's casement; and running up to this, one of those exterior flights of stone steps, so common in Cleveshire stable-yards.

Melicent felt sure that it would not be difficult, if there were something to hold by, to swing herself out of the window, upon the rectangular slab of stone, which was only a little to the left. In this way she could get out, if ever her longing for a solitary ramble overcame her. The gate of the yard was locked at night, but she knew were the key hung; and at times her longing to be free and away on the magical moors was like a voice calling, or a force drawing her.

There were only four windows overlooking the stable-yard; one was on the landing, one was her own, and the remaining two belonged to the boys' room, which was of course, during term, untenanted.

On Thursday night, her head full of what Mr. Dow had said about Gwen, she found herself unable to sleep, and actually carried out her plan. There was a staple, securely fixed in the wall, just by her window. To this she firmly attached a bit of rope's end with a loop. Sitting on the sill, and jumping lightly to the left, she alighted on the verge of the stone slab, and, holding firmly to her rope, swung herself round, got her balance, and stood safely. It was easy to slip round the two dark sides of the yard and open the gate. When it was shut behind her, and she stood under the wall, in the grass of the church meadow, she felt herself swallowed up in the immensity of the night.

For an hour she wandered in the little wood, and sat by the side of the tributary beck, rushing noisily over its stony bed to join the trout stream below. Then, no longer restless, she quietly returned, accomplished, not without difficulty, her re-entry, and creeping into bed, was instantly asleep.

It so happened that she mentioned her exploit in the course of the following day to her cousins. They were all cross and out of sorts, their mother having forbidden a walk to Bensdale that day—Bensdale, where there awaited them an instalment of a new serial—Phyllis and the Duke having been duly united by an archbishop in the bonds of matrimony, amid a blaze of splendour and a pageant of ancestral halls.

"We might just as well live in a prison," grumbled Maddie.

"Prisons are not so easy to get out of," replied Melicent: "If you dislike it so, why don't you run away, and decline to come back unless they make terms?"

"Run away!" they all cried; and Gwen added, with a sneer: "Why don't you try, if it's so easy?"

Melicent answered in all good faith:

"Because I don't want to seem ungrateful. I know it was good of Uncle Edmund to ask me here. Only, you see, I don't fit, and I never shall, because I don't want to be the kind of person that Aunt Minna wants to make me. So I shall not stay; but I don't want to run away in the night, as though they ill-treated me."

The girls clamoured to know how she would set about running away, if it came to that; and she simply told them that she had been out the night before, and explained how she managed it. They listened with deep interest.

"Shall you tell them you went?" they asked.

"No; not unless I am asked. I don't think myself bound to account to them for every minute of my time."

"Yet you played the Pharisee yesterday, and would not join our game."

"I think that's different. To do what we were specially told not to do, in front of other people, is publicly to shame Uncle Edmund and Aunt Minna. Now my going for a breath of air was quite private; there was nobody to be scandalised."

"Well," observed Babs, "if you had been seen, half the village would have been scandalised."

"That's true," said Melicent thoughtfully. "I think I had better not do it any more; but it was very tempting, just to try."

On the following day, Gwen had neuralgia, and was in great pain.

"It's her bed," said Maddie, "it's in such a draught; and mine's no better. Mother says it's all right if we keep the window shut, but we can't sleep with the window shut, so we always get up and open it, after she has been in. I wonder we're not both blown away! I tell you what, Millie, I wish you'd let her sleep in your bed just for one night, to get rid of it. We don't want to tell mother, or she'll keep her indoors, and perhaps stop her from going to Clairvaulx on Monday."

"Why, of course I will!"

"Yes; but remember, we mustn't change till after mother has been round last thing."

"All right; Gwen had better slip in when the coast's clear," said Melicent unsuspiciously.

The change was duly effected, without detection, and next morning there was no doubt that Gwen's neuralgia was cured.

It was Sunday morning—a warm, sunny, October day, and the golden light streamed into the Vicarage breakfast-room. The girls were all assembled, waiting for breakfast, with newly brushed hair and clean frocks. All looked healthy, cheerful and glad. But the vicar's face, as he walked in, was in sharp contrast to the gay morning. More than the customary hush descended on his entrance.

"Melicent," he said, greeting nobody, "oblige me by taking your breakfast into the study. Eat it there, and wait till I come."

Melicent stood up, staring in surprise. "Why do you say this? What have I done?"

"What you have done cannot be so much as alluded to before your young cousins. Leave the room at once."

Melicent drew herself up. She looked round at all the furtively dropped eyes—at Gwen's cheeks, oddly suffused with sudden scarlet—then at her uncle.

"I have done nothing to deserve to be so spoken to," said she. "When you find out the truth, I hope you will apologise to me."

"We wish to hear nothing from you, Melicent. Go in silence."

Tommy behind the tea-tray, and her pupils seated round, were well-nigh paralysed with terror. What had been found out? Were they implicated? Would Melicent obey?

She took up her cup and plate, tossed back her hair, and walked out, white and speechless. The vicar shut the door, sat down in the dire silence, and began his breakfast. They all chewed their way through chunks of pork-pie in unbroken gloom.

When his daughters had filed away to learn their collects, their father betook himself to his study and the culprit.

Melicent had finished her breakfast, and stood by the window. He sat down at his table, and fixed his eyes upon her.

"Well," said he, "I suppose, before condemning you, it is only right to ask you what you have to say."

"I don't know what you mean," said Melicent. "I have nothing to say. I am waiting for you to explain why you treat me in this manner."

"Unfortunately," he said, "all is known. You will hardly deny that you got out of the window of your bedroom, when I happened to see you do it."

"I do not deny that I did," she returned quietly.

"Perhaps you will tell me why you did so?"

"It was partly that I wanted to see whether I could, and partly that I was restless. I am used to be out of doors a great deal more than Aunt Minna likes me to be."

"When I tell you, Melicent, that I know what happened last night, you should see how much worse you are making things by quibbling like this."

"Last night! But—"

"We are speaking of last night."

"I am not. The only time I got out of the window was on Thursday night."

"Do you seriously mean to tell me that you did not get out of the window last night?"

"Certainly! I did not."

He sat staring; and in the pause that followed, enlightenment came to Melicent, and she wondered at her own blindness. Gwen had asked to sleep in her room, in order to get out of the window!

That being so, she could not clear herself without incriminating her cousin; and in a flash she saw that if she said Gwen and she had changed beds the previous night, the others would all deny it. Her mind, travelling with the speed that comes in moments of crisis, discerned the strength of the case against her. Even Tommy did not know of last night's escapade. Both she and Mrs. Cooper could say with confidence that all the girls were in their own beds at half-past ten on Saturday night. She wondered at herself for being deceived by the flimsy pretext of the toothache, when she thought how unlikely the story would sound.

The girls must deny everything. They had no other course. They had to go on living at home, and such a thing, if known, would make life impossible, and turn their prison into a veritable dungeon keep.

She, on the contrary, had no intention of remaining where she was. Her uncle had already a bad opinion of her. To allow it to grow worse seemed the only course in the dilemma so suddenly developed.

After long thought, her uncle spoke, in a gentler tone than he had ever used to her.

"Confession, Melicent," he said, "is the only possible way to lessen my extreme displeasure. Last night, or to be more correct, at two o'clock this morning, I heard a casement flapping in the wind. I got up, believing it to be the landing window, and left my room without a light, to shut it. I found it closed, and was on the point of pushing it open, to look out, and see whence the noise came, when a movement in the yard below caught my eye. Two people were seated, side by side, upon the stone steps near your window, the window of which was no doubt causing the disturbance. One was a man, the other was my niece. I saw that the man had his arm round your waist. His face I could not distinguish, but in the light of recent events, I consider myself justified in supposing it to have been Alfred Dow."

The girl's short, indignant laugh, naturally increased her uncle's idea of her shamelessness.

"I saw you"—he went on—"I saw you escort him to the gate, shut and lock it after him, return and scramble in, by means of a piece of rope, into your bedroom. I stood there, broad awake, and saw all this. After hearing my story, will you persist in your denial?"

"No," she said, after a minute's thought; "I do not persist in it."

"You admit," he said, with righteous indignation blazing under the even surface of his voice, "that you did all this?"

"No," said the girl; "I do not admit it. If you saw it, there is no question of my denying it or admitting it Either the thing is certain, or you have made a great mistake."

"Why not confess openly, Melicent?"

"I have nothing to confess."

"This is mere quibbling," he said, still temperately. "But what you have said I consider tantamount to a confession. One thing, and one alone, you can do to lessen your guilt. Give me the name of the man who has violated my home, insulted my office and degraded my niece."

She was silent

"You will not?"

"I cannot."

"You mean you will not."

"I mean that I cannot."

He almost wished that she were a boy, and could be caned.

"I believe you to be wilful and undisciplined," he said, almost appealingly, "but I am most anxious not to judge you too harshly, Melicent, for I know what your bringing up has been. I will not make too much of what I hope and pray may have been merely a wild, rebellious prank. If you will tell me frankly what you did, and the man's name—"

"I can't do either."

"Then, Melicent, most unwillingly, I must require of you that you remain in the schoolroom while we are at church. Think things over, and by the time we return, God grant you may be of a better mind. Come with me, please."

Melicent followed him without a word.

CHAPTER XVII
A CRISIS AT THE VICARAGE

> "She said sometimes: 'Aurora, have you done
> Your task this morning? Have you read that book?
> And are you ready for the crochet here?'
> As if she said: 'I know there's something wrong;
> I know I have not ground you down enough
> To flatten and bake you to a wholesome crust
> For household uses and proprieties.'"
> —ELIZABETH BARRETT BROWNING.

The schoolroom was empty. Tommy and her brood were preparing to go to church. The vicar laid a little book upon the table and addressed a few sincere words to the girl. Narrow he was, prejudiced he might be; but a man who, however mistaken, is quite sincere, has always some power. Melicent felt that, had she been to blame, she might have repented at his bidding.

It was not expected that the party from the Grange would be at Fransdale Church that day. Mrs. Cooper was inly disconcerted when she saw that they were there. She found their inquiries after Melicent, when service was over, difficult to parry.

"A little *disagreement*?" she murmured, smiling, meaningly, and speaking as though taking Mrs. Helston into special confidence—always her manner when she was not telling the truth—"just a little question of discipline between dear Melicent and her uncle. We must hope for the best; but it needs much patience and kindness to eradicate the results of such training."

Mrs. Helston, though furious, realised that no indignation on her part would help Melicent's cause. She longed to ask questions, but knew she had no right to interfere in the matter at all. Mrs. Cooper, smiling and chattering, got away with adroitness on which she prided herself, with no questions asked as to whether Melicent would be allowed to go to the picnic next day.

Meanwhile Tommy and her pupils were in a terrible panic. They dared not guess what had been found out. Gwen, on considering the matter, could not believe it possible that it could be her last night's escapade, because, if her father had by some mysterious means seen anything, she felt sure that he would have taken the culprit in the act. By no means a student of character, she forgot that he never took action in the heat of the moment. They all crept home from church with shaken nerves, fully expecting that the storm would burst on their return. But nothing happened. Whatever Melicent's offence, she had certainly not incriminated them.

They were all so burdened by guilty consciences that, had it been their custom to be natural before their parents, anybody could have seen that something was wrong. However there was nothing unusual, at the Vicarage, in embarrassed, sulky silence, or monosyllabic answers: so all passed off without disturbance, and they were free to stare at one another in the seclusion of the schoolroom, from which the captive was now removed, and ask what could possibly be "up."

Mr. and Mrs. Cooper were meanwhile at a loss. It was certain that they could not keep their niece among their own children, but what other course was feasible? They could not afford to support her at school. She was too young to be turned out to get her own living, not to mention the probability of her disgracing herself and them, wherever they placed her.

Her aunt went in during the afternoon, and tried her blandishments, but was confronted with a steady, cold assertion that the girl had nothing to say.

That night, Melicent slept in another room, with a screwed-down window and a locked door; and in the solitude she broke down utterly, and wept pitifully for her dead father. She yearned for the presence of somebody she knew—somebody that believed in her; she even thought, with a gust of something like tenderness, of Bert Mestaer himself.

But in the morning, when her aunt brought her breakfast, she was self-contained and proud as ever. She heard the waggonette from the Grange drive up to the door, in dazzling sunshine. From her window she saw it pass out of the gate, after a twenty minute's delay caused by Mrs. Cooper's not being ready—saw Maddie, Gwen and Theo, in the new blouses she had made and hats which she had trimmed.

They had not been long gone before the key turned in the lock and Tommy crept in. She looked flurried and eager.

"Oh, my dear," she gasped, "at last I have a moment! Do tell me what has occurred!"

Melicent laid down her book and looked up, "Has Uncle Edmund not told you anything?"

"Not anything!"

"Then of course I can't."

"Really, Melicent, you are an impracticable girl! How can we help you if we don't know the scrape you're in?"

"You can't help me."

"Oh, very well!" huffily. "I came to let you out, and say that of course Babs and Bee and I should not tell, and you might just as well come and sit in the schoolroom with us."

"You are very kind, Miss Lathom, but I shall stay here. I don't cheat."

"I can guess what it is," observed Tommy, with an air of penetration. "Your uncle has found out that you got out of window!"

There was no reply.

"I thought so!" said Tommy triumphantly. "I was sure of it! That would be just the thing to make him angry. But I must say, I think they're punishing you too severely, considering you were shut up all yesterday. However, cheer up, my dear! These things blow over, you know."

"You're very kind," said Melicent wearily, "but I think you'd better go away. I feel sure they told you not to come and talk to me, didn't they?"

Tommy grew red.

"You're an ungrateful little cat," she said. "I come here trying to be kind to you, and I daresay you'll go and tell tales of me!"

"You ought to know by now that I don't tell tales," said Melicent; "but as I can hardly ever speak the truth here without telling tales, the only thing I can do is to hold my tongue."

Miss Lathom flounced out of the room in a rage.

Meanwhile, the Vicarage party met with a very cool reception when they arrived at Clairvaulx.

Lady Burmester clearly showed her displeasure.

"Surely you are too hard upon a girlish fault," she said stiffly. "If Melicent was in punishment all yesterday, you might have relented to-day, when you knew how anxious we all are to have her."

"If you knew the gravity of my niece's fault," said the vicar, in his most distant manner, "you would, I believe, think differently. She has proved herself altogether an unfit companion for innocent girls, and must, I fear, be sent to some institution where the moral sense may be developed by constant supervision."

"Good Lord!" said Sir Joseph.

The six elders were standing together, the girls having strayed off in company with Lancelot and Mr. Freshfield.

Mrs. Helston's cheeks were crimson.

"Will you think we ask too much if we beg to be told what she has done?" she inquired, in a voice that shook.

"Our claim to know is a strong one," put in her husband, "as, if Mr. Mayne consents, we should like to undertake the child's education, and give her a home. We hoped that, as you have plenty of daughters, and we have none, you would perhaps spare her to us, who have grown attached to her. But we ought to be in a position to know what tendencies in her to guard against."

"I presume," said the vicar, "that you would rather that we did not speak before Sir Joseph and Lady Burmester."

Her ladyship laid her hand on her husband's arm, and led him away across the grass.

"If I were a girl," she said, "the very sight of Mrs. Cooper would make me wicked. She makes my flesh creep. I wish somebody would take out her ear-rings."

"You are an ungenerous, ill-regulated woman," said Sir Joseph placidly. "I daresay they've had a sweet time of it, trying to break in Harry's precious African filly. He hints at her having had a past already. I expect she's a bit of a fire-brand in a peaceful parsonage."

The four others strolled in an opposite direction. The vicar, with real reluctance, and with brevity, described what he had seen Melicent do.

"I do not believe it!" cried Brenda Helston hotly.

"Brenda!" cried her husband, while Mrs. Cooper grew pink, and trembled visibly.

"It was one of the maids masquerading," went on Brenda, unheeding. "The very idea of Melicent doing such a thing is outrageous! One of the maids used her window to get out by! I daresay she sleeps soundly."

The vicar had had his moment in which to collect himself.

"Unfortunately," he said, "my niece does not deny it."

CHAPTER XVIII
A NEW HOME

> "— —Many, I believe there are,
> Who live a life of virtuous decency,
> Men who can hear the Decalogue, and feel
> No self-reproach; who of the moral law
> Established in the land where they abide
> Are strict observers; and not negligent
> In acts of love to those with whom they dwell,
> Their kindred and the children of their blood.
> Praise be to such, and to their slumbers, peace!
> —But of the poor man ask, the abject poor;
> Go and demand of him, if there be here,
> In this cold abstinence from evil deeds;
> And these inevitable charities,
> Wherewith to satisfy the human soul."
>
> —WORDSWORTH.

It was getting dusk—too dusk to see to read the "History of Europe"; and Melicent, who had scarcely slept all night, stretched herself upon her bed and fell asleep. The flash of a light in her eyes awoke her, and starting up, she saw her uncle come in with a lamp, followed by Mr. and Mrs. Helston.

She gave a low, thrilling cry, like that of a babe who sees its mother. She had not expected this. The vicar had never seen her look as she did when running to her friends' arms. He set down the lamp and left them together.

It was long, however, before they could persuade her to tell them anything. They were obliged to make her clearly understand the serious nature of the charge against her. They showed how essential it was to remove such a stigma. They guessed at once that she was shielding someone; and after much urgent entreaty, she was induced to tell them all, and leave the upshot to their discretion.

"I am sure," she said, when she had related the whole story, "that it would not be the least use to tell them the truth; for two reasons. First, they would think the bare idea of Gwen's behaving like that simply ridiculous.

Aunt Minna thinks they are all babies, and talks to them as if they could hardly understand what she says; and they mimic her afterwards. Second, because all the girls would deny it. It would be my word against Maddie and Gwen. Which do you think they would take?"

"There would be somebody else," observed Harry Helston firmly. "Young Freshfield. I know Sir Joseph has been dissatisfied lately, and he will have about settled his hash if any of this gets about. The thing is—how to trap him? There will be no more chance for Gwen to use that window, I take it?"

"He would still go on writing to her at Bensdale under cover to Tommy, I expect—but oh, you must not say anything about it! You don't know how awful it would be! Tommy would be sent away; they would lead the most weary life—wear chains on their ankles, I should think."

"But, dear," said Brenda gently, "what is to happen if this is allowed to go on? Gwen does not know what she is doing. Suppose she came to harm, what should we feel, who had never warned them of her danger? Now I think of it, I noticed little things between her and that man once or twice to-day. But she is so unformed, and—to me—so unattractive, that I never thought of such a thing."

"She's rather a handsome girl," said her husband.

And now Melicent exhausted her eloquence to implore them not to say anything.

"You see, it will only make them worse," she said. "If they were trusted, they would be all right; if they were given credit for good sense and good feeling, they would be quite different. But they are treated like fools, who would be knaves if they were allowed their own way, and it just makes them treacherous—they must have an outlet! It's only for adventure and frolic that Gwen did it—it's the only thing they have to think about—they're not allowed to read or think, or do anything but just vegetate; how can such a life content them? And now, if this is known, they will be all the more shut in and tied up, and crushed down, and I shouldn't wonder if it drove them to do something really wrong."

This view of the subject constituted a real difficulty. Revelation would merely tighten the prison-bars, and would so increase the very evil it was intended to remove. A more perplexing problem had never been offered to the Helstons.

They put it resolutely away from them for a time, in order to tell Melicent about their own plans for her future. They told her that they hoped to receive, in about a fortnight's time, Carol Mayne's formal permission to take charge of her for the present.

They had some private means, but did not consider themselves rich enough to justify them in adopting her entirely. In all respects, they thought it would be doing her a truer kindness to educate her with a view to making her independent. Harry Helston, artist and dreamer by temperament, was architect by profession. He had spent so much time in travelling the world, and absorbing the idea of all the masterpieces of his great profession, that his fortune was by no means made. It was perhaps a drawback to him professionally, that of him it might be said as of a certain statesman who "thought in continents," that he, Harry Helston, "thought in cathedrals." The ornamental suburban residence, with its nurseries chopped away in chunks to make the external elevation picturesque, was his pet abomination. He would do no work, where cheapness was to be the marring key-note. Simplicity and the best craftsmanship were his mottoes. His work lay in London, where he and his wife, after their travels, were about to take a flat. But he was also now determined to fulfil his youthful ambitions, and build for himself the house of his dreams in Fransdale itself.

Sir Joseph, who was a byword in the district for his stern refusal to sell or lease land for building purposes, had relented in his case; and the home of his imagination was to arise in a level meadow half-way down the Dale—a pleasure house for holiday hours—a final refuge for old age.

For the austere mystery of the North had made him as completely a captive as was Melicent herself.

The girl could hardly believe that she was to visit every year, in the company of those she loved best, the Dale which had gripped her fancy so powerfully. The Helstons were to rent, until their own house should be built, the tiny cottage upon which Melicent had looked down, when she sat upon Tod's Trush. The darkness of her misery was all changed into pure joy by the time her friends took leave.

Before Mr. Helston lay the formidable necessity of seeing Mr. Cooper. He was fairly perplexed. Should he speak, or not? He found himself wondering what advice Mr. Hall, of Ilberston, would be likely to give. But there was no time for reflection. He left his wife still with Melicent, and found himself in the study without having made up his mind as to his duty. His intention flickered to and fro like a candle in the wind. Was he shirking truth because it was disagreeable? Or was he contemplating an unwarrantable interference into another man's affairs? Was he justified in giving information which would result in deeper mismanagement of those unaccountable beings, young girls? Or if he stood aloof, was he guilty of Cain-like indifference to his brother's peril?

He sat down in more discomfort than he ever remembered to have suffered before. His indignation that Melicent should suffer under any kind of stigma made another powerful factor in his desires; and he did not know for how much he ought to let it weigh. As he looked at Mr. Cooper's cold, dark face, he was conscious of a desire to demand that, as it had been publicly announced that Melicent was in disgrace, so it should be publicly known that she was cleared. But he felt pretty sure of the difficulty there would be in establishing the truth. He saw a distinct likeness between the vicar and his niece; he had seen the same hard glint in Melicent's eye when she was on the defensive. The Coopers gave him the idea of being always on the defensive — on the watch to parry and frustrate any attempts upon their confidence or their intimacy.

"I shall be glad to hear that you have elicited any information that may tend to Melicent's rehabilitation," said the vicar, in tones wholly devoid of expectancy.

Helston found himself speaking without having in the least determined what he meant to say.

"Melicent has told us what she knows," he said. "We think it clears her. But we respect her motive for silence, and are inclined to think that no good end could be served by telling you what she told us."

The vicar looked stony. "But I think I must ask to hear it," he said.

"It was told us in confidence. Melicent is—is content to feel that we know it. I—I am not sure that I am entitled to let it go further."

The cold, blue eye still fixed him.

"You convey to me the idea that Melicent is shielding someone else. Is this so?"

Helston twirled his soft hat idly in his hands, and looked at the ground.

"I do not feel at liberty to say," he said at length.

"If that be so, the person shielded must be a member of my household," said the vicar, in a voice which sounded to Helston like the crackling of ice in a hard frost. "I suppose you can scarcely be venturing to insinuate that it was one of my daughters?"

"I insinuate nothing; I do not know who it was. It was not Melicent."

"Far be it from me," said Mr. Cooper, after reflection, "to traduce or speak ill of my sister's child; but if she has resorted to the desperate expedient of trying to fasten blame upon one of my poor girls, I must reluctantly lower still further my opinion of her. I fear you and Mrs. Helston are altogether deceived in her."

"We are willing to take the risk," said Helston immediately, "and to relieve you of the charge of her to-morrow, if you are willing." His eyes twinkled as he added: "We have no daughters to be contaminated."

"Had it not been so, I could not in honour have allowed you to undertake the charge of her. I am quite frank with you. I tell you plainly that I will in no case keep her among my own girls; and I do not know how to meet the cost of maintaining her elsewhere. If you, knowing what you know, are willing to take her, my feelings can but be those of gratitude and relief."

"Then we may consider it settled!" cried Helston, rising.

Perhaps his haste betrayed how he was yearning to get away, for a look of suspicion crossed the vicar's face.

"Do you not think I have a right to ask you to be more explicit?" he said.

His visitor looked down, and it was after an interval that he slowly said:

"You have a right. I ask you to waive it. What I have heard rests wholly upon Melicent's word, which, I understand, you do not trust."

The vicar could not say that he did.

"You would not take her word against that of your own children?"

"Certainly not!"

"That is natural enough; but it convinces me that there is no more to be said."

The vicar looked down, thinking deeply. Then abruptly, and perhaps with the deliberate idea of taking the other by surprise, he demanded:

"She would not tell you the name of the man?"

"There is no man in the world to whom she would accord a clandestine meeting."

"Perhaps you forget that I was an eye-witness, Mr. Helston."

"Would you swear in a court of law that the girl whom you saw was Melicent?"

The vicar hesitated.

"Why," asked Helston, "did you not at once enter her room, and convince yourself?"

"I never act in haste; besides, there is no doubt. She wore Melicent's hat—a kind of broad, flat cap which she wears in the garden; and she entered her room! Mr. Helston, I fear I must ask you to be explicit. You have said too much, or not enough. What is it you suggest?"

"I suggest nothing, for I know nothing, except the fact, of which I am sure, that the girl you saw was not Melicent. Had you gone to her room, and confronted her then and there, you would have known more than I do at this moment."

"I think you are bound to tell me what my niece has told you," said the vicar; and a new uneasiness was in his voice.

"No; I am not bound to, and I have no wish to. But there is a further question, as to whether I ought to. I—I can't speak without inflicting great pain, which I am very loath to do. But I can't get away from the feeling that perhaps I ought not to allow you to go on in ignorance of the true state of affairs. Perhaps I have said enough to put you on your guard. Let us leave it so."

"No;" the answer came at once and firmly. "We cannot leave it so. You must tell me the tale which my niece has poured into your ears, in simple justice to me and mine. If Melicent has slandered her cousins, she should be punished."

"Equally, if they have allowed her to suffer for them, they should be punished," said Helston, stung at last. "May I ask if you have made any sort of inquiry among them?"

"Decidedly not. I have not allowed them even to know the way this misguided girl has behaved."

Helston hardly knew whether most to pity or be enraged at such blindness. He turned away and walked to the window. The girls were just passing through the garden on their way from feeding their rabbits. They all glanced in a furtive way at the study windows, and Gwendolen met his eyes fully. She averted her face in confusion, and hurried on. The visitor turned abruptly to the vicar and took leave. He could not trust himself to say another word. Mr. Cooper accompanied him to the hall door, and they found themselves suddenly face to face with Gwen, coming in.

Her father, in a marked way, encircled her with his arm, as if to show his confidence. The girl was trembling, scarlet, deeply moved. She turned upon Helston.

"Then she held her tongue?" she gulped out. "She has not split, even now?"

Helston's face lit up.

"Does that touch you, Miss Cooper?" he asked kindly.

"It does. I'm most things that are bad, but I simply can't be such a sneak as this. Father! It was I, not Melicent, whom you saw in the yard! And you may thrash me, or starve me, or do what you like with me, but I will never tell you the name of the man who was with me! Oh, Melicent isn't the only person in this house with any sense of honour! She's—she's—taught me a lesson! You tell her from me, Mr. Helston, that if I'm ever any good in this world, it'll be all owing to her."

The vicar had not said one word. He stood where he was, the arm which his daughter had shaken off rigid against his side. His face grew bloodless, his expression a marvellous exhibition of self-control.

It seemed to Helston kindest to say good-bye and leave the house hurriedly. His admiration for Gwendolen was great; after what Melicent had told him, he could partly guess the effort it needed to make her confession—a confession which must expose not only her own wrong-doing, but the whole working of a long system of deceit; for the matter could now hardly be allowed to rest where it stood.

Contact with Melicent's honesty and courage had stimulated this girl to show herself honest and courageous. He felt very hopeful of her future, though he himself winced at the ordeal now before her.

CHAPTER XIX
AN UNMARKED FESTIVAL

> "Day of days! Unmarked it rose,
>   In whose hours we were to meet;
>   And forgotten passed. Who knows,
>   Was earth cold, or sunny, sweet,
>   At the coming of your feet?"
>
> —MRS. MEYNELL.

As her visitor departed, Brenda Helston turned from the door and let herself sink into an easy-chair by the fire with a gratified laugh.

Five years had not changed her, except that her soft, abundant hair was whiter. No wrinkles marred her smooth pink cheeks, her eyes were still bright, though her forty-fifth birthday stared her in the face.

The room in which she sat—the drawing-room of her flat in Collis Square—was an unusual room. Harry Helston strongly held the theory that Londoners must live inside their walls. The pictures which hung on these were all originals and all good. A line of bookshelves encircled the room like a dado, the top forming a shelf for the reception of rare bits of pottery, brass, *cloisonné* and curios. In one corner the line of books was broken for the admission of a large secretaire. With this exception, and that of a roomy writing-table near the fire, the room contained no furniture but chairs of every variety of comfort, and small solid tables, holding no ornaments, but convenient for the reception of cups, books or papers. There were flowers in every place where they could be put without risk of being knocked over.

The visitor who had just left the room had gone unwillingly, but gladdened by a cordial invitation to return later. His hostess thought of him with pleasure and satisfaction. He was immensely improved by his term of foreign service, and it was gratifying that his first visit on reaching London should have been to her. She had always liked Lance Burmester; and the fact of his having proved himself so emphatically all that a Special Correspondent ought to be—of his having chosen to have a profession, and to work hard at it, being, as he was, the eldest son of a wealthy man—had by no means lessened her good opinion.

She rang the bell, gave some orders to the maid who answered it, and was still in reverie—perhaps building castles in the air—when her husband came in, chuckling.

He held an evening paper in his hand.

"Brenda, here's something that will amuse you," he said, stooping to kiss her affectionately.

She looked up eagerly.

"I have news for you, Harry! Guess who has been here to-day!"

"I'll guess afterwards, but first I must read you this. It's about Melicent. Won't she be furious? She did think she had dodged the halfpenny interviewer." He unfolded his copy of the *Hauberk* and read aloud:

"'THE LADY ARCHITECT

"'The decision of Miss Lutwyche, three years ago, to complete her course of architectural training by acquiring a practical knowledge of building, caused a considerable flutter of the dove-cotes at the Polytechnic when she applied personally to be enrolled. There was no rule, however, by which she could be excluded, and she has been ever since, the only lady among six hundred male students.

"'Having completed her course, she is now taking steps to set up for herself, and is to begin by superintending the erection of two labourers cottages from her own designs, upon the Cleveshire estates of Sir Joseph Burmester. Miss Lutwyche has an intimate knowledge of the tastes and requirements of the natives of the district in question, and it is understood that she is strongly of opinion that the question of the housing of the poor will ultimately be successfully tackled by women and not by men.

"'Simplicity, durability and convenience are the keynotes of her work. It is known that she had much to do with the erection of the wonderful house which her adopted father, Mr. Helston, F.R.I.B.A., has just completed in Fransdale, which has been described as the most imaginative specimen of domestic architecture produced by an Englishman during the last three hundred years. It has been seriously suggested that the house in question may revolutionise the idea of the English country house, and that the day of gables, barge-boards, rough-casting and timbering is over.'"

They looked at each other in mischievous amusement.

"She *will* be angry," said Brenda; and, after a moment's silence, burst out laughing.

"Think I'd better not show it?"

"Oh, you must let her see it; because, if you don't, someone else will—inevitably."

Helston leaned back in his chair, with reminiscent eyes fixed on the glowing fire.

"You and I were right, Brenda, when we believed her to be above the average: she ought to go far."

"Never for a moment have I doubted it," his wife answered. "She has power! Her smallness, her silence, her strength—it is a wonderful combination. Many a time I have thanked God for her."

"I fancy," said Harry reflectively, "that Mrs. Cooper to this day believes that we shall repent, and that it was Melicent who corrupted her entire household, girls, maids, governess, all in the space of two or three weeks."

"If she does, the vicar knows better," returned his wife, "and is glad enough for Gwen and Theo to come to us whenever they can."

"I believe we made one mistake," thoughtfully pursued the man. "I have often wished that I had not complied with the vicar's written request that the Burmesters should be told nothing. I don't want them to think there is anything to conceal, as far as Millie is concerned. You see, Mayne doesn't like the circumstances of her leaving Africa talked about, and Cooper doesn't like the circumstances of her leaving the Vicarage talked about. At this rate, it seems to me that she may become a Woman with a Past, if we don't take care."

"Oh, pooh," said Brenda; "don't make a fuss about nothing. Everybody knows what the Coopers are."

As she spoke, a gay voice, a dog's bark, a scuffle, was heard without; and the girl they both loved whisked in, waving a roll of vellum in her hand.

"Behold," said she, "the result of my labours! A certificate about the size of an ordinary table-cloth, signed by about a dozen men whom nobody ever heard of. If that doesn't convince people of my competency nothing ever will!"

She tossed the document in Brenda's lap, and sat down on the fender-stool, a little out of breath.

She had not changed greatly since her early teens; but she had improved. She was still small, though not too small; still pale, but with the clear, rose pallor of a Malmaison carnation. Her soft, fair hair was becomingly arranged, her movements graceful, her manner decidedly good.

"It's going to snow," cried she. "March is going out like a lion! Pater, I hope the wind won't nip our crocuses."

"A Cleveshire crocus laughs at frost," said Helston. "But will a Cleveshire maiden laugh at an impertinent newspaper paragraph?"

"Paragraph! You don't tell me! Where? After all my trouble!" She stopped short, indignant, her cheeks suddenly rose-colour. "Well, I don't care," she concluded defiantly. "Ne'er a reporter of them all shall flout me out of my humour."

"Shall I read it?"

"Certainly!"

Helston did so, not without relish. When he had done, the girl made a sound of disdain.

"Charming!" she said. "But what does it matter? Does anybody whose opinion I value form that opinion upon the *Hauberk*?"

"If you will start doing what nobody has done before,—"

"Well, somebody must start," said Melicent composedly, "or nobody would ever get anywhere. After all, these things matter so little. People very soon forget; and one is not nearly so important as one believes."

"Your common-sense and self-possession are getting quite odious, miss," said Brenda languidly.

Melicent was thoughtful.

"Very likely it is true what they say—that a business woman has got to sacrifice something. But I always was practical, you know."

"So little do we know ourselves," gasped Helston.

"Why? Am I not practical?"

"Dreamer, idealist, dweller in Utopia, believer in the Fourth dimension and in the sum of the really important things that nobody can classify—go to!" said he gravely. "Tell that to the reporters, but not to the unfortunate pater who had to hold you in when designing a house! 'Bridling the Tweed with a curb o' stane' would have just been an interval for light refreshment."

Melicent, her arms about her knees, laughed blithely.

"For sheer power of vituperation, you are hard to beat," she said. "Well, mater, what have you been doing all day?"

"When you have done railing at each other, you shall hear. I have news of a really exciting character, but I shall not tell it until there is a suitable demand."

Melicent whirled round and clutched her.

"What has happened? Speak instantly! Something nice? Something to take out the taste of that par.?"

"I have heard news and received a visitor: who but Lance Burmester?"

She had no reason to complain of lack of interest in her hearers. They rained questions upon her.

"He is in town for one night only," said she. "Goes down to Ilbersdale to-morrow; so I implored him to come back and dine. He demurred, on the ground that he had two friends with him, whom he could not desert One is a Captain Brooke, a friend picked up in Africa. The other is—guess, Melicent!"

There was a peculiar intonation in her voice.

Melicent looked up quickly, and met a mischievous look; and suddenly colour flooded the girl's face. Quite unexpectedly to herself, she did what she was never wont to do—she blushed; and she felt as though the blush covered her like a garment to the very feet.

The sensation made her furious. Why should she blush? At the memory of a period of her life now so incredibly remote that it seemed like a previous incarnation? She sometimes felt, in the infrequent moments when she recalled her amatory experiences, as though she had merely dreamed the savagery, the bestiality, of her African days; as though she had first awakened to life when her uncle drove her out upon the high heathery Nab that overlooked the moorlands.

Brenda's hint evoked a rushing stream of unpleasant, importunate memories. Was it possible that Bert had bridged the five years' silence? That he was still in pursuit—still claiming the promise made in a half-delirious moment?

Her inmost being sickened. It could not be! Not now, on the very threshold of her career—now that she had grown used to happiness and love and England. Disgust was so acute that she grew actually faint.

With a craving for air she sprang from her low seat by the fire, stood up, drew a long breath, flung back her head. What useless panic! She was free: no promise could be said to bind her! Why should she fear?

The shock, the overwhelming spasm of apprehension, passed away so quickly that the Helstons had barely time to wonder what was amiss when she took calmly on her lips the name that haunted her.

"Do you really mean that it is Bert Mestaer?"

Brenda laughed.

"Bert Mestaer! What a notion! You would hardly expect Mr. Burmester to make friends with him! Oh, no; it is someone whom you will really like to see—surely you can guess!"

"Mr. Mayne?"

"Of course!"

The relief, the reaction, were extraordinary. Melicent's head swam. With more demonstration of feeling than was usual to her, she clapped her hands.

"Oh, that is good! I am pleased! What a pity he did not get back in time for my twenty-first birthday last spring! I wonder whether he will think that I have changed!"

"Your wonder will be speedily set at rest. As it appeared that Lance was inseparable from his friends, and that this was his only night, I told him to bring them both back to dinner at eight. I sent Elizabeth for fish and cream, and I wish you would go into the dining-room on your way upstairs, and see that the flowers on the table are all right."

"Well!" cried Melicent, and heaved a sigh. "Things are happening tonight in the bosom of this peaceful family. Pater, just put away that odious newspaper in the table drawer, so that nobody can see it. To think of Mr. Mayne being in England! Why didn't he write and say he was coming?"

"I fancy he only quite suddenly found that he could get away. You see, all his plans are changed. He is to be Bishop of Pretoria."

"Bishop! Oh, lucky Pretoria!"

Melicent paused again, her eyes full of memories. She saw an open grave, a long black procession of uncouth people winding down the rough fields, past the Kaffir huts—the sun blazing down on Carol Mayne's sharp-cut, ascetic face.

"*I am the Resurrection and the Life. He that believeth on Me, though he were dead, yet shall he live.*"

The thought of what her heart had been then, torn with hatred, racked with grief, savage, sullen, lonely, arose in sharp contrast with the thought of all that had been since, all that she had come to understand, believe and hope, in these full years of growth that lay between.

Moved by a rare impulse, she stooped and tenderly kissed Brenda's forehead, before going to inspect the flowers upon the dinner-table.

CHAPTER XX
CAPTAIN BROOKE

"What man would risk the danger twice,
  Nor quake from head to heel?
Whom would not one such test suffice?"

—A. C. SWINBURNE.

Not Melicent herself looked forward to the moment of meeting with more eagerness than did the Bishop elect of Pretoria. He had been through many anxieties during his first months of guardianship; and his gratitude to the Helstons was immense. It was most natural that he should look forward with interest to a sight of the girl he had saved.

She was not present in the drawing-room when the three men arrived, but the cordiality of the Helstons' reception was delightful. Lance was grateful to them for including his friend, a big, silent man, who had been with much difficulty persuaded to come. Brenda assured him that six was a far better number than five, and made him welcome with sincerity which could not fail to please.

"But he wouldn't have come at all; he would have held out obstinately," said Lance gaily, "but for one thing, one mysterious reason, which will transpire later. You needn't blush, Brooke."

"Haven't the least intention of it; don't play the fool, Burmester. I suppose it was natural for an outsider to feel that he was intruding on a party of friends who were meeting after long separation."

"Just as well for you to become acquainted now, for you'll be sure to meet at Fransdale," said Lance easily. "I suppose you are going up for Easter, Mrs. Helston, and I am taking Brooke and the Bishop to Ilbersdale."

As he spoke, the door opened, and all three men turned to watch Melicent as she came in.

She had rather more colour than usual, and her expression was strangely arresting. Her evening gown was white, and trailed over the soft carpet with a delicate rustling. She walked straight up to Carol Mayne, her eyes shining, her two hands outstretched: and he caught them in his, meeting her glance with the piercing, deep-set eyes she remembered so well of old.

"Well!" he cried. "So this is you! How thankful I ought to be that my responsibilities are over! Ah, well, I don't think I should have known you, if I had met you in the street, but I am beginning to recognise the eyes, the brow! The smile is new. I never saw that in Africa; did I, Miss Lutwyche?"

She looked up gravely, but with a certain kindled enthusiasm, far more impressive than a girl's laughter.

"*Miss Lutwyche!*" she said reproachfully. "I shall not allow that. As for you, you are not a bit changed. I should know you anywhere—Bond Street, or darkest Africa."

"What about me, Miss Lutwyche?" cried Lance pleadingly.

"You have improved," she said, with an air of critical appraisement. "You are not nearly so—lady-like as you used to be."

They all laughed.

"Are you still a crack shot, as you used to be?" he cried.

"I shoot every autumn. I have improved," she replied demurely.

When Captain Brooke had been presented, they all sat down, and the talk hung fire a little.

"It is too big," said Melicent, with a little sigh. "There is so much to say, we don't know where to begin. Mr. Mayne, I know, is thinking of me with my hair in a pig-tail, and a calico frock, slouching across the yard with a copper bucket; and Mr. Burmester is thinking of a time when I was locked up in disgrace in the Vicarage schoolroom, and not allowed to go to a picnic; and Captain Brooke is thinking how disagreeable it is of people to have reminiscences he cannot share."

Captain Brooke smiled a little.

"I am thinking that it is hard to fancy you in a calico dress with a copper bucket," he said.

Melicent was suddenly grave.

"People who have always lived in England don't realise," she said absently. "We dwell in a kind of Garden of Eden here, and nobody appreciates it. They should go to some place such as I was brought up in, and learn what thorns and briars lie outside the garden gates."

"I saw a good deal of it during the campaign," the soldier answered. "A good deal of outer darkness, I mean."

"Does England seem good after it?" she asked.

"Exactly what you say. Like the Garden of Eden."

At the moment dinner was announced, and they went into the dining-room.

"I suppose," said Melicent, who was seated next Mr. Mayne, "that it is of no use to ask you after old acquaintance? It is so long since you left Slabbert's Poort?"

"Well," he answered, "I have kept up with one or two of the folks there. But the general scatter, when the war broke out, made great changes, though, as you know, the place was never in the line of march. Marten Brandt still owns the Vierkleur."

"I often meant to ask you in my letters what became of Otis?"

"The great Amurrica? It is reported that he made himself notorious in the Boer Irish brigade, but later on—after the capture of Kroonstadt—he turned up on the British side, got a commission in a scallywag corps, how I know not, and is quite a great person now."

"Not sure he ain't a colonel; I knocked up against the beast," said Lance. "Remember hearing about Gouverneur J. Otis, eh Brooke? Remember the story of Sal's Drift and the stampede of the gun mules?"

The two men laughed, as at a common memory.

"Worst of him was, the brute was so witty," said Lance. "I believe all our officers knew he was not to be trusted, but they made no end of a fuss with him. Daresay he'll be turning up in England soon, in some swell house that's been lent as a convalescent home, and flirt with all the titled girls as bold as you please."

"Let's see; he was the chap who got his head punched by Millie's Boer champion, wasn't he?" asked Mr. Helston.

His wife gave him a warning glance. Young Burmester was present, and he knew nothing of the girl's vicissitudes, nor was it desirable that he should. Besides, there was a stranger among them. She could see, by the way he instantly began to speak, that Mayne was as desirous as she to turn the subject; but Lance had caught the word.

"Hallo, Miss Lutwyche! had you begun breaking heads and hearts, even before you came over?" he asked gaily, across the table.

"Boers don't trouble about hearts," said the girl, with composure. "We were a pastoral people, and never did anything interesting. It is you from whom we expect tales of prowess. Did you never escape in a goods train, or scale a prison wall, or—"

"As to that," said Lance, "I've a magnificent yarn, all ready for telling, only this beggar"—indicating his friend, who sat next to him and opposite Millie—"tried, before he would come here to-night, to get me to promise not to tell."

Melicent had wholly succeeded in turning away the subject. The silent captain reddened, looked morose, and was heard to murmur that Burmester was a rotter.

"I hope you were not so rash as to make the promise in question?" cried Brenda.

"Well, do you know, as far as to-night goes, I'm afraid I did!" owned Lance.

"You did," said Brooke distinctly.

"But the fact of it is," said Lance lightly, "that he saved my life. Ever heard it said that if you save a man's life, he's sure to do you a bad turn? Look out for me, Brooke."

"I'll look out for myself," was the unamiable reply.

"But it's only if you save from drowning that the proverb applies," said the host.

"Well, this was drowning. River suddenly rose while the column was crossing; and the last men got washed away. But this is spoiling my yarn. I'll keep it for when Brooke isn't about."

"I told you I should spoil sport if I came," said Brooke grimly.

Melicent looked at him with some amusement

He was a fair man, severely tanned by exposure. He was clean-shaven, and the salient feature of his face was his large, finely-cut, strong yet delicate mouth: a mouth which lifted his otherwise rough-hewn face up to a different level, and made it full of possibilities. With such a mouth a man might be a poet, a soldier, a statesman; but whatever he was, that he would thoroughly be. He was also shy, to an extent that was amusing in such a Hercules. When he spoke, he muttered: and he hardly ever raised his eyes.

The gentlemen did not linger over their wine. Mayne was anxious to talk to Melicent of her future, and Lancelot was astonished at himself for the anxiety he felt to return to the drawing-room. He remembered a day when he had seen a slip of a girl seated on Tod's Trush, and how he had said to Helston: "One is conscious of a personality." He was vividly conscious of it now. It was the "indefinable something" that Melicent possessed. She never spoke much, but always gave the fascinating impression of vast reserves behind, of a boundless store from which she could give more, and always more.

He was vexed with Mrs. Helston for engaging him at some length in talk, which she did advisedly, to allow Carol to talk to the girl.

It was with interest and satisfaction that Mayne listened to her, and found out how soon she hoped to be self-supporting, and how close were the ties that bound her to her friends. There seemed no cloud upon her horizon; life, which had begun so stormily seemed, like many a rainy English morn, to be breaking out into a cloudless sky.

"But there is one thing I want to ask you about," said Melicent presently. "I have one wrinkle among my rose-leaves. It is only a little thing, yet at times I fear it I have a constant dread that ... you know who ... may turn up. I expect it is very silly of me. Men soon forget these things; and in so long a time, he is sure to have forgotten. But I have wished to see you, to make sure. I didn't like to write about it. I can't help a dreadful kind of feeling rushing over me at times, that he..." she looked round. Nobody was in hearing but Captain Brooke, idly turning over music on the piano; she dropped her voice—"that Bert Mestaer—may still think he has a claim on me."

There was a silence, which the chat of the group by the fire did not seem to break. Captain Brooke earnestly studied the song he was reading.

"That idea—the idea that Mestaer might still think of you—would not be pleasant to you?" asked Mayne.

"Pleasant?" the word was a gasp. "But you see the life that is mine now," she said tremulously. "You remember the house of bondage—the darkness and shadow of death."

"Bert Mestaer wanted to loose your bonds."

"Oh, no! Only to bind me to another master!"

"I think you wrong him there, Melicent."

She turned towards him, put out one hand, and laid it on his.

"It was you who saved me; you delivered my soul from the snare of the hunter," she said. "If Mestaer let me go, you were the only man that could have persuaded him. You know it; we need not discuss it. What I want you to tell me is, whether you have seen or heard anything of him; whether he is alive or dead."

"He was certainly alive when I left Africa. He did splendidly during the war. I believe he is considered the finest scout in the British army. I feel sure I may take it upon myself to say, on his behalf, that he will never make himself obnoxious to you. You need be in no fear of him."

"He has forgotten all that nonsense about me?"

"I don't exactly know what you mean by nonsense, Millie. If you mean his love for you, I don't think I can truly say that he has forgotten."

She made a little sound of dismay.

"But he is in process of forgetting—he must be!" she cried. "Anyhow, he doesn't expect me to start off to Africa to keep the promise he says I made?"

"Nothing could be farther from his thoughts, I assure you."

"Well, that is what I wanted to be sure of! Now I shall breathe freely again. I will confess to you now, that I had a terrible moment this evening. Mater said Mr. Burmester had come home, and laughed and asked me to guess who was with him! I leaped to the conclusion that it was Bert Mestaer, and I suddenly found myself in the grip of a blind terror. I thought I should faint, all the horror of that dreadful time came back so clearly. I don't think I could have faced him...."

But Lance was no longer to be held back. He broke away from his captors, and came towards Millie, calling for a song. Captain Brooke, who still stood forlorn and rigid by the piano, leaning his chin on his hand, was roughly pushed away. Melicent sat down without shyness, and sang two or three ballads in a voice that—like herself—was small and flexible and very distinctive. The last thing she sang was that wonderful little piece of inspiration,

"The night has a thousand eyes."

Captain Brooke was turning over for her.

"That's very true," he said,

"'The mind has a thousand eyes,
The heart but one,'"

he repeated thoughtfully.

"Yes," she answered; "yet many people seem content with the one! I suppose all women used to be! Think what an awful fate, to look on life merely as a matter of sentiment! The thousand eyes are better, don't you think so?"

"I never tried," he answered simply.

The reply struck her as remarkable, but she had no time to reflect upon it, for Lance again struck in:

"Seems to me wonderful, with a profession of your own, that you should find time to learn to sing so beautifully," he said.

"The singing is my recreation," she replied, "the other my serious work."

"Ah!" cried Lance, "and that reminds me of old Brooke's business and the reason why he came here to-night! Do you know, Miss Lutwyche, Brooke wants to build a house, and he's been reading a paragraph in the *Hauberk* about a lady architect."

Melicent grew pink, and looked down.

"Captain Brooke won't want to give his work to such a complete novice," she said demurely. "Now that he has seen me, he will want to retire gracefully from his intention, and you put him in a cruel dilemma by mentioning it."

"I like trying experiments," said the Captain, with more animation than he had yet displayed.

Everyone was now crowding with interest around the music-stool where Melicent sat.

"What and where would your house be, Captain Brooke?" asked Helston.

"It would be in my—my—the place my people come from," he replied. "It's in Wiltshire."

"Wiltshire! That's a variable county; on Salisbury Plain?"

"No; it's a pretty village. Clunbury, they call it."

"What kind of house do you think of building?"

"I should leave that entirely to Miss Lutwyche."

"I say, Melicent, here's your chance!" cried Helston mischievously. "You'll be able to send another paragraph to the *Hauberk*?"

"How dare you?" she cried, threatening him in mock rage. "Oh ... but this is wonderful! Are you serious, Captain Brooke?"

"Quite. I have bought the land. Only about twenty acres. I should like your advice about the actual site of the house."

"Well, Millie, if you give satisfaction over this, your career is made," cried Brenda.

"But what kind of house do you want?" cried the girl. "You must tell me that!"

"No; that's what I shall pay you to tell me," said Millie's client calmly. He smiled for the first time, as he added: "You have the thousand eyes."

"Well!" said Melicent, "the agitations of this day have been quite too much for me!"

"Do your people live at Clunbury?" asked Helston of the Captain.

"Oh, no; not now. They sold their last acre in my grandfather's time. A churchyard full of their graves is all that is left. It is, however, a part of their land that I have bought back."

"That is the kind of thing I would like to do myself," said Carol Mayne.

"Now, Miss Lutwyche, is the house rising before your mind's eye?" cried Lance, pleased at the intense interest created by the scheme.

"Not yet," said Melicent; but her eyes were dreamy. "What kind of people were your forbears?" she asked the Captain.

"Merely yeomanry," he answered, "and wholly Philistine; people with one eye."

"And do you want the house to resemble them in tone?" she asked, smiling at his allusion.

"No. I want it to be the typical house that is in your mind; the house you would live in, if you could choose."

She laughed.

"Take care! You don't know how lordly my ideas may be! You will have to bring them down to the level of estimates."

"Do you want the thing put in hand at once?" asked Helston.

"Yes, I do. I should like Miss Lutwyche to come down and look at the site before I go to Ilbersdale for Easter."

"Well, Millie, you must make up your mind! Do you accept the order?" cried Carol Mayne.

"I should like to come down and look at the site before I finally say Yes," said she. "And ask Captain Brooke all manner of questions."

"That will suit me well," he replied gravely. "To-day is Monday. Shall we say Thursday?"

CHAPTER XXI
MIRAGE

"He who has seen a city in the skies
Knows he may never cool his tired eyes
At the fair waters of that Paradise.
But the one moment when he thought his feet
Would enter that dream-city, was so sweet
That he can bear the noonday and its heat."

—ALICE HERBERT.

The sky was clear and starry; the night was swept by the strong, clean current of the March wind, as the three men stepped out into Collis Square.

"How shall we get back?" asked Burmester, lighting his cigar. "Train, tube or bus?"

"I shall walk," said Brooke, with brevity.

They were standing just beneath a street lamp, whose strong light, falling on his face, showed it haggard and strained. Burmester did not observe it.

"You don't catch me!" he cried jovially, flinging away his light. "Come on, Bishop—leave that maniac to his own devices. Here's a hansom, the very thing."

The jingling cab pulled up at his signal, and he sprang in. "Rhodes Hotel!"

"All right, Burmester, I'm walking a bit with Brooke," said Mayne.

"The deuce you are! Nice trick to play on me!" cried Lance, as he was bowled away.

"Why can't you go with him, and leave me to myself?" growled Brooke, lighting a pipe with a hand that shook.

"Because I want your society, though it seems the desire is not mutual."

There was no reply. They tramped eastwards in silence, past the Marble Arch, down Park Lane into Grosvenor Square, and on into Berkeley Square, where suddenly Brooke said:

"I wish you would go."

"You're not playing fair," quietly replied Mayne. "Conspirators ought to share confidences."

"Confide away then."

"All right, I will. I am as pleased as I feel sure you must be, though you don't show it, at the result of your idea."

"Pleased!" echoed Brooke. "Pleased! ... Great Heaven! Pleased, are you? But then, you see, I am not you. Bishop, I know every line of her face, every tone of her voice, though I never heard but one in the old days! I know her as a man knows the land where he was born; and she could sit looking full at me across the table, and not know she had ever seen me! ... Man! How have I come through it?"

"Excellently. I don't understand you. Surely it is what you were hoping for, planning for—complete non-recognition? What would have happened if she had known you? You heard what she said to me about you?"

"Every word;" his voice sank to a despairing whisper.

"She is at least consistent," said Mayne.

An inarticulate murmur of assent.

"I don't think the non-recognition wonderful," went on Mayne. "You see, she never thought about you, or even looked at you attentively in old days. And think what you were like then! Not only the outer man has changed. Remember that I myself, when first I saw you without your beard, and without your slouch, and without your oaths—in your uniform, drilled into a self-respecting Englishman—I did not know you."

"But you did, as soon as I said: 'Don't you remember me?'"

"Exactly; because you did say so. But you have not said so to Miss Lutwyche; and don't you see that your very failure to do so would banish the idea of your possible identity from her mind? You come before her with looks, words, manners, your very nationality—all changed! An English landed proprietor! Doubtless she knows nothing of the great diamond find on the High Farm, nor of the fortune you have realised. The idea that you should adopt such a method of gaining access to her, would never strike her, it would not seem characteristic of her preconceived idea of you."

"I don't know how I got through," said the Captain brokenly. "When she came in, looking like an angel from God ... and passed me by and went up to you! By George, Mayne, she was right! It was you who saved her! But for you—"

"She was wrong; it was you," said Mayne. "She will probably never know the fight you made; women don't understand these things, and it is as well they don't. Things go like that in the world."

"She's beautiful, Mayne; don't you think so?"

Mayne laughed.

"I don't think her at all angelic," he replied, "but I will own that she seems to me less unlovable than I used to think her in Africa. Don't punch my head! ... Burmester admired her, I thought."

"Yes, confound him!"

"But you have made a splendid opening. The idea of the house was a masterly one. It gives you endless opportunities and a common interest. Only remember, you must keep yourself well in hand. As I warned you, the game is a dangerous one. One false move may cost you all."

"The worst is over now," returned the Captain. "The awfulness of feeling that she's everything to me, I a nightmare to her! I can still hardly believe she didn't know me."

"Everything was in your favour. She was full of my return, and of relief that it was I, not you. The silent Captain Brooke was a negligible quantity."

"She never looked at me squarely but once. That was in the middle of dinner. My heart nearly stopped. I had to lower my eyes lest they should say things. Ah, well; you're a good sort, and no mistake. I'm glad we've talked it out, though I was a sulky brute at first."

"H'm! Yes; Melicent might think the change in you not so deep if she had heard your way with me this evening," said his friend drily. "The old Bert is still there, in spite of all the polish."

Bert laughed as he strode on, with his long, swinging step. He made a fine tribute to the creative powers of Sergeant What's-his-name. There had been good material to work upon, and the right kind of training; and the result was something like a miracle.

In the old days, Mayne had realised that this man was something out of the common: but even he had not been prepared for his persistence, nor for his wonderful *flair* for knowing the right men, reading the right books, doing the right thing. During all these five years, no week had passed without the exchange of letters between those two. Mayne had sent up books, had cheered and inspired his pupil, had never let him feel that nobody cared. Bert had bent all the powers of his strong mind and still stronger will towards the attainment of his one idea. His life had been a life of monastic purity, of iron self-control, of self-denial and constant effort. It was hard for the priest to believe that such a wonderful thing could fail of its reward. But he had been troubled at what Melicent said that evening. He almost made up his mind that he would tell her something of what her influence had meant to Bert. But his final decision was for complete inaction in this most delicate matter. Bert must fight his own battle, and win his own victory. The time had come for his friend to stand aside.

Far into the night Mayne was considering the case. He, with his unusual insight into souls, had found a certain egotism and hardness in Melicent. The hardness was inherent—it had always been there; and her present life of independence and success was likely to foster it. Did she know, at that moment, that a man was in London who had spent five laborious years in fitting himself for her conquest, as a nation may equip itself for a great campaign—and who was bent solely upon that quest—he felt pretty certain that her only impulse would be to escape from him, to guard her own freedom, to determine resolutely never to be enslaved.

Would the constancy and persistence of the man be a match for the hardness and self-will of the woman?

He thought Bert might stand a better chance of winning, were it not for the bitter memories which were bound up in the girl's mind with him. That she should long remain in ignorance of his identity was inconceivable: and when she recognised him—what then?

Bert was his own spiritual son; his desire for his success was intense. But now that he had seen Melicent, he was full of doubts. Carefully as Bert had educated himself, the gulf between them was still wide.

He could do nothing but pray.

CHAPTER XXII
RECOGNITION

"Go from me. Yet I feel that I shall stand
Henceforward in thy shadow. Nevermore
Alone upon the threshold of my door
Of individual life, I shall command
The uses of my soul, nor lift my hand
Serenely in the sunshine as before."

—SONNETS FROM THE PORTUGUESE.

It had been arranged that the fledgling architect should be accompanied by Mr. Helston, and have the benefit of his knowledge and experience when she went down to look at Captain Brooke's estate at Clunbury. But fate decreed otherwise. On Thursday morning Mr. Helston was in bed with a high temperature and sore throat. A railway journey on a raw, gusty day in early spring was out of the question for him; and Melicent was obliged to go alone.

Brenda suggested something about her being unchaperoned, which was met by the young lady with unspeakable scorn.

"Better throw up my profession at once, if Mrs. Grundy is to have a say in my business arrangements," she remarked; and caught her train at Paddington with professional composure.

She alighted at a small station on a branch line, which was the nearest point to the village; and as she stepped from the compartment, Captain Brooke approached, in a suit of country tweeds, gaiters and knickerbockers. In such guise he reminded her of her beloved Dalesmen, and the idea gave kindness to her smile of greeting.

As he approached, she noted that he looked pale under his tan, and seemed not perfectly ready to speak at once.

"So Mr. Helston was unable," he brought out, after manifest hesitation.

The girl looked surprised.

"I am so sorry! He is in bed with a severe chill. I bring you his apologies. But if you think he is indispensable—" she added, as an afterthought, puzzled by the disturbance visible in his face.

"Oh! by no means. It is good of you to come alone," he said hurriedly. "This way, please; I have only a hired trap at present, and am putting up at the inn near here, which is two miles from the village. I've ordered lunch, but it won't be much good, I'm afraid; these English country inns are astonishingly bad."

"Please don't apologise," she said. "I am used to roughing it, and I like it."

He smiled, as he tucked her into the dog-cart, and remarked, as he climbed to his seat beside her.

"Collis Square didn't seem very rough to me."

"Ah! But you haven't seen me at work. I can lay bricks, mix mortar, point walls—it's delicious."

He laughed. "I feel sure you could do anything you tried," he said.

They drove on briskly, through a lane whose hedges were beginning to show bronze buds upon their blackness. The sky, after some boisterous sleet storms, was washed a clear, pure blue. A faint golden haze of willow catkins brooded over the adjacent brown copses, and the wet sparkles on the bare boughs threw back the sunbeams. Here and there the lazy reek from a cottage chimney hung pearly against the indigo fir woods—a typical English April, and a typical English landscape.

"Do you like this country?" he asked abruptly, and his tone seemed to imply that he thought anybody must.

She made a conventional answer that it was very pretty.

"Perhaps you don't care for scenery?" he inquired anxiously.

She turned to him laughing.

"Oh," she said, "scenery is my particular fad. But this is too tame for me. You should see my Cleveshire moors and dales!"

His silence, in some inscrutable way, conveyed to her the idea of extreme mortification.

"Do you mean," he presently asked, "that you wouldn't care to live in this part of England?"

"I shouldn't choose it," she replied carelessly. "But then, I have no links with it. I quite appreciate your reason for choosing it."

"You do?"

"Undoubtedly. Your ancestry drew their living from this soil; they ate the corn it grew, the cattle it fed. In a real sense, you are part of this little bit of little England. There must be something in you that is in mysterious sympathy with it."

"That's how I feel," he replied, as though gratified to be so interpreted by her. "But I admire the country for itself too; it seems a great pleasure-ground—a sort of park laid out by God Almighty."

"I like more mystery, more wildness."

"I've had enough wildness," he answered very determinedly. "I like this because of its cultivation and fertility and order."

"I'd like to show you Fransdale," she said, smiling.

"I hope you will," he replied. "I'm going to Ilbersdale, you know." He reflected for some minutes, then said: "Should you advise me not to decide on this till I've seen the other?"

"What!" cried Millie, "when you've bought your land, and found your ancestors and all! I never heard of such a thing."

"I might put up a shooting-box on the moors," he said reflectively.

"You must be very rich," commented the girl, in wonder.

"I suppose I am. I did a big deal in land out there," he replied.

Privately she thought he had more money than wits; but perhaps he would make none the worse client for that.

They reached the inn, and he ushered her into the quaint, low parlour, with the usual stuffed birds, coloured almanacks and corner cupboard.

During the interval before the appearance of the roast fowl and boiled ham, she unrolled the drawings she had brought, spread them on a table in the window, and described them to him. The sun streamed in at the lattice, gilding her hair where it curled over and about the edges of her wide, flat, dark-blue cap as she sat absorbed in her plans and ideas. Her companion drank in the details of her dainty presence—from her fine skin to her firm, little hands, from her natty, embroidered collar to the strong, laced boots appearing below her short blue serge skirt. He was considering whether he found her more adorable in the lamplight in her white gown, or in the sunshine, in her workmanlike, country suit Suddenly he was conscious that he had failed to answer a question, and that a severe, surprised little face was being lifted to his.

Their glances met; he had a moment's awful apprehension. It seemed to him that she had caught him unawares without his mask. He had no notion what was the question she had asked, and he floundered desperately.

"You were saying—I am such a thundering ass—my mind had gone off. I was thinking that you can see the Lone Ash, where I want to build—from this window—there. That hill to the left—"

The inn maid-servant, bringing in the lunch, saved him.

But his moment of confusion, so much greater than the occasion seemed to warrant, had jarred the smooth, impersonal nature of Miss Lutwyche's opinion of him. There had been so remarkable a look—almost of consternation—in the man's eyes as he faced her. She had been at some pains to expound the main principle of the Lee-Simmons system of drainage for isolated houses, which was her special fancy, and which she was most anxious to have him adopt; and it was certainly annoying to find that she had been speaking to deaf ears. But his curious expression when she had looked at him! He had seemed like one suddenly caught in the act—taken red-handed. What could the thought be which had absorbed his attention, and reddened his brown cheek?

She was so kind as to repeat her information while they sat at lunch together, and had no cause this time to complain of lack of attention. But his momentary lapse had occasioned in her a subtle change of mental attitude. She was, without knowing why, suddenly on her guard—all at once concerned with this man, about whom before she had not thought at all.

Of course she did not say this to herself. Like all deep-seated motions of the mind, it was spontaneous, unrealised. But it was there; and the man encountered it, felt it with his alarming sensitiveness where she was concerned; and by degrees there arose up within him a profound uneasiness, which made the simplest sentence an effort.

Melicent soon settled, in her positive way, what was wrong. She thought the Captain, being rich and eligible, was nervous of being *tête-à-tête* with his youthful lady architect. She spoke with elaborate ease and unconcern, determined to show him there was nothing to fear; but he seemed each moment more self-conscious.

There was, nevertheless, no doubt that he was interested—not only in the speaker, but in what she was saying. By the time lunch was over, he had practically decided upon the Lee-Simmons idea, and was eager to transport his architect to the scene of her enterprise at once. He went outside to the little rough plot of green before the inn to find the ostler; and urged by an impulse of such curiosity as she seldom felt, Melicent went to the window to watch him.

A few village children were at play upon the green; and one little girl, probably inspired by parents who hoped for some advantage from the rich man who was going to make his home among them, shyly approached him as he stood.

He had put his hands behind him, and forgotten himself in staring at the hill crowned by the Lone Ash, where he meant his fairy palace to arise. The little fair girl advanced diffidently, shyly holding out a big round bouquet of primroses, tightly tied together. He turned, looking down at her, half-amused; and Melicent thought that the big, fine man and the blushing child with her flowers, illumined by the crude spring sunshine, looked like the coloured supplement to a Christmas Number.

The Captain accepted the flowers, felt in his pocket for a penny, and turned back towards the inn door, with the intention of presenting the floral tribute to Miss Lutwyche.

Now, what was there in that action — what sudden thrill of memory — of recognition — of pain, like a sharp blow on a raw spot — darted to the brain of the girl who watched in the window?

She had seen a man come into a room once, with a bunch of flowers in his awkward, unaccustomed hand; she had heard the slapping thud with which they had been hurled into the grate.

"*So you'll break your word!*"

It seemed to her that the words were spoken aloud, now, at this moment, in the room. And a blinding light illuminated her. She knew, as completely as a moment before she had ignored, that Captain Brooke was none other than Bert Mestaer.

Waves of cold and heat, sudden dizziness clutched her. He was coming in — in a moment he would be there — she could not face him.

Terror prevented unconsciousness. Catching at the furniture, she staggered across the room to the inner room leading to the kitchen.

"Take me upstairs — a bedroom — I must lie down!" she gasped; and as the maid-servant, scared by her white face, rushed forward and encircled her with a strong arm, she gasped: "Don't say anything to Captain Brooke ... please. I shall be ... better directly."

The girl half supported, half dragged her up the narrow stair.

"Dear miss, what shall I do? Burnt feathers? Key down your back?" cried she distractedly.

"Is there—cold water? Yes, that's all. Go away please. Go! Come back in ten minutes. Leave me alone now."

Melicent turned the key in the door, and sank upon the scanty feathers of the rocky bed. For several minutes her one overpowering, paralysing sensation was fear. She could not think at all.

She lay prone, while the surging currents of her nerves slowly settled themselves and adjusted their balance. Her sense of outward things came back to her by degrees. The fine cold air flowed through the little casement with the sunshine. Wheels crunched upon the gravel below; a dog barked; someone spoke; in the distance a cow lowed. The world went on as usual, lapt in afternoon, rural peace. But from her skies the sun had dropped. The nightmare that had pursued her for years was now beside her in bodily shape, dogging her steps. Mestaer had come back.

How came it that she had not known? She answered herself bitterly that it was because she had trusted Carol Mayne, and he had allowed her to be deceived. Not for one moment did she now doubt Captain Brooke's identity. The marvel was that she had not detected him at once.

This had been the first time of her looking at him, he being unconscious of the fact of her observation; and in that moment he had betrayed himself, she could not have told how.

And now in what a net was she caught! The thought of the man's persistency turned her cold. She was committed to his acquaintance, involved in a business transaction with him—he was going to Ilbersdale. Even in Fransdale she should not be safe from him! And Carol Mayne had connived at this betrayal!

It did not take her long to form a decision on one point; namely, that her only hope lay in going on as if nothing had happened.

Surely she was capable of that! She, the self-contained, self-reliant professional woman!

Reaction had set in. Passionate anger, active defiance succeeded fear. It was quite simple, after all. She had stolen a march upon the conspirators and surprised their plans. It was the best thing that could have happened. She knew now what to guard against—could avoid intimacy and repel advances.

Springing from the bed, she dashed water into the basin, bathed her hot forehead, and was once more her own mistress, all her spirit, all her force, summoned up to defend her liberty.

She peeped from the window. Captain Brooke stood waiting by the trap below. His attitude betrayed a subdued impatience. Undoubtedly he was much changed—completely altered from the man she had known. There was real excuse for her non-recognition. But that he should have imagined that such an incognito could be sustained! No wonder he had betrayed nervousness that morning when he faced the idea of a day alone with her!

Well, they were equals now! He knew, and she knew. If she could prevent his knowing that she knew, all would be well.

She snatched up her gloves, and ran lightly downstairs, not allowing herself time to pause, but passing straight out into the sunshine to meet him.

CHAPTER XXIII
REBELLION

"— —You knew not me
Master of your joys and fears;
Held my hands that held the key
Of the treasure of your years,
Of the fountain of your tears.
For you knew not it was I,
And I knew not it was you.
We have learnt, as days went by.
But a flower struck root and grew
Underground, and no one knew."

—MRS. MEYNELL.

"I'm afraid I've kept you waiting," she said a little breathlessly, as she sprang into the cart.

"Oh, that's nothing, to a fellow who is always waiting," was his calm reply.

"Always waiting! What for?" cried Melicent, wonder overleaping discretion.

"For the future, I suppose," he answered, after a short hesitation. Adding, as though suddenly conscious of being eccentric: "You know—that endless chivying of De Wet got on one's nerves."

"I can quite believe it," said Melicent cheerfully. "But now, to-morrow has come, as I used to say when I was a small child. You've made your pile—you're an English landed proprietor. You're not waiting any longer."

"Oh, yes, I am. There's one thing I haven't got yet," he said, a slow, curious smile curving his fine mouth.

He did not look at her as he spoke, which fact was her salvation. She could rule her voice, but not the rebel blood that waved live banners in her cheeks.

"Obviously," she returned lightly, "there must be a mistress for Lone Ash when it is built. Is this what you're waiting for?"

Her own daring dazzled her. It was a thing that he could not possibly conceive her saying had she had any notion of who he was.

"Yes," he answered quietly, "that's what I'm waiting for."

"And that's just what you'll never get by waiting!" she cried gaily.

He turned sharply upon her. "How do you know? What do you mean?" he asked, amazed.

"If you want a wife, you must go in search of one," she answered mischievously. "They don't drop into people's mouths."

"Well, that's what I will do," was his tranquil answer; "but one thing at a time, you know."

"One thing at a time," she echoed, lightly; and as she spoke, he checked his horse at the gate of a field.

"Here begins my property," he said, "and my idea is to have the drive entrance-gate here, and the house over yonder, just below the brow, screened from the road by those trees. The ground falls away to the south and west, you will notice, but the Lone Ash hill would keep off the wind. I want to know what you would think."

He had alighted, opened the gate, and led the horse and cart through. Now he proceeded, striding over the grass, and Melicent, her arms round her knees, forgot nervousness and bravado alike in her professional enthusiasm. They passed a large cluster of barns.

"The house was here," he said. "The man who bought it found it too far gone to repair, and knocked it down, leaving the outer shell for barn walls. Not much of a place, you see. I don't know why they put it here, except for the well. But there shouldn't be any difficulty about getting water. I sank a shaft up yonder, where I am going to show you, and we struck good water at thirty feet."

She found herself chatting to him about subsoils and surface water in a wholly professional manner.

When he reached the place where he proposed to build, she found herself unable to suggest an improvement. It was an ideal site—near the village, yet secluded, sheltered, but not shut in—overlooking a bit of broken ground which gave quite a prospect; and a regular trap for sunbeams. There was little she could suggest by way of alteration; she grasped the main features of his thought with instant appreciation. They sat down side by side upon the trunk of a felled elm; she brought out her sketch-book, and drew suggestions. By degrees a house shaped itself to her mind's eye—a house full of pleasant detail.

The south front was to face a terrace; the drawing-room to be at the western end, with two sunset avenues, converging upon the large door-window. One was to focus the dying sun in winter, one in summer. Both were to be grass walks, cypress-bordered, and they were to lead to a rectangular fish-pond, set with lilies, and reached by shelving steps. Beyond the fish-pond, a warm brick wall, with deeply alcoved seats.

The cypress-edged grass walks were her special fancy.

"But don't have them unless you like," she earnestly advised. "Some people think them sad."

He would have had hop-poles at her recommendation, but he managed to appear genuinely convinced.

Then, in fancy, his architect wandered back to the house—to the hall, with its two-branched staircase, and the windows in the gallery above.

"This house will be plain grey stone," she said, "and its roof will be of tiles, to prevent the effect being too cold. We shall try to pick up tiles that are already weathered, so that it may not look too new. I will not introduce anything that is a deliberate imitation of what was old, such as timbering, barge-boards, or painted woodwork. You shall have no grotesques; you must not yearn for a letter-box shaped like the Ace of Spades, as they have in Hampstead, nor for garrets with the window set at the end of a tunnel, as one sees in all the new toy suburbs. Our gables will be few; our roof shall not be cut to pieces. All our lines shall be simple, and our chimney-stacks things of beauty."

Her face was rapt as she sat looking at the bare ground where in fancy she saw her creation taking shape. Captain Brooke, sitting at her side, let himself go for a brief moment, gazing his fill upon the face that was always graven on his heart. It did not take her long to become conscious of the scrutiny of his steady eyes. The moment that he saw she had come out of her dream, he rose, and walked away to the excavations his workmen had made, returning with lumps of marl and chalky soil in his hands, and quietly making a remark about foundations.

As they plunged into the discussion of builders, estimates, contracts, etc., she realised that she was full of reluctant admiration for him. How well he bore himself! How completely he was master of his feelings! She felt, she knew, that he was entirely to be trusted. His speech was correct, his bearing dignified; nobody would now take him for anything but an English gentleman. Five years had wrought all this in him. How persistently he must have striven; how hard he must have worked!

And all this, she must conclude, had been done for her—for one whose heart was wholly untouched by any answering feeling—to whom the mere thought of him was pain and humiliation—who asked nothing better than never to see him again.

As the thought of her present position flooded her again, she felt so strong an impulse of resentment that for a long moment she was inclined to throw down her plans, rise and denounce him—repudiate his claims, break the chain that seemed to hold her, leave him where he stood, and flee from him for ever. How could she go on like this, now that she knew? Did not every moment that passed leave her more deeply committed to the incredible situation?

Never did she remember before to have been the victim of indecision. Now she, the self-poised, self-sufficient Miss Lutwyche, was swayed to and fro like a reed in the grip of opposing passions. Terror drew her one way, pride and ambition another. Under all, the mainspring of all, though she knew it not, the desire to defy Bert, to pay him back in his own coin, to seize his masquerade and turn it into a weapon for her own use, to punish him withal.

And all the while the rollicking April wind sang in the tree-tops, the sun moved westward, the light grew mellow, till the lump of earth in the captain's hand gleamed like a lump of gold. And his architect walked to and fro beside him; paused here, moved on again upon a new impulse; measured out the dimensions of things with her long builder's tape, and caused the owner to stick little white bits of wood, marked with weird symbols, into the ground at certain intervals. So they stood and talked, each ignorant of the storms that swept the other.

The surface of the girl's manner—easy, impersonal, remote—was never once impressed by the tremendous undercurrent that lay below the man's cool utterances. She was thinking: "After all, this is quite easy. I could keep it up for ever."

He was telling himself—"This sort of thing can't go on. Could I bear another day like this?"

Suddenly, it was over. She looked at her watch and announced that she must catch the 5.10. For a moment the thought that the strain he had been feeling so acutely was to be forthwith relaxed, gave him so sharp a sense of loss that he could not immediately speak. When he did, it was to beg her to come back first to tea at the inn. She firmly declined this. The inn, to her, was horror-haunted. The ghost of her past had risen there to dog the footsteps which she had believed were free. She replied that she would have an hour at the junction in which to get tea, and must not stop now.

They returned to the dog-cart, and drove back, in so brooding a silence on his part, that she dashed into small talk, lest he should be contemplating some rash words. As they drove past the inn, she averted her eyes that she might not see the green, or recall what had stood there. The vision of poor Bert, with his bashful, uncertain smile, his ridiculous flowers, his hesitating advance, rose before her, creating sheer nausea. Once more she was lying in the parlour at High Farm, once more she felt the agony of her wounds, the scars of which must to this day be hidden from her dressmaker. The crimson of shame suffused her. Oh, if he could but have kept away! Usually she managed to forget all this—to forget that she was branded, physically and morally, by the searing flames of degradation. He was the living reminder of all she hated and rejected.

She fell silent, unable to continue her babble; and Bert was silent too. But as they neared the railway, and he found moments running short, he made a spasmodic effort at conversation.

"You were brought up in Africa, were you not?" he asked, as casually as he could. He might as well have held a match to gunpowder.

She turned upon him with a deadly quietude.

"Never speak to me of it," she said, almost between her teeth. "I have forgotten it all. Every memory, of place or people, revolts me. There is nothing that ever happened there, and nobody I ever knew there, except Mr. Mayne, that inspires me with any feeling but horror."

They were turning into the station yard. He made no reply to her words until he had brought the pony to a standstill; then, turning fully to her, he said, very simply:

"I beg your pardon."

Something in his dignity shamed her. He helped her down in silence, collected her odds and ends, felt under the seat, and brought out the fatal bunch of primroses, which he carried to the platform.

As they stood waiting, she said, hurriedly and nervously:

"I am sorry, Captain Brooke. I didn't mean to speak so horridly about Africa. I hope I didn't hurt your feelings."

"My mistake," he returned good-humouredly. "We're such slight acquaintances, I expect it was pretty cool cheek of me to ask you a personal question. I'm afraid there are a good many holes in my manners."

No man could have shouldered the blame more naturally. The train came in. He found her a carriage, and handed in her things to her; then shyly offered the flowers.

"A little village kid gave me these," he said; and she thought, as he spoke, how fine a head and shoulders he had, framed in the square of the open window. "I thought you might like to take them to town with you."

She just managed to say, with a vague smile, "Thank you." Then the train started, he had raised his hat, stepped back, and she was in solitude. For full five minutes she sat motionless, crouched together, her two hands gripping the seat, her eyes fixed on the unoffending primroses, whose delicate, mysterious fragrance stole towards her on the evening air.

At last, with a strangled cry, she sprang to her feet, seized them, hurled them with all her force through the window; and then, sinking back into her corner, burst into wild, ungovernable tears.

CHAPTER XXIV
UNREST

"Let me alone! Why must you claim me? I
Am woman—do you tell me I must lie
All passive in Fate's arms until I die?
I must not care for Art, nor crave to be
A force in this fair world—'tis not for me
To live my own life. Was I made for thee?
No! I am rebel! Through life's open gate
I pass alone, and free; you come too late!
Or is't too soon? I know not; let us wait."

Carol Mayne passed all that day in a state of feverish anxiety. In the evening he suggested to Lance that they should go round to Collis Square. It was late, but it was their only chance to call upon Mrs. Helston before leaving town. They arrived about half-past eight, and found Brenda in the drawing-room, and with her Theo Cooper, who was a frequent visitor.

It was now twelve months since this young lady had defied parental authority and gone on the stage.

She was conspicuously unfitted for such a life, being pretty in a showy way, forward and giddy. But her parents' very natural opposition did not weigh at all with her. They had so often objected to what was wholesome, reasonable, and harmless, that their opinion had no weight with any of their children. With their habitual reserve, they suppressed entirely their deeper reasons for objection, and the only one they ostensibly urged was: "What will people say?" To a girl whose one hope was to be notorious, this was no deterrent.

The affair of Gwendolen and young Freshfield had produced a curious effect in the Vicarage family. The strenuous efforts of Mr. and Mrs. Cooper to hush it up had been successful as regards their neighbours; but this success had been dearly purchased at home at the cost of lowering their children's estimate of them. These merciless critics had now discovered that whatever they did would be condoned, sooner than let the world suspect a family breach, or a family scandal. Mrs. Cooper's own theory of her perfection, and of her success as a wife, mother, and leader of conduct in the village, must be preserved at any sacrifice of truth.

Gwendolen and Madeline were despatched to school, the governess was dismissed, and all went on as usual. But from that moment each child took his or her own line.

George, the eldest, whose sulky protest against taking orders had been wholly ignored by his father, ran into debt at Oxford, failed to take his degree, and finally bolted to America, whence he wrote for funds at frequent intervals.

Willie, the next boy, who had some ability, after various letters and conversations which left the vicar enraged, humiliated, well-nigh heart-broken, had gone to reside with an agnostic community in East London. He was just the man they wanted—his intellect exactly of the calibre which quickly assimilates specious argument, and reproduces it in an attractive form; and the Fraternity of Man paid him one hundred pounds per annum to teach men brotherhood, while denying meanwhile the one great antecedent fact of common Fatherhood.

Gwendolen, on leaving school, found herself unable to live at home, and had gone to teach English in a Russian family at St. Petersburg. Madeline remained at the Vicarage, nominally as governess to Barbara and Beatrice; she was the weakest of the five, and the most deeply influenced by her mother.

Theo would have been a very pretty girl, with a little good taste to guide her. But, coming up from the lonely spot where her life had been spent, she, with quick receptive capacity, imbibed notions of dress and *coiffure* from the girls in the omnibuses in which she travelled. She wore, as Melicent once remarked, a quantity of cheap clothes, extravagantly put on.

A bright-coloured silk blouse, low in the neck, beads, artificial flowers, a becoming hat, but too large—atrocious boots and a reek of scent—these must have convinced anybody of the good ground Theo's parents had for thinking her unsuited to go about London independently. Without conscious intent, her whole appearance laid her open to the chance of being mistaken for quite other than she was; and she had all the vain-glorious self-confidence of a very young, very ignorant girl. If she came off scatheless, it would be because her type is so plentiful, and by no means because of her discretion.

Carol Mayne, when presented to this young lady, as one of Melicent's Fransdale cousins, was guilty of the rudeness of staring. He could not believe that he had heard correctly, as he contemplated the lithe figure, the lounging attitude, the lumpy hair, the cigarette.

"Not—one of the Vicarage cousins?" he asked, in amazement.

Theo was delighted as she saw him visibly trying to adjust her with his preconceived notion of the strictly brought up Miss Coopers.

"My father being a priest doesn't make me a priestess!" she cried. Her voice was a little too loud at all times. "That's where the English make their big mistake. My mother thinks she has every bit as much right to go round lecturing the parishioners as my father has; but that's just tommy-rot, you know. We're always telling her she hasn't any official status. You're not married, are you, Mr. Mayne?"

"There isn't any room in the colonies for the English provincial vicarage life," he replied good-humouredly, mentally contrasting this flower of modern girlhood with his late ward, and trying to realise that this young lady's parents had thought her contaminated by Melicent's companionship.

"Are you living in town?" he asked.

"Yes; I'm on the boards," said Theo, leaning forward to toss her cigarette stump into the fire. "Keen on the theatre?" she asked casually.

Carol looked at Burmester, who was enjoying his friend's consternation. The Cooper girls were the young man's horror and annoyance.

At this moment the door was pushed open, and Melicent came quietly in.

She had been told who was there, and was on guard.

She knew why Mayne had come. He wanted to know how his conspiracy was progressing. Very well; he would get nothing out of her.

Lance hurried to her. "So you've been to look at old Brooke's ancestral acres?"

"Yes." She sat down after greeting the company. Her tone was colourless.

"Dear," said Brenda, "I hope you've had some food; I told them to keep it hot."

"Oh, yes, thanks. How's Pater getting on?"

"He's very anxious to hear what you've done."

"Oh, I don't know that I've done very much."

"You look tired."

"I am. Such a horrid journey. I wish Pater could have come."

"Why, was Captain Brooke not cordial?" asked Brenda, in surprise.

"Oh, quite, thanks. Only I don't know that I shall undertake the commission after all; it's such a big thing."

"Millie!" Brenda almost gasped, for this speech was wholly out of character with the habitual utterances of Miss Lutwyche, among whose failings diffidence could not be reckoned.

"Well, you'll never get on," said Theo earnestly. "Hitch your waggon to a star, my dear. You might live to be fifty, and never get such another chance."

"That's very true," said Melicent, with curious emphasis.

Then she remembered Mayne's presence, and could have bitten out her tongue.

"What do you think of Brooke, eh, Miss Lutwyche?" asked Lance, eager to have his friend approved.

"Well, I thought him rather—what shall I say—capricious, unstable," she said, and was met with a simultaneous protest from both men.

"You couldn't say that of Brooke!"

"Oh, you both know him, of course, and I don't," said she composedly. "But I thought him a little undecided. Seemed quite ready, at a moment's whim, to throw up his idea of building in Wiltshire, and try another county, after he had bought the land."

"If he is like that, it would be better not to undertake his work, I should think," said Brenda, in tones of disappointment.

"But, Mrs. Helston, I assure you he's not like that!" cried Mayne, with warmth. "And he's rich enough to build two houses if he wants them."

"He seemed to like the ideas I suggested," said Melicent, leaning back restfully in a corner of the sofa. "I daresay I shall get on all right. I'm a bit tired to-night, but I feel better already for the comforts of home. I know how it is that men often come home of an evening as cross as two sticks. How goes the world with you, Theo?" she went on, as Brenda left the room to see if her husband wanted anything.

"Oh, not so bad! Bates"—her agent—"thinks he knows of a crib for me. Gertie Gordon's got it; but she's too stumpy, and they're going to sack her; and it lies between Lillie Billington and me. I'm going to see Freeman to-morrow."

"Freeman? Then it's musical light comedy? I thought that wasn't your line."

"My dear, when you're a beginner, you take what you can get," said Theo coolly.

"That's the worst of it, I should think. Is it a good part?"

"Ra-ther! Principal boy!"

"Principal boy!" Melicent thought of the Vicarage at Fransdale. But her attention was diverted by the gentlemen rising to go. Evidently Theo meant to stay, and her presence prevented either of them from carrying out the design with which they had come.

Lance's manner, as he spoke of their early meeting again, was so significant, so obviously fraught with admiration, that the girl could not mistake it. As she stood by him, near the door, while he took his leave, an idea darted into the back of her mind.

Bert would be powerless to pursue her if she were married to someone else.

It was very different from the career she had planned. She wanted to build up a future, not to resign herself to a level, monotonous domesticity. But under the pressure of her present scare, the bare notion of any way of escape was welcome.

Carol departed with a distinct sense of disappointment. He hardly knew what he had hoped. But the impression he took away with him was that Bert had wholly failed to please or interest Millie. Not for a moment did he guess that the secret was out. Under such circumstances, with the state of feeling which she had so lately confessed to him, he would not have thought her self-possession possible.

Slowly Melicent walked back to her seat by the fire, where Theo had lighted another cigarette. On her homeward journey she had had time to decide upon her plan of action. She was not going to say a word of her discovery to anybody.

Her first impulse had been vehemently to reproach Carol Mayne for treachery; but reflection had showed that she could not do this without Bert being made aware that she knew him. To tell the Helstons would be to subject herself to the continual fret of knowing herself observed. They might even urge her to tell Bert that she knew; or counsel her to give up this building scheme, to which her ambition turned with fierce longing. She felt sure, in spite of her diffident words, that she could design and build at Lone Ash a house which should make her reputation. To do this in peace, she must keep her own counsel. After all, this was nobody's affair but her own. If Bert had come for her, as seemed fatally obvious, it all rested with him and with her. Single-handed he had engaged on the contest, and single-handed she would fight him. There seemed something a little cowardly in calling in the Helstons to her rescue. She did not mean to marry him. Well! He would soon find that out. There were plenty of girls in England for a man of property to woo successfully—Theo, for instance.

She leaned forward.

"Theo!" she said abruptly, "you've got to mind what you're about. There was a girl at school with me who went on the stage, and she did what you are doing—signed an agreement as principal boy—and she found she had done for herself. Ever after, she had only boys' parts offered her. 'Oh,' said they, 'you can't object, you have done it before.' She left the stage in consequence. Of course, for all I know, you may prefer being boy, but I thought I would just warn you what to expect."

"Awfully good of you," said Theo. She smoked in silence for a minute, then broke out: "Anyway, I'm not going another tour with Tarver's Company. After that Minnie Leslie's husband turning up, as I told you, at Crewe, when she was in rooms with—"

"'Tsha!'" It was a little soft sound of disgust that Millie was prone to make. "Look here, Theo, if you really are going on with this kind of life, your only way to keep clean is to turn your back on all that kind of thing. Don't be mixed up in it—don't talk about it."

"It's the agent that counts," said Theo evasively. "Bates is a right good sort, and he isn't going to see me let in, you bet I was pretty careful what agent I went to. I know the ropes, though you think me a country bumpkin. I can't help knowing that Batey's going to give me every lift he can."

"Why?" asked Milicent bluntly.

"Because he thinks there's money in me."

This was unanswerable.

CHAPTER XXV
THE WAY OUT

"Can it be right to give what I can give?"
—SONNETS FROM THE PORTUGUESE.

The mild spring weather made strolling in the garden pleasant, even in the keen air of Fransdale. Carol Mayne strolled accordingly, in company with Mr. Hall of Ilberston, and forgot manifold preoccupations in the pleasure of his company.

The last fortnight had been a curious and trying period in his life. He had become a mere bystander, where he had previously been a confidant. He was in the position of the trainer who has coached his man and sent him into the ring, and now has no more that he can do but to watch the conflict. Bert had stepped down into the arena, and had ever since ignored Carol to the point of rudeness. He had refused interviews, shirked even looks; had borne in total silence the daily rebuffs inflicted by Melicent—the continual pin-pricks of indifference under which he smarted.

Carol would have liked to hold the sponge between these preliminary rounds, but this was denied him. Perhaps, when some knock-out blow was dealt, his champion would have need of him. Just now, he was nowhere in the scheme of things.

But so deeply had he grown attached to this man that there was an unexpected degree of suffering entailed by the sight of his pain. Day by day his eye detected more and more of the old Bert surging up baffled, dogged, passionate, under the fine bearing of Captain Brooke. He remembered so well how things had gone in the old days—how long the big man would endure, and then suddenly, the oath that showed him goaded past bearing, the brief rage, the wild repentance. Twice he had seen Melicent—as he believed, unconsciously—bring things to this point, and Bert only save himself by immediate departure. But not a word of complaint, or of any kind of feeling, was to be got out of him afterwards. The thing seemed too deep, too momentous for comment to be possible. A kind of terror grew in Mayne as the days went by. What would happen if Bert were ultimately foiled? He could not foresee it, even dimly. He looked at the slip of a girl who swayed the man's wild blood, and tried to choke back his secret fear that tragedy might be the outcome of it all.

For Bert had encountered a rival on the very threshold of his enterprise; and the rival was the man whose life he had saved, at risk of his own, because he knew that through him he could get the introduction to Millie which he craved.

That Lance should admire Melicent was in itself no bad thing. It was no doubt well that Bert should not find himself alone in the field. But as the days went by, it was clear to Carol, who thought of nothing else, and watched all that went on, that Millie was, by her own conduct, whether of set purpose or no, leading Lance on to be serious, where at first he had merely been making holiday.

For Lance she broke through the crystal armour of "stand-offishness" which she usually wore. She talked to him; as a rule, she listened only to men, saying little. But she gave to Lance looks, smiles, and low tones.

To Bert her manner was quite friendly, even cordial, as from an unknown artist to her first patron. But of good fellowship there was not a trace. So clever was she that in all this fortnight Carol had not been able to determine whether it was by accident or design that she had never for one minute been *tête-à-tête* with Captain Brooke. Had he known the girl as thoroughly as he knew the man, the underlying strain must have been visible to him as it was to two who loved and understood her—Brenda Helston and Mr. Hall. Brenda thought she knew its cause—that it was the result of the sudden fulfilling of the girl's hopes, the terror lest her first great effort should end in failure, and her professional prospects be injured by her having undertaken what was beyond her powers.

This was in a measure true. But not the whole truth. Melicent's real preoccupation lay deeper; it was more complicated. How could she build Bert's house, and keep clear of Bert himself?

If she meant to have nothing to do with him, as she vehemently did, was it honest, was it wise, was it even sensible, to go on with the building?

But pride was at present a far stronger factor with Millie than self-sacrifice. At the first suggestion that she should design a really big thing, her ambitions had flown skyward. In spite of her secret knowledge, she knew that she meant to go on.

"That's a fine fellow, that friend of yours, Captain Brooke," said Mr. Hall musingly to Carol, as they paused to look at the first game of tennis that season, now in progress on the Helston's court at Glen Royd.

"Yes; he's an unusual person," said Mayne. "He says odd things at times. Last night, up at Ilbersdale, we got talking in the smoking-room about the different things men mean when they speak of love. Most of the things said had the materialistic tendency which I find to be characteristic of English thought to-day. Then suddenly Brooke, who seldom argues, came out with his opinion. He said that the difference between passion and love was comparable to the difference between fact and truth. They asked him to define the difference between fact and truth, and he answered without a moment's hesitation that he thought that was obvious; fact is temporal and truth eternal. How does that strike you?"

"Then he suggested that passion is temporal, and love eternal, just in the same way?"

"Yes; I have been thinking it out, and there's a deal of truth in it. One of the men asked him how you were to distinguish between the temporal thing and the eternal, and he quite simply answered that you could only tell in the result. They then said much what was said to Christ on the subject—that it is not good to marry. He replied that we were in the same case with all big things. We have to take chances in life. Nobody can say how anything will turn out until they try. He said, in love, as in religion, as in art, as in all big business undertakings, you don't have to hold an opinion merely, but to live a life. They chaffed him tremendously about being a devout lover, but it had simply no effect at all upon him."

"He must certainly be unusual! I should like to know more of him. He might be strong enough to tame my wild bird."

"Your wild bird?"

"I mean your ward, Miss Lutwyche. She needs a deal of taming. She is full of fine qualities, but has no chance to exercise them, all things being well with her. She is spoilt, as the only child proverbially is. However, as your friend says, we must leave it to life to teach her various things that she will have to learn."

As he spoke, Carol's eye was following Melicent, who had finished playing, and was arranging another sett. She had not once played in the same sett as Brooke. Now she put him to play with Theo, against Sybil Ayres and a curate. She was sorry for Theo, who had, after all, not succeeded in obtaining Gertie Gordon's "crib," and was still "resting" according to the language of her profession—a euphemism which ought to have delighted Mr. Cooper.

Lancelot had been Melicent's partner, and was at her heels.

"You promised to show me the latest treasure-trove," he said, "and I've been waiting all the afternoon."

"We found it at Citta della Pième," she said, "and I really do believe it is valuable. Pater is wonderful, he has such an eye for the real thing."

She led the way to a little garden-house which was Harry Helston's workshop, and lifted a cloth carefully from an object which lay on the table.

It was the oaken figure of a winged child, with dimpled hands and feet, and exquisite face. It had evidently been wrenched from a frieze or mantel-carving of leaves and flowers. Great part of the surface was still coated in grey mould, but the face and throat had been skilfully cleansed.

"He is treating it with glass paper, and it's slow work," said Melicent, touching the angel with soft, appreciative fingers. "It was broken in two places, but he has mended it perfectly. When it is polished, it is going to be the finial of the baluster in the hall."

"Jove, he is clever!" said Lance. "What a house this is! One feels that a mind created it! Brooke's a lucky chap if he's going to have such another."

Melicent laughed:

"We shan't exploit Tuscany for him, unless we get a special commission to do so," she said. "But he is so rich, he can have what he chooses."

"How go the plans?"

"He seems to like them very much. But I have made two alternative elevations, and he has not yet decided between them. Pater has helped me tremendously, of course. But I'm afraid I'm neglecting your father's cottages."

"He is very pleased with the drawings, I can tell you. Who would have thought you were such a genius? But do you know, I feel very proud of myself. I said so from the first."

"Said what?"

"That you were something wonderful. Do you remember"—his voice grew soft—"how you sat up on the Rigg, on Tod's Trush, and we came by, and you shot a grouse with my gun?"

"Yes; I remember."

"I said afterwards, to Helston, that there was something wonderful about you, I felt a power in you..."

He broke off mute, like most of his countrymen, in face of an emotion. Putting his hands in his pockets, he strolled round the little room, idly taking up bits of carved wood and stone, tools and drawings, and laying them down again. Melicent neither moved nor spoke. She stood silent beside the oaken angel.

"It's wonderful," he suddenly began again—"don't you think it's wonderful, how sometimes one's identity seems to come up against someone else's, and a response sounds, as if we were two Marconi instruments, and were in tune with each other. Have you noticed that?"

"I know what you mean."

He came nearer and stood beside her.

"The thing goes on a long time, before you're conscious of it; at least, it did with me. When I got to London, I didn't realise why I wanted to go straight and call upon the Helstons, until—until I saw you come into the room. Then I knew that all the while I was in Africa, I had been thinking about you.... Are you angry?" for she had turned away a little.

"No, I'm not angry. But ... you know very little of me. I ... never thought about you like that."

"No, I daresay not. But as to knowing—when two people are tuned together, intimacy comes, one hardly knows how. This Easter has been the jolliest time I have ever known. I feel like the chap in Locksley Hall, who thought the grass was greener than usual, and the birds brighter coloured.... This spring is like that to me, because of you—because of you! ... *Melicent*!"

The girl looked up. She was of those whom excitement renders pale. Her cheek was white, but as if a fire shone through the whiteness. Here was the way definitely open to her, out of the intolerable strain of the past ten day. But she was honest.

"I'm going to disappoint you," she said slowly. "I must. I don't feel like that. I don't believe I ever should. My enthusiasm seems to be for things, not people. I am ambitious and selfish. I suppose, to be ambitious is always to be selfish."

His voice was uneven and broken now, as if it fell over rough edges.

"You can only disappoint me by saying that you care for ... some other fellow ... more than for me."

"I like you better than anybody else," said Melicent simply, raising her eyes to his agitated face.

She was quite unprepared for the result.

Her hands, her waist, were caught, she was in his arms; before she was fairly conscious of what he was about, he had kissed the ineffable, smooth rose whiteness of her cheek.

"I'm content," he whispered. "You like me better than anybody else! Oh, you darling! What is it? Have I frightened you? There, I will be good, I swear I will! I'm not a brute ... only I lost my head! I never thought you would, or could, but now—"

She edged away, sick and trembling. To her virginal aloofness, the fact of his embrace clinched the matter. He had stolen a march on her. Unless he were her betrothed, how could she face him again? He would become a second incubus, like Bert Mestaer. Yet still her honesty fought for liberty.

"You did not let me speak," she cried. "I mean to say—I like you better than anybody else, but that is not enough!"

"But it is enough," he cried triumphantly. "You say yourself that you are cold—I don't care a shot for that, I want you as you are. And if you like me best, what more is there? I'm not as clever as you, but I can give you money and a title, and I did well in the campaign.... By the way, I shall be more deeply indebted than ever to old Brooke! If it hadn't been for him—!"

The mention of the name was opportune. It stiffened up the girl's resolution.

"Oh, yes; he saved your life! Tell me about it!" she said, with an idea of gaining time to collect her thoughts, which seemed to be circling in a kind of whirlpool, nearer and nearer to complete surrender.

"Would you like to hear?" he cried; and fell to musing for a moment. "We were crossing the Vaal, you know," he said. "It's celebrated for its rapid risings. The ford was quite easy when the first chaps went over, and in half an hour it was impassable. There was a commando not far behind us, and we knew, if we could get across, they couldn't follow, so we made a push for it I, as you know, was correspondent, not combatant; and it so happened that I had been with another column that morning, and had ridden hard to pick up with Lacy's. My horse was completely done. I was hardly knee-deep when I knew she would be washed away. Swimming against that current wasn't possible; I just grit my teeth and prepared to drown. But by instinct I worked my feet out of the stirrups, and we worried on, until the poor beast's foot rolled on a big stone and she slipped away, with an awful, human-sounding scream. There was a big trooper riding just above me. His eyes had been on my face, and he had ridden all the way, so as to try and break the force of the water for my mare. His horse was magnificent; and, just as I was going under, I found his arm round my body—Jove, what a grip! I wonder he didn't crack a rib or two.

"'Strike out with the other hand' he said in my ear; 'strike out for all you're worth, and I can hold you up.' And he did! My head was mostly under water, but I gave all the support I could, and his horse got through with us both! It seemed to me as if it went on for days, the fighting with the current, the struggle for breath; till all at once the water gave way under me, as it were, and my legs flopped down, and he literally hauled me out, holding me with his right arm, and I just clutching on as I best could. I faintly heard the cheering as we came ashore, and half a dozen chaps rushed to catch me, and then I fainted. They gave him his commission chiefly for that, I believe, and jolly well he earned it. And that was the beginning of our being chums."

She drew a deep breath. The long arm of coincidence had not been kind to Bert Mestaer. But how could she help that?

For ten days now, she had not known a moment's peace. Her usual profound, dreamless sleep had changed to white, wakeful nights of vague, dreadful apprehension of she knew not what. This would put a stop to her nameless fears. But it had come too suddenly. She was not ready.

Lance, however, would have no half measures. He had not, it is true, come there that day with the deliberate intention of clinching matters; but a fine opportunity had presented itself, and he had risen to the occasion with a success which bewildered and delighted him. Melicent's suggestion that he should give her time to think things over was impetuously scouted. Life was not long enough for hesitation, he told her, and his intense confidence did to a certain degree infect her. They would be married in the summer, and go to Greece, Sicily—India, if she liked, to see the architectural treasures of the world. Melicent told herself that it would be very nice indeed. He was already embarked upon an idea for their own house, if she chose to build one, when voices were heard, and steps on the gravel, and Captain Brooke and Theo peeped in.

"Oh, here they are, looking at some wonderful relic of the past!" cried Theo. "What a ridiculous, mouldering thing!" gazing with a laugh at the oaken angel.

Melicent took up the cloth, without a word, to cover her treasure from further insult. Captain Brooke arrested her hand.

"Won't you let me look?"

She laid down the cover and moved aside. The atmosphere thrilled with a sense of something unusual. Brooke had no suspicion of the truth. He knew Lance, but he thought he also knew Melicent. The idea of her taking a husband as a weapon of defence against himself had not as yet occurred to him. He looked quickly, searchingly, into her eyes, to ascertain what the matter was.

The result was curious. She met his gaze; and there rose up and revealed itself to him, the feeling always uppermost in her when he was present, fear. She did not know that she betrayed it: defiance of his unspoken question was what she meant to convey. But he saw fear; and the result was a flood of light which fairly dazzled him. He knew that he was recognised, and his heart rose within him. If she feared him, it was because she felt him dangerous. For the first time since he came to England, he saw a chance, a loop-hole for hope to enter by.

He let his eyes rest upon the angel lest their radiance should betray him. In the thrill of consciousness which his new knowledge—the knowledge of their mutual secret—gave him, he could hardly keep from smiling.

"Is this the treasure you found in Italy?" he asked somewhat hoarsely.

"Yes; do you like it?"

"I think it beautiful! I am learning to know beauty when I see it, you know."

"Learning to know beauty when you see it, Captain Brooke! Didn't know gentlemen had to be taught that, as a rule!" cried Theo, laughing affectedly.

"You make a great mistake, Miss Cooper," said Lance. "Beauty requires a trained eye. Which do you suppose a ploughman would rather hang on his cottage wall—a Rembrandt etching, or a chromo-lithograph of the Royal family on an almanack?"

"Oh, aren't you confusing beauty and art?" said Melicent, finding her voice again.

Theo, who had never heard of a Rembrandt etching, looked blank.

"Mrs. Helston sent us to fetch you in to tea," she said. "Come, Mr. Burmester, we had better let Melicent continue her treatise on beauty."

"She's well qualified to teach, by precept and example," said Lance, with tender gallantry, standing aside to let his betrothed and Captain Brooke pass out.

"Yes," said Theo, when she had procured a minute's delay by stooping down to disentangle slowly a wisp of her flouncing from a splinter of wood on the table-leg. "It's wonderful how well she's turned out, isn't it? Does her such credit, poor thing, and the Helstons too. Mother was obliged to send her away, you know; fortunately Mrs. Helston had no girls. She seems to be quite all right now, doesn't she? You would never guess what she came from."

Lance was so astonished that for a moment he could not speak. At last he said:

"I don't understand. Are you talking of your cousin, Miss Lutwyche? I thought her mother was the vicar's sister?"

"So she was; but you see, poor Aunt Melicent married a brute. It was a runaway match, of course. I can't tell you what he did—drank himself to death, or something of the kind. I believe my aunt died of a broken heart It's a wretched story. But oh, I forgot! Papa does not like us to speak of it, on poor Millie's account. He thinks it would be so bad for her if such a thing got about, so you must try and forget what I have said! I am so heedless!"

She laughed boisterously. Lance was furious. He had always disliked the Cooper girls, this turned his dislike to positive rancour. He felt sure that almost the whole of what he heard was mere ill-natured calumny. Still, there is no smoke without fire, and his self-esteem received a jolt. He was the eldest son of a baronet, and though the Burmester blood was not blue, it was very respectable. What would his parents say to a bride whose antecedents were shady?

His discomposure was momentary. His eye fell upon the proud, careless grace of Melicent as she walked along the path before him. She was giving Captain Brooke a fluent account of the finding of the oaken angel, which left him no chance to put in a word until they reached the others.

CHAPTER XXVI
THE END OF THE FIRST ROUND

"Go, if you will! Let continents divide us,
And put the seas between, and sink the ships!
What space shall sunder us, what darkness hide us,
What force shall keep apart our meeting lips?"

One of Captain Brooke's first purchases when he came to England was a motor; and it had since been Carol Mayne's fate to be driven hither and thither by a driver whose want of skill at first was only equalled by his recklessness. Now he had mastered the art, as he mastered most of the things he cared to try; and it fell out that he drove Mayne and Burmester home from the Glen Royd tennis-party, the early spring air being chilly, and the ladies of the party all preferring Sir Joseph's motor, which was closed.

He took his seat at the wheel, with Mayne beside him and Lance behind, in the *tonneau*. They had not gone far before Lance brought out his secret. His people had not been told yet, he said, but these two were his very good friends, and he must make known to them the great news that he had proposed to Miss Lutwyche that afternoon and been accepted by her.

To Mayne the thing was like a bomb exploding in a non-combatant country. It was utterly unlooked for. He had seen that something was afoot, of course—had had vague fears that by the end of the summer perhaps...

And now it was suddenly all over. His champion had been knocked out in the first round. To such a man as Carol the announcement had all the effect of a hopeless finality. Melicent was betrothed; then Bert's chance was over. He almost expected to see him reel visibly under the blow. Of course the ordinary man is not openly affected by such things. We most of us in our time have to listen politely while somebody cheerfully calls upon us for congratulation upon the circumstance that is defeating our hopes. But to Bert this news meant the loss of all things. His money, his lands, his education, all he had and was, existed for Melicent....

The Bishop elect felt himself turning cold. Visions of possible tragedy had brushed his eyes with their dark wing that afternoon, and behold, already the darkness was upon them. Once before, after Bert's long patience, at the moment of fruition, Carol had stepped in and asked him to forego. He remembered the effect of brute strength in leash, the impact, almost physical, of this man's will against his own. And then he had been able to hold out hope, to say: "Wait, and try again when you have proved yourself."

But this time it was final!

What would Bert do? Would his civilisation, his Christianity, even his manhood, be proof against this stroke of Fate?

It had been better far for him to present himself avowedly to the girl, to say: "Behold the result of my long effort to be more worthy of you. Will you try to learn to love me?"

Mayne had counselled this all along; but Bert had, as usual, taken his own way.

Mayne's eyes were fixed apprehensively upon the firm hands grasping the wheel. He almost expected some explosion, some display of violent resentment, of ungoverned temper, that should shoot them all down into the ravine on their left, where the limekiln smoked blue against the dark moor beyond.

There was not even a change of colour. Bert continued to look out keenly along the road, as his manner was when driving.

"Asked Miss Lutwyche to marry you?" he said, in a preoccupied voice. "What on earth d'you do that for?"

Lance was silent for a moment, in something closely approaching stupefaction. Carol stared at Bert, in whose temples he saw a pulse visibly throbbing; no other sign of discomposure.

"Surely you've seen, Brooke, that I was hard hit in that direction?" said Lance presently, in a hurt tone.

"Saw you admired her, of course; but so do I," said Bert shortly. "Had no idea you had made up your mind."

"You must forgive our lack of warmth, Burmester," said Mayne. "It seems to me very sudden. But you know they say, 'Happy's the wooing that's not long a-doing.'"

"You don't know enough of each other," said Bert, still in that preoccupied tone, as though his mind was concentrated on the road before him.

"Well," said Lance, "but what were you saying last night in the smoking-room? One has got to take one's chances. It is true, and it was that that gave me courage to speak to-day."

Mayne saw the blood slowly overspread Bert's face. Lance, behind, could not see the sardonic grin which accompanied the manifestation.

"Well, it seems I've made myself responsible for a big order," remarked the *chauffeur*.

"Don't you think she's charming?" said Lance anxiously. "Charming in such a very unusual way? You know, lots of girls are pretty, but you feel you'd so soon get tired of 'em—run through 'em, so to speak, if Mayne will pardon the expression. But with her—" his voice broke and softened.

Bert put on power, then jammed down the brake, as an opportune cart came galloping downhill towards them; opportune, because it enabled him to say "Damn!" with expression, to violently control the rocking car, and to be occupied with it busily. When he spoke again, which was not for several minutes, during which Mayne vainly searched his own mind for a suitable remark, it was to say:

"What are you going to do about St. Petersburg?"

"Oh!" said Lance, unpleasantly reminded.

It was only a fortnight since he had been rejoicing in the offer, made to him by his newspaper, of going to Russia under very favourable conditions.

"Well," he said, after a pause, "that will have to be referred to—" Bert made his whistle hoot so noisily that the final word was lost.

When they drew up at the door of the Grange, Bert said to Mayne, upon whom he had not bestowed glance nor sign:

"Mayne, like a good chap, see if there's any post for me before I send this machine away."

Mayne went in, and sent out the servant with a bundle of correspondence, of that unclassified kind which the rich man and the buyer is always burdened withal. Brooke sat in the car, opening envelope after envelope; and after a minute, Mayne came slowly down the steps again and stood near, his eyes soft with sympathy, but no words on his tongue.

"Ha!" said the Captain at last, as though to himself. "Yes; that's what I expected. Well, I think I shall be off at once, and take my machine to Wiltshire by road."

After a moment's surprise: "A good idea," said Mayne heartily.

Bert looked at him as if he had never seen him before.

"Oh," he said, "you think so, do you?" Then turning to Sir Joseph's *chauffeur*, who waited: "Tell my man to be ready in an hour to take me to London," he said laconically, getting out of the car as he spoke. "I must go and apologise to Lady B." he remarked, with a grin, as he passed Mayne. "See you later, old man. These are my builders' estimates, and I must get on with that house of mine."

"But"—Mayne was so mystified that he followed him through the hall—"but if your architect is—what I mean to suggest is, that she may not be able to carry out—"

Brooke turned and faced him with clear grey eyes that had the effect of a locked door.

"She's signed her contract," he said, "and if she don't keep to it, I'll go to law and make her. But this is business: women aren't so unbusiness-like as you seem to suppose. Forman, where's her ladyship?"

There is little doubt that her son's engagement would have been wholly unpleasing to Lady Burmester had it not been for one fact which, curiously enough, made her look more favourably upon it. This was nothing else than the total lack of enthusiasm with which the Helstons regarded the new idea.

The thing was sudden; on Melicent's side they had noticed no symptoms. They thought it rash and ill-considered. No doubt many young people made up a match upon equally slender acquaintance; in fact, one way and another, before Lance went abroad, he and Melicent had seen a good deal of one another. Undoubtedly, from the worldly point of view, it was an excellent match for their girl. The thing that distressed them was that they felt sure her heart was not in it.

"But in that case—why?" they asked each other blankly.

They thought they knew her too well to imagine that the social advantages weighed enough in her eyes to turn the scale. They were simply mystified, without a clue.

"Are you sure you are wise, my child?" said Brenda earnestly, when first discussing it with her adopted daughter. "You know we have always spoken out frankly to each other. Don't let us forego that habit. Tell me plainly. You care for Lance deeply? He's a charming fellow, I know, but weak. Have you realised that he is weak, Melicent?"

"I don't like strong men," said the girl, with a perceptible shudder. "There's something brutal about all strength, even moral strength. I fear it."

This speech deepened the darkness in which Brenda groped. She could not fathom it.

"Of course I understand his feeling for you," she said slowly. "You are just the woman for him, and he has penetration to see it—"

"But you won't give me the credit for like penetration? Why shouldn't I see it too? Isn't that kind of thing generally mutual?"

"Well, if you tell me it is so ... but it seems to me so rapid."

"It was unexpected to me," said Melicent thoughtfully. "I did ask him to give me time to think. But he seemed so sure. You know, mater, I don't think I should ever smile and cry and bill and coo. I'm not that kind. But I know I like Lance better than anybody else. If I find that we don't get on, I could break it off, you know."

"Lady Burmester would never forgive that."

"Oh, bother Lady Burmester!"

"There! That's the mood I distrust!" cried Brenda. "Melicent, you're behaving like a child! You will have to consider your husband's relations, and especially his mother! This is real life, remember. You are not going away to live in an enchanted castle."

"Well, it seems to me that you want me to act as if I were, and doubt me because I speak sensibly!" cried Melicent, hurt.

Brenda began to see that she had made up her mind. For the first time—the very first time since she took this orphan to her heart—she was conscious of feeling jarred. She ceased to argue, but went instead to her own room and wept.

This was early in the day. Lancelot and his parents came to lunch.

Mr. Helston was quite outspoken. He said his position briefly was that he was a man of moderate fortune, with two brothers, both with large and needy families. He could not feel justified in leaving much to his adopted daughter, as he had carefully explained to her uncle when he first took her. He had carried out his plan of giving her a first-rate education and a means of livelihood; and as long as he or his wife lived, she had a home. But she was a poor match for a prospective baronet.

Sir Joseph asked a few questions as to her birth and parentage, which Mr. Helston answered as fully as he could. Her father, Arnold Lutwyche, was a member of a reputable family which had gone to the West Indies, and there gained, and subsequently lost, a large fortune. He had no near relations, being the last of his line, and had been brought up in a luxury which, after the early death of his parents, had been found to be wholly unjustified. He had married Mr. Chetwynd-Cooper's sister, against the wish of her family, the opposition being solely on pecuniary grounds. Melicent had been sent to England on his death, her mother having predeceased him.

In his brief account of her home-coming, and Mr. Mayne's guardianship, Helston made no mention whatever of the Boer half-brothers and sisters, simply because he never thought about them. From the day of Melicent's first arrival in England, no word had come from Tante Wilma. Melicent herself never seemed to realise that the Boer woman's children were in any way akin to her. The stupor of coldness which had congealed her heart in the old days had seemingly rendered her incapable of loving anybody. Even now she loved but few; and those slowly, and, as it were, with difficulty. She repudiated her African life so wholly that Helston and his wife had hardly ever heard her speak of it.

But Brenda was urgent in recommending delay. She thought Sir Joseph ought to bring pressure to bear upon his son not to go forward in the matter at present. She owned that she was not altogether certain of Melicent's feelings. It was then that Lancelot's mother showed cold surprise. Naturally she did not find it difficult to believe that her son's attractions had proved fatal.

"Lancelot himself seems to have no doubts," she said. "It is possible he may understand the woman he loves better than you yourself, Mrs. Helston."

"That is very possible," said Brenda.

"His particular reason for wishing the engagement announced," said Sir Joseph, "is that his newspaper wishes him to go to St. Petersburg on a three months' commission. He would like to be married on his return, in the summer. His mother and I have every desire to see him settled, and he is by no means a boy who has given trouble in the way of flirtations—I mean, that I feel tolerably sure of his knowing his own mind; and that being so, I should not feel justified in putting obstacles in his way."

Brenda was aghast. She tried to say that her main objection to the engagement was the insufficient knowledge of each other possessed by the contracting couple; and that, if they were to be separated during the whole of their betrothal, and married with little chance of improving acquaintance, she felt considerable anxiety for their chances of future happiness.

It ended by Lady Burmester taking up the cudgels definitely on behalf of Romance. She naturally felt it most unlikely that, quite apart from the question of position, any girl could ever possibly repent marriage with her boy. She seemed inclined to treat Mrs. Helston's hesitation as an implied slight upon an exemplary son.

When Brenda found that Melicent herself was against her, she surrendered. The arrangement was in truth just what the girl had wished for.

Her engagement would be merely nominal for the next three months while Lone Ash was in building. It would be there, an impregnable barrier against Hubert Mestaer, and in no sense a drag upon herself. The calmness with which she faced the idea of parting from her lover added the final touch to Mrs. Helston's conviction that there was something desperately wrong. She began to think she must be mistaken in her girl after all. Was her head really turned on finding herself the chosen of one of the county eligibles? It must be so. Doubtless the girl herself did not realise it. Excitement lent a glamour to the situation, and Melicent, like many another silly maid, mistook the glitter for the rainbow glory of the wings of the Love-god whom she had never seen.

Not even her husband could understand the full depth of Brenda's disappointment. It seemed to her that she would have to learn Melicent all over again. She brooded over the subject continually, searching and searching for a motive for conduct which nobody but herself found in the least unnatural.

CHAPTER XXVII
THREE MONTHS' TRUCE

"Red marble shall not ease the heartache..."
"Why should I rear me halls of rare
Design, on proud shafts mounting high?
Why bid my Sabine vale good-bye
For doubled wealth and care?"

—C. S. CALVERLEY.

There was, however, much in Melicent's new position which was irksome, and to her inexperience, wholly unexpected. She had not foreseen that the event would make a stir in the county, and bring her into a prominence much accented by the fact that she was a qualified architect, now occupied in building a gentleman's country-seat.

Sir Joseph's paternal kiss was an infliction which positively scared her; and the influx of congratulatory visitors still worse.

"Capital, Melicent darling!" was Mrs. Cooper's honeyed sting; "you are quite a lesson to us all in overcoming unfortunate tendencies! I always quote you to anybody who complains to me of children that are difficult to manage."

Lancelot was out of earshot when this amenity was uttered; but Mr. Helston heard it, and, being unregenerate, hit back.

"Talking of children that are difficult to manage," he said, "what news have you of George?"

"A most amusing letter," promptly replied the vicar, who was always ready, with armour girt on, to defend his own. "He gives a capital account of the colonial method of pooling labour for harvesting purposes. Had you that custom among the Boers, Millie?"

"I don't know," said Melicent. "Ask Captain Brooke."

"Brooke's gone back to town," said Helston. "He went off last night on his motor. He is going to take it to Clunbury by road."

"Oh," said Millie, "I wish he had taken me! Travelling all night too! I should have enjoyed it!"

"Oh," cried her aunt, "we must really tell Mr. Burmester this! You must remember, Melicent darling, that you are appropriated now. It would never do to make Mr. Burmester jealous."

"Really, Aunt Minna," said Melicent disgustedly, "one would think you were the under-housemaid."

She walked away, with her head in the air, after this unpardonable speech, and told Lancelot that she could not stand Fransdale now that she was engaged; they must go back to town at once.

"Well," said Lance, "of course I ought to be back, only I was waiting till you went. We'll travel together."

"Captain Brooke's off, I hear."

"Yes; the builders' estimates for that confounded house came in, and he was off like a shot; thinks of nothing else but his house and his motor car; hardly took any notice when I told him we were engaged."

"Oh, well," said Melicent vaguely; "one wouldn't expect him to be interested in that."

"I did. I do. He's my friend."

"Ah! That's why, I expect! You see, he knows me better than you do."

Until Lance's blank stare faced her she did not realise the thing she had said.

"I mean," she hastily subjoined, "that he may have heard all about what a naughty girl I used to be from Mr. Mayne. You know, they are great friends."

"Ah," said Lance tenderly, "but Mayne thinks the world of you."

"Does he?" said Melicent, rather wearily.

In the train, on the way to town, she felt happier. Things were falling out as she wished. It was unconsciously that she was acting with such surpassing selfishness. She did not tell herself that she was fencing herself with an engagement in order to be free to gratify her ambition. She did not even know that at the back of her mind lay the treacherous thought that, when Lone Ash was built, Lance might be thrown over. But a deeper self-knowledge would have shown her that this was what she really intended. Her mind just now was full of dreams: but they were in stone and mortar. Visions of corbie-stepped gables, of oriel windows, of mullions, drip-stones and other bewitching details, would keep coming in between her and

Lance's scholarly, boyish face opposite. She and he were at one end of the carriage, the Helstons, with newspapers ostentatiously spread, at the other.

Lancelot was a good deal elated and somewhat thrown off his balance by the great fact of his engagement. He arrived at the railway station brimful of the idea of writing to his paper to decline the St. Petersburg mission. He was terribly dashed at first by his *fiancée's* warm opposition to this idea.

"You can't care for me, if you can coolly face the idea of my being away till the end of June!" he cried.

"I never pretended to care for you in that emotional kind of way; I'm not emotional," said Millie, with calmness. "I care with my mind, and I like a man to go and do his duty, not to hang round a woman's apron-string. Look how soldiers and sailors have to part from the women they love! You have your name to make in the world."

"I see your point of view," said the lover wistfully, "but it is a little hard to go off and leave you so soon. I'm—I'm very much in love, you know, darling. You are the kind of girl men do make fools of themselves for."

Melicent sighed. Perhaps she was thinking of a certain cup of coffee streaming down a man's face and shirt, and the fight that ensued on that swift insult.

"I tell you honestly, Lance, I'm not in love with you," she said. "It's no use pretending."

He was silent, giving her only an ardent look—a look that she resented.

But she told herself, a man is only in love for such a short time. It is the kind of thing a woman must tolerate and allow until the brief madness passes. Now with regard to Bert, she doubted if such well-recognised rules would hold. He might easily prove capable of being in love all his life, which made him inexcusable. Her fancy ran off again upon this tack, till she was recalled by hearing Lance say:

"If you knew how awful it is to think of leaving you. Words don't convey the horrible feeling, the craving for you, when you are out of my sight."

"Perhaps you don't trust me," she said, with a little supercilious smile. "Perhaps you think I shall not keep faith if you leave me?"

"Melicent!" He insisted upon taking her hand, unbuttoning and removing her glove, kissing the palm and holding it to his cheek. "I shan't say another word. I'm the happiest man on earth. I shall look on my exile as the proof of my manhood."

"I am more likely to value you correctly if you go away," said Melicent, withdrawing her hand when she had borne his caress as long as she could. "I shall grow used to the idea of you. I can't adjust my horizons at present, with you in the foreground. It used to be so empty."

"And you will spend all to-morrow with me, won't you? We will lunch, shop, dine together, go to the theatre—we will have one day of happiness, and then part."

One day of happiness! The girl looked wistfully at him.

"Lance, will it truly make you very happy to spend the day with me?"

"I wonder you can ask," he said. He added a string of lovers' folly—tender names and protestations.

"Well, then, we'll try it!" she cried recklessly. "I want a day of happiness too. You shall take me where you like, and I shall try and be happy. I think I am too cold and selfish. I'll try and let myself go to-morrow, and enjoy things, and be sweet to you. You shall have a memory to carry to Russia with you—the memory of a day as happy as I can make it."

The day of happiness was a pitiable failure as far as Melicent was concerned. She did her best, honestly. She wore her prettiest clothes, and tried hard to be really interested in jewellery, and to persuade herself that driving down Bond Street in a hansom, purchasing a smart diamond ring, lunching at the Trocadero, and so on, in company with a good-looking, well-dressed, clever and agreeable young man, constituted the elements of enjoyment for her. But it would not do. She would rather have been wandering alone on Fransdale Rigg in a storm and a mackintosh; or, better still, superintending the foundation-laying of the first child of her genius.

After their final leave-taking, and the passionate demonstration on the part of Lance which she had not been able to evade, she was almost determining to put an end to the whole thing. But when he was gone the tension relaxed at once. She liked him very well at a distance. Perhaps—almost certainly—by the time he returned, she would find that her affections had progressed in his direction. Meanwhile, she blindly felt the protection of her engagement to be an imperious necessity in the present circumstances.

And three days after the sailing of her lover, the idea of her approaching wedding had grown dim and far; for Captain Brooke came to Mr. Helston's office to consider the builders' estimates.

Melicent was at her drawing-board when he came in, her fair head bent over a piece of delicate work. The meeting was expected on both sides, and both were thoroughly on guard. Mr. Helston was present, and after the usual greetings had passed, the Captain, without pause, offered Melicent his congratulations on her engagement.

"Mayne seemed afraid that you would throw up your commission and leave me in the lurch in consequence of more pressing interests," he said. "I am glad to find you are more business-like than that."

She smiled.

"I'm afraid Lance knows that he will have to go shares with architecture in my heart," she said, slightly shrugging her shoulders.

Helston had gone for a moment to the outer office, to carry a paper to a clerk: the two were alone.

"*What a fool Burmester must be!*" said Brooke hurriedly, under his breath.

She looked up, angry, amazed; but his eyes were in another direction, and it was impossible for her to answer him, because Helston immediately returned. They plunged into business; and thereafter her client's manner was wholly natural, quiet and business-like.

In the course of two or three interviews, the raw surfaces of Melicent's susceptibilities were healed, her apprehensions lulled.

Fired through and through with professional enthusiasm, she gave herself heart and soul to the difficulties and the fascinations of her profession.

The glory of it! To see her Idea taking shape in material that should endure for ages! To see dreams and thoughts reduced to dimensions and proportions and traced upon the bosom of the ground in foundations that would be still young, years after their designer was dust!

The circumstances were exceptional. Her client gave her *carte-blanche*, and was to the full as enthusiastic as she. The spring was a glorious one. As the fruit trees in the old orchard of Lone Ash Farm burst into flower, the outline of Melicent's creation began to rise imperishable, on the hill-side.

CHAPTER XXVIII
THE GATES OF SPRING ARE OPENED

"For rest of body perfect was the spot,
All that luxurious nature could desire;
But stirring to the spirit; who could gaze
And not feel motions there? ...
        But the gates of Spring
Are opened; churlish winter hath given leave
That she should entertain for this one day,
Perhaps for many genial days to come,
Her guests, and make them welcome."

—WORDSWORTH (The Recluse).

There was a little ceremony when the foundation-stone of Lone Ash was laid.

Mr. Harland, lord of the manor of Clunbury, had an aged grandmother living in his house, who actually remembered Captain Brooke's grandfather, and the departure of the family to South Africa when the old place was sold up. This venerable dame, as forming so interesting a link with the past, was at the Squire's suggestion, asked to lay the stone; and on the first of May the ceremony was performed, before quite a concourse of spectators.

It was a fine opportunity for the county to show sympathy with the eligible owner by being present; and there was many a pretty girl who would have dearly liked to preside at future gatherings on the same spot.

For the few with whom he was personally acquainted, the Captain provided champagne luncheon at the primitive inn, where he still had his unpretentious quarters. Melicent had feelings to contend with on entering that inn once more.

The health of the architect was proposed by Mr. Harland, and enthusiastically drunk by those present, among whom the slight young girl, whose talent was undeniable, was an interesting figure.

Mayne was among the guests, observant but aloof. He was shut out completely from the confidence of both those who were dear to him. He could see that the girl was wholly possessed and dominated by her one absorbing interest. He imagined that she had accepted Lance simply because he asked her, and because she was young and undeveloped, and did not know exactly what she wanted; or because Lance admired her, and the admiration of the young male will always for a time influence the warm blood of the young girl. But Bert he found more inscrutable. The man lived within himself to a quite incredible extent. But as far as Mayne could see, he was not unhappy: certainly not in despair. He seemed to have accepted, without one kick, the hardest stroke of Destiny. In such submission, to one who knew Bert, there was something ominous.

Mayne knew nothing of one electric moment in which Bert had torn from Melicent's eyes three secrets. First, that she knew him; second, that she feared him; third, that she was going to entrench herself against him.

These things lay unspoken in the man's dogged heart.

In the late afternoon, the Captain turned to his architect, who had been saying good-bye to the Harland party, and took out his watch.

"You have three quarters of an hour before your fly comes to fetch you," he said, "and Mayne has taken the Helstons to look at the church. I want to show you something, if you would stroll down the lane with me."

To refuse would have been ridiculous; but as they went, she was acutely conscious that this was the first time they had been alone together since the day she had recognised him.

They were walking towards Lone Ash, and the wonderful beauty of the May evening breathed incense about them as they went. Orchards everywhere made the whole earth seem a-bloom. A glory of distant gorse blazed on the horizon line.

After a few moments Melicent grew nervous, and felt she must speak.

"Is the first consignment of dressing-stone delivered?" she asked.

"Up at the station," he replied eagerly, as if the question pleased him. "We bring some down to-morrow; it ought to be on the ground at ten o'clock. I took a look at it to-day, and thought it was up to sample; but I should like you to see it."

"It's a pity the journey from London is so long," she said regretfully.

"The very point I want to raise," returned he, with unconcern which was not overdone. "I think I need my architect on the spot, and I'm prepared to pay to have her there. Ah!" as they turned a corner and a charming cottage faced them, "this is what I want to show you. How do you like it?"

She stopped short, with a certain glow of feature and glint of the eye, which was characteristic. As usual, when very pleased, she did not speak. He watched her eyes as they dwelt on the rustic English beauty of the place.

The white smother of cherry-blossom melted against the mellow red tiles. By the garden-gate a big Forsythia bush bore a burden of honey-coloured flowers. The garden was a tangle of periwinkle, woodruff, and forget-me-not, with the all-pervading sweetness of wallflower; and the glowing coral of the ribes nestled against the tumble-down porch.

"It will be a mass of lilac-bloom in a fortnight," said the girl, hardly knowing she spoke.

"I want you to come in," Brooke told her.

The door was ajar. It opened upon a kitchen, beautifully clean and tidy, evidently for ornament, not use. Within was a tiny parlour, with gate-leg table, grandfather's clock and oak dresser.

"This is what I would ask my architect to put up with now and then, to save her a good deal of going to and fro," said Brooke. "I have taken it for three months, to accommodate my visitors, as there is no room in the inn."

Carried away by the sweetness of the place, she sat down upon the window-seat.

"This is Arcady!" she said.

He leaned against the print valance of the mantel, looking very large in the tiny place.

"Do you like it? Would you like to stay here now and again?"

She turned her little head, its outlines sungilt against the light without, and looked at him; and she answered like a child, accepting unconsciously the suggestion of an older person.

"I like it very much. It would be a great convenience to be able to stay. I am so anxious about the house."

"If that is so, you shall wait here and talk to Mrs. Barrett, and ask her to show you the upstairs rooms, while I go and fetch the Helstons to look at it. There will just be time."

CHAPTER XXIX
THE FRIENDSHIP GROWS

"A whole white world of revival awaits May's whisper a while,
Abides and exults in the bud as a soft hushed laugh in a smile.
As a maid's mouth, laughing with love and subdued for the love's
    sake, May
Shines, and withholds for a little the word she revives to say."

—A. C. SWINBURNE.

For three weeks, Melicent came down to the cottage on Tuesday and stayed till Friday. The first twice Brenda had accompanied her; but Pater grumbled, and the third time she came alone.

She was growing bold. Brooke's behaviour never varied. He was courteous and easy, but never confidential. He would come down the lane with his dogs, whistling, and lean over the gate among the lilacs until Melicent appeared from the cottage door, and they went on to Lone Ash together. His first greeting always was:

"How are you? Good news of Burmester, I hope?"

He was in great social request, and dined out most nights, often hurrying away from the absorbing spectacle of the rising walls of his home to lunch with some neighbouring magnate.

During the third week, except for their morning chat together, she scarcely saw him at all until Friday afternoon.

The week had been wet and cold, and she had been tramping about in a mackintosh and gaiters; but to-day was brilliantly fine, and she was lunching *al fresco*, up at the works, being immensely interested in some fresh boring operations then in progress in connection with her beloved fish-pond. She was sitting upon a pile of dry planks, making a dessert of almonds and raisins, and deep in a book, when she saw the Captain drive up. He seldom brought the motor up to the works. He had his own cart now, and a fast cob; and a trim young groom to look after them.

He sprang out, came up to where she sat, and began asking eager questions about the boring. They talked shop for several minutes, he sitting among the planks a little below her perch, bare-headed, and with his gaze upon the long foundation-lines.

Then a short silence fell, while the exhilarating May air sang about them. Looking straight before him, he said unconcernedly:

"Came to see if you cared for a drive this afternoon. It's a jolly day, and I've got to go to Arnstock. Care to come?"

She hesitated. Why not? She had evicted Mrs. Grundy long ago, and on what other grounds could she refuse? Yet something within said, "Don't," so loudly as to drown the voice of calm reason.

"I think I'd better not. I'm waiting here to see them begin to lay the damp course. Thanks all the same."

He looked at his watch. Then turned to her with a gleam in his eye.

"They quit work in an hour, so that reason won't do. Don't you trust me?"

"I have no notion what you mean," said Melicent, instantly frozen.

"Well," he said, "of course I know you despise conventionalities or you would not be following your present profession. When a girl steps down into the arena and joins the wrestling, one takes it for granted that she doesn't mind what folks say. So, if you refuse to let me take you a drive, I have to conclude that your objection is personal, don't I?"

"Then you don't consider it possible that I really may not wish to take a drive this afternoon?"

"Seeing what the weather's been this week, and what it is to-day, and the way you've been sticking to work, I think it's unlikely," he said calmly. He rose. "Pity you won't come," he added. "They're enlarging Arnstock Churchyard, and they've unearthed the head of a Saxon cross." Melicent sprang involuntarily to her feet. He looked at her steadily. "Knot-work," he said firmly. "As clean-cut as if it had been carved last week. They have got several bits. Harland thinks they may find it all. That's what I'm going to see."

She laughed a little uneasily. "I don't believe I can resist that," she said.

"Come along then," he replied coolly, picking up her warm coat from the planks. "There's Alfred to play propriety, you know."

"I don't believe you've ever been to Arnstock," he said, as they bowled lightly along the firm high-road. "You do nothing but stick to work. It isn't good for you."

"I have been to tea with the Harlands, and I am going to dine there next week. I don't know what more you can suggest in the way of dissipation. I'm sorry if I am ridiculous about Lone Ash, but you must consider the fascination of it. My first house—my dream! To see it taking shape before my eyes!"

She gazed before her with eyes that saw visions, and Hubert looked at her.

"I feel great scruples about monopolising you so much," he remarked. "Ought not all your energies just now to be concentrated on your *trousseau*?"

He was in a position to see the full play of expression in the face she sought to avert He marked the instinctive repugnance, the effort at concealment, the cold annoyance.

"Lancelot understands that I must first do what I undertook to do," she said stiffly.

"Then I am actually postponing the wedding arrangements? This is serious. My only excuse must be that there was no one who had a prior claim when you pledged yourself to me."

For just one moment she misunderstood—for one second she was on the verge of self-betrayal. It was on her tongue to say: "I never pledged myself to you!" when she saw the trap laid for her. Was it intentional? Swiftly she flashed a look at him. No babe could have been more innocent in expression.

"My private concerns will never be allowed to clash with business arrangements," she said haughtily. "What man would postpone, or throw up good work, just because he was going to be married?"

"Marriage is a mere episode nowadays, isn't it?" he said. "Just a holiday experience. The English fashion of it wouldn't content me."

"Marriage is not a thing you can talk about in the abstract," she said irritably. "One marriage is not a bit like another. You can choose your own kind, I suppose."

"Can you?" he asked urgently, in the candid tones of one seeking useful information.

There was a shadow of emphasis on the pronoun. She made no reply, and he went on:

"People's circumstances are so different I can imagine that *you* might face the idea of marriage as a mere interlude, because your life is so full, and holds so much else of love and fame and what not. Now in my case ... will you allow a lonely man the luxury of talking about himself for five minutes?"

"I am interested," said Melicent, quite politely.

"Well, you see, here am I, alone in the world. I can hardly remember my mother. I never had but one real friend—a man. I don't think I can remember a woman speaking one solitary kind word to me until I turned up in England with money. Now do you see, that friendless as I am, without human ties of kith or kin, what seems to you just a convenient arrangement, is to me the one possibility life offers? ... I wonder if you have ever thought what it must be to live altogether without intimacies, as I have done, for thirty years?"

There was a quiet, earnest simplicity in his voice which disarmed her. Suddenly she saw him in a new light. He was no longer the relentless pursuer, the man who hunted down a girl as his desired quarry. He was a lonely, heart-hungry fellow, who had been starving for kind words, thirsting for feminine sympathy. Seeing him in the light of what he had since become, she revolted from the memory of her own hardness. She had been the only English girl—the only creature with whom he felt affinity— in Slabbert's Poort. Among all the degradation and savagery of the place, he had stretched out appealing hands to the one woman who might have understood. And she had never given him one kind word! He said he could not remember one!

Without her own volition she felt her heart assailed with a rush of pity and tenderness wholly new in her self-centred, balanced experience. Without a word of reproach, with an almost bald simplicity, this man had opened the flood-gates of compassion. He had done more; made her ashamed of herself. She felt her face suffused with colour—she knew that her eyes swam with tears. The brilliant sun, facing them as they drove westward, almost blinded her. She felt she must say something; but the effect of his words had been so unexpected, so overwhelming, that she could not control her voice at once. At last, feeling that her lack of response must seem unkind, she faltered out:

"I—I am so sorry for you. I never guessed you were so—lonely!"

And to her rage and fury, her eyes over-brimmed and two tears—rare indeed with her—splashed down upon the rug that covered her knees.

Hubert made some kind of an inarticulate exclamation, and an abrupt movement, abruptly checked by the consciousness of the neatly apparelled back of Alfred, the groom, almost touching his own. He maintained complete silence for a long minute, then, bending towards Melicent:

"Were those tears for me?" he asked, very low.

She had hastily found her handkerchief.

"I—I think so. I can't quite explain; what you said recalled something else ... and I suppose I'm tired."

"Nevertheless," he replied, still below his breath, "I have had, at least for a moment, the sympathy of a woman. I shan't forget that. I hope you don't think I am in the habit of puling and drivelling about my lonely lot. I don't know what impelled me to sentiment, but I assure you it is all over now. See, there is Arnstock Church! We will have tea at the inn, and then the workmen will be gone home, and we can have the churchyard to ourselves."

They pulled up at a little low inn, covered with wisteria and honeysuckle. As he helped her down, she realised that her fear of him had suddenly disappeared.

Seated by a little table at an open window over-looking a quaint garden, she poured out tea for him, and enjoyed home-made bread, and honey from the row of hives which stood before the hawthorn hedge.

They talked easily and naturally, like two between whom a barrier has been swept away. Hubert told her of his search among his mother's papers, his discovery there of the name of his grandfather's native village, his coming to England, and his quest of what Lance called his ancestral acres.

Tea over, they proceeded to the churchyard, and spent a vivid half-hour with the fragments of the Saxon cross and its knot-work. Melicent was in a fever of eagerness to discover runes, but there were none. However, they found what was almost as good, a series of grotesques down the sides of the shaft.

The workmen had turned up almost all the pieces, and when Melicent suggested, in a moment of inspiration, that the Captain should pay for its restoration and erection in the churchyard, by way of inaugurating his reign at Clunbury, he took up the idea with avidity.

They drove back almost in silence; but a silence so full for both, that they hardly realised their lack of words.

At the lilac-decked cottage gate, Hubert jumped out, and as usual held his hands to help her down. She had just drawn off her leather gloves, and there seemed something significant and wonderful in the warm contact of their bare hands. The light was not good. That, or something else, caused her foot to slip on the high step.

For just one moment she felt an instinctive tightening of his grasp, and one arm went round her so swiftly that all danger of a fall was over before recognised. She was set on the ground ... she felt dizzy, and almost staggered when released. For in that arresting instant, his mouth had been close to her ear, and she thought a sentence came to her—that he said, so low that she could scarcely hear:

"Hadn't you better give in?"

She had regained her poise, drawn herself away, her eyes shot a bewildered glance at him in the twilight. He did not look at her, but seemed in a tremendous hurry to be off. He had jumped back into the cart and was spinning down the lane before she had time to draw breath, or to ask herself if he had really said what she thought she heard.

She stood there, listening to the brisk beat of the horse's hoofs on the dry road, for quite a long time. Not a twig stirred in a stillness which seemed almost portentous. The dampness and fragrance of earth and growing things rose about her like incense. In a thicket not far distant, a nightingale began to bubble and gurgle into song.

Had he said it? If so, what did he mean? To what was she to give in? To the influence which that afternoon had softened, and as it were, dilated her heart? To the new kindness which she felt for him?

It must be illusion. Would he have asked a question of the kind and ridden away without an answer? Was it an inner voice that had spoken? If so, what was the purport?

Anger and self-will awoke. Her understanding, her emotions, her will were and should remain in her own keeping. What was the sensation she had experienced a moment ago, with his arms about her? She felt herself blush scarlet in the darkness.

Next morning she went back to London.

CHAPTER XXX
THE TREACHERY

> "Doubt you if, in some such moment
>   As she fixed me, she felt clearly
> Ages past the soul existed,
>   Here an age 'tis resting merely,
> And hence fleets again for ages,
>   While the true end, sole and single,
> It stops here for, is this love-way,
>   With some other soul to mingle?
> "Else it loses what it lived for,
>   And eternally must lose it;
> Better ends may be in prospect,
>   Deeper blisses (if you choose it);
> But this life's end and this love-bliss
>   Have been lost here; doubt you whether
> This she felt, as looking at me,
>   Mine and her souls rushed together?"
>
> —ROBERT BROWNING.

Melicent only came down to Clunbury for one day the following week; and Mr. Helston was with her. The week after, she came for two days, and brought Brenda.

This was not the result of any scheme of self-defence; it simply happened in the ordinary course of events.

For she no longer disliked Hubert. Her mental attitude had changed.

The enlightenment which his simple and sparing speech had brought to her had been a veritable shock. She saw herself again as she had been at the time of his early devotion—the despised Cinderella, the half-grown slattern, the insolent, self-absorbed little upstart. Her own dulness of perception and ingratitude began to show themselves to her in a strong light. She marvelled at his constancy, and stood amazed at his insight. He had seen her, not as she was, but as she might be. It was she who had been blind.

So she thought of him: and yet, at the bottom of her mind, lurked a mysterious reluctance to go down to Lone Ash again.

She wrote to Lance more affectionately than she had ever done. She told him she meant to be less hard, more unselfish, to do her best to respond to the affection he lavished upon her.

Time was flowing swiftly past her. In three weeks he would be home!

And it was June.

At last Captain Brooke wrote to say that there was a question in the builder's mind respecting an additional support at a point where the thrust of the wall was greater than had been reckoned for. He added that the builder and the engineer were quarrelling about the Lee-Simmons man-holes. Moreover, the weathered tiles were beginning to arrive, and there was a question raised as to the condition of some of them. There was no doubt that her presence was necessary, and finally she went down, upon a day that focussed in its heart all the tender glories of an English summer.

The lilacs were fading now, but pink may and golden laburnum flaunted in beauty; and Melicent, as she cycled up the lane from the station, caught the intoxicating fragrance of syringa.

"What a garden this is! I believe it holds a bit of everything in the world that smells sweet!" she cried, as she greeted Mrs. Barrett. "It reminds me of the garden in Solomon's Song. How this sunshine does make the spices flow out!" As she spoke, she gathered a tiny spray of waxen syringa and a cluster of double pink may, like wee Banksia roses, and fastened them in her white gown. "After London, this is so wonderful!" she sighed.

"You look pale, miss. The fresh air'll set you up. The Captain was round this morning to know if you'd come. He seemed that disappointed not to find you. I expect now he'll think you're not coming down till to-morrow."

"Is he up at Lone Ash now, do you think?"

"I believe he will be, miss. Tommy, have you heard the Captain drive back, down the lane?"

No, Tommy had not; he was sure the Cap'n had not returned.

"I'll have a glass of milk now, please, Mrs. Barrett, and then go up and find him," said Melicent.

"There's been a gentleman had your rooms this week-end," said Mrs. Barrett, as she provided refreshment. "Mr. Mayne, a clergyman. They do say he's to be made a bishop. He was fine and took up with the building, and as friendly as ever I see. I'm sure we oughter be grateful to the Lord for sending of the Captain down here. A godsend to this village he be. There's Carter down the lane, talked of drowning hisself, he did; wife and three childer, no work to be had, nowhere to live if he got it. Now he's to have head gardener's place, and Captain's going to build him a cottage, four rooms and a kitchen! He just goes about, does the Captain, and finds out truth about everybody. Nobody's going to get over him, not they! Keeps his eyes skinned, and no mistake about it. Been into the bar of the Hearty Welcome night after night since he's been staying there, and found out all he wants to know about they chaps. He's got the whip-hand of the lot by now; knows twice as much about 'em as what vicar does; and it's my belief, he'll be the best served master in this county."

Melicent drank her milk absently. She wished, yet dreaded to see Hubert again. Her novel mood of self-abasement craved humiliation. Since realising how unlovable her conduct had been, she was invaded by unreasonable desires to let him know that she was really not such a beast as she seemed. A wish to tell him that she knew who he was, and would like to be friends, assailed her like a temptation, though she knew that such confidences would be the very height and apex of folly.

There was nothing for it, she firmly told herself, as she put on her shady hat and mounted her bicycle, but to remain upon business terms.

It gave her a little shock of joy, as she neared the gate leading to the Captain's property, to see the grey walls high enough to be clearly discerned from the road.

She rode noiselessly over the pasture, dismounted at the hill, wheeled her bicycle forward among the trees, and propped it against the trunk of a big beech.

The workmen were gone. She could see Hubert sitting there, on the pile of planks where she had sat last month. How long ago that seemed! How far she had travelled since their drive together!

He did not appear to be doing anything but meditating. His arms rested on his knees, his hands hung down between; he was looking at the ground. Melicent was taken with a sudden conviction that it would be wise to turn and run before he saw her. She combated the feeling with indignation. She remembered how loath she had been to go that drive. And how glad she now was that she went! It had made so vast a difference to her, she felt something as Gareth felt when he unhorsed the dread Black Knight, and found the rosy child within.

Why not go forward?

The alternative no longer remained: he looked up and saw her.

She came towards him from among the trees, in her white gown, wearing a look he had never seen upon her face before in life, though he had dreamed of it now and then. Her eyes seemed to have grown larger, darker, softer. Her face was of that warm rose whiteness which relieves itself so vividly and strangely against a white dress.

He stood up; but absorbed in the picture she made, he did not advance to greet her.

"I thought you had not come," he said; and even to say so much was an effort.

"I had things to do." She smiled. "Some of that shopping you reminded me of the other day! I came by the later train."

He recollected himself.

"I hope you have good news of Burmester," he said mechanically.

"The best," answered Melicent quietly. "He will be home in less than three weeks."

He had been staring at the grass, but on that he raised his eyes.

"And when shall you be—married?"

"The day is not fixed; only that it will be at Fransdale." There was a pause, and to fill it she said: "I hear Mr. Mayne has been here."

"Yes; I suppose you are going to his consecration next week?"

"Oh, yes; he sent us tickets. Do you know how long he stays in England? He ought to wait for my wedding."

"So I told him," said Captain Brooke slowly, balancing a long screw-driver with which he was playing across one finger of his left hand.

"What did he say?"

"Oh!—well, he said several things; but he didn't mean me to repeat them, so don't ask me, please."

She gave an odd, excited laugh. "I don't ask; I order you to tell me."

He gazed upon her, so absorbed in his thoughts about her, that the subject in hand faded out of sight. She could not meet his look. Tossing her head, she turned a little away.

"So you won't tell me?"

"Tell you what?"

"What he said."

"What who said?"

"Captain Brooke, what is the matter with you? We were talking of Mr. Mayne. We had better leave off if you are not attending, and go and look at those tiles."

"The more serious matter is the water," he said, shaking off his preoccupation and sensibly relieved by the change of subject.

He led the way from where they stood to a pit four feet deep, with a stand-pipe projecting from the newly-turned soil. Kneeling down on the edge, he bent over, and turned on the union tap, which had been fixed for connection with a rubber hose. The girl gave a mortified exclamation:

"Why, it's dry!"

He acquiesced.

"That's where Shepherd's rage against the Lee-Simmons engineer comes in, and why he wants to wipe up the floor with him. The supply was all right the first two days, dribbled for two more; then stopped. The engineer says it is simply that Shepherd's men have fixed the thing so carelessly that the pipe's blocked down below. I think I'll get the jointed rod and probe it."

"Oh, my fish-pond, I thought I had secured you!" said Melicent sadly.

"You shall have it, if there's water in Wiltshire," he began; then stopping dead—"I mean, the thing must be made to act somehow. By the way, there's Alfred with the cart. I'll send him back for the rod; he can bring it in a few minutes."

"Lend me your wrench, then, and I'll get the tap right off," said the girl.

He handed her the tool she asked for, and went off across the field to give his directions.

She jumped down into the muddy pit, and set herself to unscrew the tap. It was not very easy, but she managed it at last; and then, with the thing in her hand, remained in her crouching attitude, examining it to see if there was any obstruction.

There was a sound like a deep sigh—a rush like heavy rain—a jet of yellow water flew from the pipe, hit the opposite side of the pit with great violence, and before she knew what had happened, she was over her ankles in water. In a calmer moment, she would have scaled the miry sides of the pit, regardless of appearances; but she was not calm, and she lost her head. The unexpected nature of the thing scared her—she had the idea that if once she let the pit fill, they would be unable to stop the flow; and so, with a spring, she flung herself upon the pipe, clasping her two hands rigidly about it, and stanching the most part of the rush. But the strength of the pulsing water was great, her footing slimy, her purchase feeble. Raising her voice, regardless of all but the emergency, she cried aloud:

"Bert! Bert! Bert! Quick!"

He had only just dismissed Alfred on his errand, and was hurrying back, when that sound smote his ear. He broke into a laugh of pure joy as he heard it, but he ran with all his might.

The moment he got to the brink of the pit, he saw what was happening; and he, too, lost his head. Instead of calling to her to let go, and holding down his hands to draw her up, at the expense of a drenching, he forthwith sprang down, placed himself beside her, and locked his hands over hers.

The fact of his doing this bereft her of all power of speech.

She was totally unconscious of having called him by name; she did not know the reason of his kindled, glowing look. Neither, for a few long-drawn seconds, considered what was to be done. They simply stood there, so acutely conscious of each other that nothing else in all the universe seemed real.

She was the first to recall her scattered wits.

"Oh, this is too ridiculous," she said faintly. "We can't hold on! We can't hold on!"

"Just long enough for Alfred to get back," he whispered. "He can't be ten minutes. He can have the thing ready to screw on, and save you a deluge—"

"Nonsense!" she uttered feebly. "We can't hold on here for ten minutes! We can't, simply."

"I wish we could hold on for ever," he jerked out, his voice sunk to a note that made her quail.

The force in his hands seemed to be communicating itself to her. She was dominated, absorbed, had forgotten everything but him. He never spoke, but she became aware that he wished her to look at him. She tore away her gaze from the sight of their gripped hands, raised her head, searched his face with pleading eyes.

Their looks met and mingled.

A dull beat was hammering through her senses. Was it his heart or hers, or the pulse of Time itself?

Their faces drew nearer, nearer to each other.

Something was going to happen—something that should explain all life and blaze the answer to every secret ... that was the thought she had as their lips met.

Was it he who bent to her, or was the impulse that drew them mutual?

The blinding sweetness of that kiss was unmarred by any thought of treachery. The world and Lance with it, had simply gone out in the ecstasy of the light that flooded her.

It was over. The world that had stood at gaze like Joshua's moon on Ajalon, swung on once more her dance among the stars.

Melicent stood there, in the fair June evening, at the side of the man who had kissed her. The wind came softly over meadows deep in buttercups, and bent the white lacy sprays of delicate wild parsley which fringed them. High in the blue sky the lark stormed heaven's gate with song.

"Let me go!" she cried, with a stifled sob. "I must go! Don't you see that I must?"

It was a moment before he replied; but when he did, his voice was perfectly composed and cool.

"As soon as you feel the pressure of my hands relax, slip yours downwards," he said.

A moment later she was free.

"There! Oh, why couldn't you do that before?" she cried passionately, as she made a frantic onslaught upon the crumbling side of the pit.

She was up and away in a minute, her white frock soaked, her feet caked in pale yellow mud. She ran across the grass, never stopping to look behind, and met the bewildered Alfred just at the edge of the plantation.

"Hurry to the Captain," she gasped. "The water has started to run and he can't stop it. I must go home and change!"

Her throat was so dry she could hardly speak. In feverish, stumbling haste she mounted her bicycle, and rode down the bumpy grass slope at a dangerous pace. Mercifully the gate into the lane stood wide, and she was through it and back at the cottage in a couple of minutes.

Alfred found his master up to the knees in what looked like weak tea with cream in it. Between them they managed to re-fix the tap, connect the long hose, and set the liquid flowing into Melicent's fish-pond.

Emerging from the pit, the Captain looked at his legs—he was wearing a cool, summer suit of light grey flannel.

"The wash-tub, Alfred, is the place for me," he said resignedly.

"Yessir!" said Alfred, who had prudently removed his own smart leg-wear before venturing to the rescue.

"Joseph was better off than I am, Alfred. His pit was dry—there was no water in it."

"Yessir! Miss Lutwyche, she was drenched, sir."

"I hope she won't take cold," said the Captain, with polite solicitude; "but fortunately the day is warm. Get on your boots, Alfred. I'll let this thing run all night, and perhaps there'll be something to show for it in the morning. There must have been something in the pipe, and the force of the water dislodged it, I suppose."

Melicent, lying upon her bed with hidden face, heard the cart go past the cottage. The beat of the hoofs was not interrupted; they passed by without stopping; and the tension of her strained nerves relaxed.

CHAPTER XXXI
THE REPUDIATION

> "Escape me?
> Never—
> Beloved!
> While I am I and you are you,
> So long as the world contains us both,
> Me the loving and you the loth,
> While the one eludes must the other pursue."
>
> —ROBERT BROWNING.

The delicate veil of sapphire which June calls night was drawn across the splendour of the sky; and it was like the device of a beauty who wears a transparent gauze to enhance the glitter of her diamonds.

In the north still lingered a supernal glow, the hint of the day that has no night.

The fragrance of unseen cottage gardens was all about Hubert as he walked slowly up the lane from the inn. There was no moon. The glimmer of starshine made mysterious radiance, yet left a soft, velvet dusk, without the clean-cut lights and shades of moonlight.

He had bathed, changed, dined. Now he was coming to ascertain the result of his daring experiment. Had he succeeded, as he hoped, in showing Melicent her own heart?

He had no remorse. The thing was necessary; it had to be done. Could he stand by and see a proud girl wreck three lives?

It was very dark among the lilacs by the cottage gate. Peering through the thick boughs, he started; for there was no lamplight, either in the parlour or the room above it. And he believed that she had fled from him.

This gave a jolt to the pleasing elation of his spirits. Walking on the grass, he approached the open door without noise. Then he halted.

The casements of the parlour were wide open to the summer night. On the window-sill lay a girl's abased head, the fair hair just touched by the star-glimmer, the face hidden in her arms.

She lay very still, and was apparently not weeping. He went up to her, resisting with firmness his great desire to lay his hand upon her hair. For the first time in years he spoke the name that stood for all his ambitions.

"Millie," he said softly.

She sat up quickly. He hardly knew what expression he had expected to see; but the indignation of her eyes was a surprise.

"Oh, I wonder how you dare come near me!" she cried.

"I won't come near you. I'll stay outside here," he said hastily, with a bewildered sense of having lost the thread of the situation.

"You certainly won't come in at my invitation."

"No, of course," he said meekly, his head fairly spinning with wonder; "but I thought you would see I had to come and beg your pardon."

She stood up, withdrawing herself into the room, as if she meant to escape.

"There are things that are unpardonable," she said coldly.

He contemplated this idea. "Do you mean that you never can forgive me?"

"Perhaps I mean that I never can forgive myself," she said chokingly. "You—you have humbled my pride to the dust. Lance ... trusts me, and I have ... How am I to face him?"

"Then you mean to stick to that—to go on with your engagement—to marry Lancelot—in spite of what happened to-day?" he asked hastily.

She stood up straight in a long, loose, pale-coloured gown, half lost, half seen in the faint light. The glint of the stars swam in her eyes.

"May I ask what else you expected?"

He was at a loss. Ready enough had he been to console her, to tell her that Fate was too strong for her, to urge her to correct her mistake before it was too late. Her present attitude stunned him, and bereft him of words. The dashing of the high hopes with which he had come bred in him a sudden sense of being wronged.

"Millie," he expostulated, "do you know what you said—up there when the water rushed out upon you? You called out: 'Bert! Bert!'"

There was silence. He saw her start.

"Did I say that?" she said slowly. "Then it is I who have betrayed myself, and you—are not so much to blame as I thought. I can believe that it excited you a little to find that I knew you, and made you think of old times." She hesitated, seeming at a loss what to say or do; her embarrassment was obvious, her distress manifest. Then, with sudden determination, she came near the window again. "If that is true, I suppose I must forgive you," she said stiffly, "and we must both forget a mad moment."

He could hardly believe his ears. "Is that all you have to say?" he demanded harshly.

"The less we either of us say the better, surely, concerning such an affair."

The man drew in his breath sharply. "After all that has come and gone?" he panted.

"Captain Brooke, for a moment this afternoon I allowed myself and you to forget that I am engaged to your friend. I must remind you of it now."

"I wish to God that I had let him drown in the drift!" he flung out. "Or that I had drowned myself—!"

"I don't wish to be hard or unkind, but I cannot listen to you. I am going to close the window."

He inserted his shoulder, so that she could not close it. The expression of his eyes was such that she dare not face him.

"Answer me one question," he commanded brusquely. There was a growl in his voice that she knew of old as a storm-signal. "I have a right to ask it, and you ought to answer—you *shall* answer! When I kissed you today ... *was it against your will?*"

Her expression made him feel as if he had slashed her across the face. Had she accepted defeat in that moment—said anything to appease the man's mounting wrath—he might have kept his head. But pain or insult had never the effect of softening Melicent, but only of stiffening her. His taunt stung her to real anger, and, in the midst of her stifled consciousness that she was fighting a losing battle, she clutched at her indignation as at a blade with which she might wound. She had moved towards the door with the intention of escape, but now she returned to the window.

"You think you have the right to ask me that?" she said, with the same ruthless arrogance that she might have used to him in Africa. "You say that to me—you, who hope to turn into something that people may take for an English gentleman! ... You did that this afternoon to get a hold over me! I know your threat! You needn't say it! You mean that, if I don't tell Lance, you will! ... And you suppose I care if you do, or what you do, or anything about you...!"

Before she had got so far, Bert had flung his leg over the sill and vaulted lightly into the room. He came quite close to her, but spoke quietly, under his breath, with an air of desperately holding himself in.

"All right!" he said. "You say you don't care, do you? Well, then, if you say so, I say you lie! You lie, do you hear me?"

"You had better go away before you grow unpardonable," said the girl coldly.

"I'll go when I've said what I'm going to say, and not before. I'm going to tell you the cold truth here and now. The Brooke farce is played out, we know each other, and you shall hear what I have to say! *You—kissed—me* to-day!—great God! do you suppose I don't *know* that you did?—and you did it because—"

Slight things decide momentous issues. Even then an appeal, the smallest sign of surrender on the girl's part, would have brought him crouching to her feet. But she flung back her head, and looked him in the eyes to show how little she feared him; and she laughed.

That let loose the tempest. All in a moment he broke off his husky, difficult words. All in a moment he had her by the waist, crushing her to him as if holding her against an army. There was no love in the fierce hold, only the determination that she should hear the cruel words that he spoke into her ear:

"Because you love me! Because you love me! Because you're mine—mine—mine!"

She disdained to struggle, as she disdained to plead. She made no effort to fling him off. Her silent, passive contempt brought him to himself in a flash.

The girl who, that golden afternoon had yielded to his spell, had weakened, had been as it were his to take, now lay like a lifeless thing in his ungentle hold. He realised what he had done.

When he let her go, she did, by an effort, stand alone. Her laugh of scorn was quenched. She lifted one hand to hide the quivering of her mouth, but did not move at once, perhaps because she feared to fall. He turned away from the still, silent, accusing figure with a kind of roar of helpless strength, of baffled will.

"The same, the same as ever," he said. "The woman's way! To make me feel a great, rough brute, when all the time it's you that are cruel. Yes! As cruel as a fiend."

To and fro he paced, to and fro upon the floor; then, with sense of defeat in overwhelming bitterness, got to his knees at her feet.

He knew that his fatal moment of uncontrolled temper had undone all that the past weeks had gained so painfully and slowly. Beneath his shame was an undercurrent of conviction that he was right and she wrong. But what was right or justice in face of Melicent's inflexibility?

"I'm sorry. I'm a brute. But it's your fault. You know what you can do with me," he said chokingly.

"Get up!" said her exhausted voice. "Get up, do! Go away. You see you are ... impossible. I thought you had improved, but you see it's all ... just as bad as ever."

"Millie!"

"Don't touch me."

"You know I am not such a hound as to think I have any hold ... or to use it, if I had?"

"What does it matter to me?" She moved: he held a fold of her gown. "Are you going to detain me?" she asked. "Because if so, I shall call Mrs. Barrett. This is not love—oh, no, nor anything like it; it's simply your fixed determination to have your own way. I've always known it, all these years—that you were not beaten, that you meant to try again. Not for love of me, but simply because to conquer me is your fixed idea. And this afternoon you thought you had succeeded. Well, you haven't, that's all."

He got to his feet, utterly humbled, reduced to abject pleading:

"Millie, see me again! Don't let it end here! I've lost my head, and don't know what I am saying. Give me a chance to talk things out—"

"Never, never, never!" she shuddered, making for the door. There she turned upon him. "You are a savage! If you knew how I hate savagery! You are a Boer! If you knew how I hate the Boers! I'll marry a man who knows how to treat a woman, not one whose civilisation is only skin-deep." He took two maddened strides towards her. "Has that hurt you? Very well, then, you can kill me, you know. I wonder you don't."

He passed a hand over his hair like one pushing a veil from his eyes.

"I can tell you why I don't," he said, in tones that rapped out sharp as a rapier thrust. "It's because you're not worth it."

Almost before he had spoken, he had turned about, sprung from the window, and disappeared. The starshine glimmered in the silent room where a moment ago had been such storm and stress.

Melicent stood alone, in possession of the field. The suddenness of the withdrawal of the besieging forces took her breath. The Parthian shot, fired in the moment of flight, reached her heart and quivered there.

She gave a strangled low cry, as if physically hurt.

At last, it seemed, the long struggle was over. Not because Bert realised that she was out of reach, but because suddenly he had awoke from his dream to find her not worth fighting for.

She told herself that, whatever the means, the thing was done, and finally done now. There would be no more vehement assaults for her to dread.

Yet something unpleasantly like remorse was gnawing at her heart. She knew she had said things she did not mean; in the heat of battle she had caught up every missile....

Well, now it was over. Silence and solitude were profound. The air which had vibrated to Bert's rage and Bert's repentance was so still that the nightingale's song sounded too loud in her ears.

"All over!" she said aloud; and the words sounded strange and horrible.

"All over!" She crept upstairs to a sleepless night; but this of late had been no rare thing with her.

In the early morning she went away to London, choosing a route to the station which should not take her past the inn.

And for weeks the grey walls of Lone Ash rose higher in their dignified beauty, unseen by the eyes of her for whom they were being raised, and whose genius had called them into being.

CHAPTER XXXII
THE FRANSDALE SPORTS

"Embrace me then, ye hills, and close me in;
Now in the dear and open day I feel
Your guardianship; I take it to my heart;
'Tis like the solemn shelter of the night."

—WORDSWORTH (The Recluse).

The wedding-day was fixed, and Melicent lived in an atmosphere of wedding presents and dressmakers.

Since her *fiancé's* return she had altered noticeably, both in appearance and manner. She was paler than usual, large-eyed and languid; and she had grown strangely gentle and yielding. She deferred to Lancelot in everything; and since two people cannot possibly continue to kneel at each other's feet, and as Melicent persistently adopted the lowly posture formerly monopolised by her lover, he had, as a result, grown the least bit dictatorial.

Theoretically, of course, the change pleased him; but as a matter of fact, he had found his lady-love more interesting when she was remote and prickly. Her new meekness was purely passive; it did not make her more demonstrative. She submitted to be caressed, but it was always obvious that it was mere submission.

Brenda was very unhappy about her. She was sure that she was suffering mentally. She knew she did not sleep. However, girls just before marriage are often restless and unsettled, and there was nothing which she could definitely take notice of.

At the end of July the Fransdale Sports took place, an annual event of the highest local importance. They were held in a meadow near the head of the Dale, not far below the Vicarage. The meadow sloped violently, but the fact was accepted by the natives as part of an inexorable law of Nature. All fields sloped; you might as well quarrel with the grass for being green.

From early morning the little heathery tracks leading down from the Riggs were black with a crawling line of folks, descending Indian file by devious ways to the scene of action. Traps of all kinds, crowded with passengers, began to arrive, and to distribute themselves in all the neighbouring stable-yards, which were soon filled to overflowing.

Streams of fine plough-horses, yearlings, hunters and little fluffy foals, moved slowly along various radii to the centre. On the ground, the chief farmers' wives were preparing a "ham tea" of vast proportions in a large tent.

As the day wore on, the whole scene was alive with colour. Exhibits of butter, eggs, vegetables and fruit, were being solemnly appraised by business-like judges. There was a cackle of fowls, a cooing of doves, the outraged cries of lordly rams tethered to stakes and with coloured ribbons round their horns.

And the band! One of the visitors remarked that it was worth coming far, if only to see that band!

The musicians sat upon boards in the large hay-cart in which they had been conveyed to the festal scene, and from which the horses had been removed. Their broad and solid backs, in every hue of weather-stained fustian, formed a study for the eye of the humorously inclined.

Then, of course, there were cocoa-nut shies and gingerbread stalls, and a wheel of fortune. For this one day in the year the austere solitude of the moorland was broken through, and Fransdale was actually noisy and crowded.

Among the throng, which grew thicker as the day wore into afternoon, was a sprinkling of gentry, conspicuous among whom were the Burmesters. Sir Joseph took a genuine interest in all the exhibits, and gave many valuable prizes. There was naturally great interest among all the natives over Lancelot's engagement. Melicent was a most popular person, and glances of affectionate admiration followed her to-day.

She wore a white lace gown, with La France roses, and her white sunshade was lined with rose colour. Brenda thought she had never seen her look so pretty, nor so sad.

"The Ayres' party are here," said Lance, strolling up to where his mother stood, with Mrs. Helston and Melicent, watching the first heats of a race run off. "They've brought their tame crowd of convalescents with them."

"Did you know," said Lady Burmester, "that the Ayres' offered their house for a Convalescent Home for wounded officers? That will arouse enthusiasm, won't it, Lance? The people will cheer, if they know there are African heroes about."

"They exhausted their enthusiasm when Lance came home," smiled Brenda. "What a pity Captain Brooke is not here, then we should have all the African contingent."

"Oh," said Lance, "I forgot to tell you, Mrs. Helston, I have at last persuaded the obstinate old beggar to leave his beloved house to build itself for a few weeks, and to come up here for a bit of rest."

"Oh, well done!" said Brenda, with animation. "I should have been so sorry for him not to have been at the wedding."

"He won't promise that, even now. You know, I wanted him to be best man. He says weddings are not at all in his line. But when we get him here, perhaps you and Melicent can persuade him."

"He ought to be here pretty soon," said Lady Burmester. "He's coming in his motor, by road all the way, I believe, and he promised to try and arrive in time for the sports. I told him they were a sight he ought not to miss."

Melicent was possessed by a most remarkable sensation, as if she were drowning. Fortunately, for a few minutes nobody noticed her; and just as the waters were about to close over her head, they began to recede again, and she drew a deep breath and made a vehement effort to collect her thoughts.

But it was not possible. He was coming. Why, why, in wonder's name, had he changed his plainly expressed intention of keeping away?

She felt sure something must have happened to cause him to reconsider his decision. Had he come to the conclusion that it was right that Lance should know their story—hers and his? Had he resolved to tell it?

If so, they must have another tussle, he and she; for somehow she felt sure that he would do nothing without giving her fair warning.

Every nerve in her quivered at the thought of seeing him. The few short words in which he had expressed his newly-born contempt said themselves over and over in her mind continually. How would he look? What should she say? What would happen?

"They're judging the foals. Such funny little rats! Come and see them run round," said Lance's voice, close to her.

She looked up at him almost pitifully, as if searching his face for visible assurance of love. He was not looking at her, nor thinking much of her apparently. His visit to Russia had been a pleasant experience for a clever young fellow—he had had his fill of flattery and attention from the English *coterie* at St. Petersburg. He was very fond of Millie, but the idea did cross his mind now and then that she hardly seemed conscious enough of the really fine match she was making. To-day, his attention was by no means hers. It was all concentrated upon the live stock.

She crossed the grass at his side, and stood by the rope enclosure, among the friendly faces of the Dalesmen. There was Alfred Dow, still unmarried, handsome as ever, if more solid; by his side, talking to him, the demure figure of her cousin Barbara. So even the Vicarage was beginning to march with the times! There was the farmer who was reckoned the best judge of horse-flesh in the horse-loving shire, and who might have served as a model for the typical John Bull, as he stood in his gaiters and beaver hat, watching the paces of the candidates. Melicent was watching them too, with real interest, when it seemed to her as though a touch were laid on her heart. Without raising her eyes, she knew who had drawn near. She shivered as she turned, and saw the Captain waiting to be greeted.

She said, "How do you do," without daring to meet his eyes; yet she longed to know how they stood, and on what terms this man was once again at her side.

"O, come ye in peace or come ye in war,
Or to dance at my bridal, thou young Lochinvar?"

As once before, at Lone Ash, she became sensible that he wished her to look at him. She knew he must read the signs of confusion on her face. The news of his coming had been too recent for her to have recovered from it. But she could not lift her eyes. Lance's cheerful greetings more than covered her silence; he was sincerely glad to see his friend. After a minute's chat, however, he was called away. He was much in request that day, and had to go off with his father and judge rams, deputing Melicent to "show Brooke round."

Alone with Hubert, her courage turned to water. For a long minute they two stood there, unnoticed in the crowd, holding their breath, dizzy, overwhelmed by the mere fact of each other's presence.

He spoke at last. "You're not looking at all well," he said.

To which she naturally replied in a hurry:

"Oh, I am particularly well, thanks, only a little tired to-day."

"How do you think I look?" he asked quietly.

She dared not refuse the challenge. Her eyes, when she lifted them, held a piteous appeal.

But it was relief of which she was sensible as she met his gaze. It was kind and gentle. He looked ill; so ill that she wondered that Lance had not cried out upon him. He was like a man who has passed through some shattering experience, she thought. There were dark marks below his eyes, he had lost flesh, and he was pale, though so tanned that this was not obvious. But in his face was no shadow of the contempt she had feared to see, and had winced from the thought of.

In her relief she smiled up at him wistfully, as a child smiles at his mother, to make sure she is no longer displeased. When he smiled in answer, it was like sunshine breaking out over a cloudy landscape. It brought all her heart to her lips, it made her inclined to say:

"Oh, I must tell you my doubts and fears, and how I have tortured myself since last I saw you!"

The words were trembling on her tongue. In blind terror of self-betrayal, she said the first safe thing that came into her head; an inquiry after the progress at Lone Ash.

"They are roofing it," he said. "The roof goes on this week."

She coloured with pleasure.

"Oh, do tell me what the effect is! Do tell me how it looks from the road below the gate!"

"It is beautiful!" he answered quietly. "It grips me afresh every time I see it. Mayne, too, admires it immensely. Did you know I have had Mayne staying with me for the past month?"

"No, indeed; but I am glad to hear it," she cried. "He was so interested in the house; and then, he is quite an authority on gardens, isn't he? You must have found him a great help."

"Yes," said Hubert absently. "That's very true; he has been a great help."

She sent a sidelong glance at him, and noted afresh the marked change in his expression. There was a look upon the mouth that went to her heart in an indescribable way. It made her long to beg his pardon for the things she had said to him that night. The indefensibility of her own conduct throughout smote upon her in quite a new way. Never before in all her life had she felt the salutary self-reproach which now reddened her cheek, tied her tongue, and seemed to leave her helpless before him.

"Oh," she thought, "if he knew how much stronger he is when he looks like that than when he is in one of those awful rages."

He was speaking, and she collected herself with a tremendous effort to listen.

"The effect of those middle windows, with the transoms, which we had such doubt about, is awfully good, to my thinking. It only needs one thing."

"One thing?"

"Which I must consult you about. I have come here on purpose to talk of it I feel, perhaps, as if my presence here may—to you—want a little explaining. I have come because I thought I ought to. When can you give me a few minutes?"

It was true then: there had, as she guessed, been a specific reason for his appearance. Strangely enough, she had never thought that it would be anything in connection with Lone Ash. Yet what more natural?

She looked alarmed. "Is it important?"

"Very."

"You had better come over to Glen Royd to-morrow morning. I do hope it's not—any mistake I've made?"

He hesitated.

"Well, I'm afraid that's just what it is. But I don't think it's irretrievable."

She was filled with consternation.

"Oh, don't tell me it's structural! We managed that thrust of the wall on the north so splendidly with the buttress."

"It's nothing structural," said Hubert.

They had moved away, talking together, from the foals' enclosure, and were crossing the grass slowly, not knowing whither they went. Sybil Ayres approached them, with two or three gentlemen, some of her military convalescents. She bowed to Melicent, whom she cordially disliked, and was passing on, when one of her companions cried:

"Why, surely that must be Miss Lutwyche! How d'ye do? Didn't expect to see me here, did you?"

And Melicent was looking into the humorous, relentless hatchet face of Amurrica. His eye wandered over her, noting every detail of her appearance and costume; from her to her companion; and Melicent, with her faculties sharpened by the emergency, saw with delight that he did not recognise Bert. Her expression did not change.

"I am afraid you are mistaken," she said politely. "I do not think we are acquainted."

"I'm making no mistakes. My name's Otis. 'Amurrica' they used to call me in Slabbert's Poort, as I've been explainin' to these ladies. You're Millie Lutwyche, ain't you?"

"I am. I remember, there was someone of your name in the place. But I do not remember that we were ever acquainted. I did not know any of the diamond miners."

"I'm a diamond major now," cried Amurrica, with an unpleasant laugh. "Look here, Miss Lutwyche, we shall be obliged to refresh your memory a little. D'you remember your father's funeral? I was there."

"The whole town was there," said Millie, with indifference. Then, with an air of stopping the conversation, she said to Miss Ayres: "Have you been in the tents? Is it worth while taking Captain Brooke to see the fruit?"

Then, receiving a dubious answer, she inclined her head in leave-taking, and walked away.

As soon as they were out of earshot, she looked up at Hubert with an altered expression—a look of comradeship—her late nervousness chased away.

"You see! He didn't know you a bit!" she cried.

"Not a bit," he answered. "Just as big a beast as ever! But do you mind my saying I think it was unwise to cut him? You've made him savage, and he may be rude."

"Let him," said Millie contemptuously. "It is quite true that I never knew him. You know, I never would speak to him. How could he be rude?"

"He might say things about you—to other people."

"Well, he can't say anything I'm ashamed of," said Millie coolly.

"You always did despise your enemies."

"Well, I haven't got any enemies now," was the careless answer.

"God grant it!" he replied, thinking of things said to him by Mrs. Cooper and her daughters one day when he went to tennis at the Vicarage.

CHAPTER XXXIII
CALUMNY

> I? What I answered? As I live
> I never fancied such a thing
> As answer possible to give.
>
> —COUNT GISMOND.

Lancelot, returning from what he called distinguishing between the rams and the he-goats, was intercepted by Sybil Ayres.

"Oh, Mr. Burmester, it is so interesting! Here is a gentleman who knows all about Miss Lutwyche! Not only that, but what do you think? Her brother is his servant!"

Lance stared blankly.

"Some mistake, Miss Ayres," he said pleasantly. "Miss Lutwyche has no brother."

"Well, if I'm tellin' lies, you can easily prove it, you know," said Amurrica jocosely. "The young lady's got a short memory, but I daresay it can be refreshed."

"Do let me introduce Major Otis," said Sybil. "He is so interested to meet Miss Lutwyche's *fiancé*."

Otis took Lance by the hand, and shook it impressively.

"I'm proud to meet a man of generosity and insight—I say, of generosity and insight," said he solemnly. "Insight to see that the gal's real grit, in spite of her family; and generosity to overlook the things in her past that are better not talked about."

"Look here!" said Lance, in a fury. "I don't know whether this is the latest variety of American humour, but whatever it is, it's deuced bad form, and you'll find you had better keep your head shut in England. Kindly choose some other subject of conversation than Miss Lutwyche, unless you want me to punch your head."

"You could easily do that," said Otis pensively. "I'm in quite the early stages of my convalescence. However, there's no need. Of course I withdraw all I said. Naturally, I thought you must know all about—well, well! Keep your hair on! Sorry I spoke. Can't say more than that, can I? Only this one thing I must say. My boy, Arnie Lutwyche, has lived in hopes of finding his sister when he got to England. Are you goin' to prevent his speakin' to her?"

"There's some absurd error," said Lance, in a rage. "I tell you Miss Lutwyche has no brothers. I also warn you, Major Otis, that there are libel laws in England."

He raised his hat and hurried off, afraid to trust himself.

Just as he departed, Madeline and Theo, who had been for a long time hanging around, in hopes of being introduced to some officers, ventured to come up, and found themselves welcomed by Miss Ayres with quite unwonted cordiality.

"Oh, do come here! Miss Lutwyche is your cousin, isn't she?" she cried. "You must be introduced to an old friend of hers!"

The girls listened spellbound to the piquant story of the presence in England of a Boer boy who was Millie's brother. "A regular, sulky Boer," giggled Sybil, "who only speaks very broken English."

They looked at each other.

"Why," said Madeline, "then I expect the Major could tell us all about Millie before she came to England—what we have always wanted to know—how she got her arm broken, and so on."

"I can tell you that, certainly. She broke her arm scrambling out through a skylight to meet her lover, when her stepmother had locked her in."

"That we can easily believe," cried Theo. "Father sent her away from the Vicarage for that very same thing—getting out of her bedroom window at night! And then she tried to fix the blame on Gwen."

Sybil Ayres listened with eyes starting from her head.

"Do you suppose Mr. Burmester knows all this?" she cried.

"If he don't, he oughter," said Otis, whose English was apt to fray, as it were, when he grew familiar or confidential. "The person that told him would be doin' him a kindness. Look here! I ought to know something about that gal, since I was engaged to marry her, with her mother's consent."

"To marry her! She was only sixteen!" cried Theo.

"We were short of gals in Slabbert's Poort," said Amurrica, with that irresistible dry grin which always fascinated people. "But the day her father was buried, Mestaer, the feller she was carryin' on with, picked a quarrel with me, fought me, pounded me into a jelly, and carried off my gal that night."

Madeline grew very red. The seriousness of this accusation was more than she had contemplated. After all, Melicent was a Cooper!

"You must mean he tried to carry her off," she said faintly.

Major Otis took out the cigar he was smoking—one of General Ayres' best—and touched her sleeve lightly with one finger.

"Cousin of yours?" He looked round at Sybil with raised eyebrows. "Better not. This pretty young English lady don't know the sorter thing her cousin came out of."

"Having gone so far, you ought to speak out, I think," said Madeline.

He shook his head, and looked sympathetic.

"This young lady is going to be married, I hear—to make what's called a good match?"

They all assented.

"Well then, why spoil her chances?" He shrugged his shoulders and replaced his cigar.

"Why, there are the Burmesters to think of," cried Sybil Ayres indignantly. "And the Helstons, whom she has deceived all these years."

"That's so," said Amurrica slowly. "That's so, certainly."

"You had better tell us what you know; we are her cousins," said Theo.

"Well, what I'm tellin' you now, I'm prepared to swear to, before any magistrate in this county," he replied, as if reluctantly. "It's simply this. Mestaer carried off Millie Lutwyche to his house and kept her there. After some days he deserted her, went off and enlisted—and the chaplain chipped in, and sent her home to her friends. Arnie Lutwyche will tell you all whether that's true or not, and you must decide whether Burmester ought to be told."

Madeline and Theo stood looking at one another.

"And she pretended to be so honest, and so disgusted with us for doing things on the quiet!" gasped Madeline at last. "Father ought to be told. Go, Theo, tell him to come at once and hear what Major Otis has to say."

Meanwhile Lance, in white heat, made his way to where his party were standing.

"Melicent," he said, "do you know there's a brute of a chap called Otis here to-day—a fellow that was notorious in Africa for all kinds of rascality—

telling everybody that he knows you, and has got a brother of yours over here with him as his servant. What does he mean by such cheek?"

Melicent turned quickly to him. "What does he say? He has one of the Lutwyche boys here?"

"The Lutwyche boys? Who are they?" cried Lance, in stupefaction.

"Why, Tante Wilma's children," said Millie disgustedly; "my half-brothers and sisters."

There was a silence. Lady Burmester turned a look of blank astonishment upon Mrs. Helston.

"Do I understand that Lance will have a family of half Boer brothers-in-law?" she said.

"But I thought you knew my father married a Boer woman after my mother died. I thought everyone knew it," said Millie. "Surely Mr. Mayne told you; he knows all about it. It was he who got me away from Tante Wilma after my father died."

Lance cleared his throat.

"Perhaps," he said, "before I again encounter Major Otis, it will be as well for you to give me further family information."

"It would have been better had it been given before," echoed his mother, very stiffly.

Melicent dared not look at Bert. She held up her little head proudly.

"I was under the impression that everyone knew," she said. "Pater and Mater certainly do, and I assumed they had told you long ago. Please believe that I have never had the least intention of sailing under false colours."

There flashed across Lancelot's mind a memory of a chance word spoken by Harry Helston the first time he saw Melicent upon Tod's Trush: *"It's not a pretty story, and I daresay would do the poor child no good in a narrow, provincial circle?"*

There were passages in Millie's life of which he knew nothing, but of which, apparently, the odious Otis knew much. It was a rankling thought.

Captain Brooke broke the silence.

"There is one consolation," he observed coolly. "Otis is such a wholesale liar, he'll soon get found out. It might be doing him a kindness if I gave him a hint to keep himself in the background. I know enough about him to make General Ayres regret his hospitality. Whatever you do, keep clear of him,

Lady Burmester. If I may count myself enough your friend to give you a hint, avoid being introduced to the fellow. He's not fit to mix with ladies."

"Really, Captain Brooke? I am extremely obliged," said Lady Burmester gratefully.

"Keep clear of the Ayres party, mother," said Lance. "Brooke's right, he's a beast. Come, Melicent, I am going to start the sports now."

He spoke irritably, and Melicent silently walked away with him, conscious of a burning, fiery resentment against him, his mother, herself, and Fate generally.

Her pride was cruelly wounded, and her conscience reiterated, "Serve you right!" She knew that had she really loved Lancelot she would have known no peace until she had told him all about Hubert. She ought to have done so. Now some kind of explanation was unavoidable. It was impossible but that Lance should return to the subject. She now felt certain that Otis would tell everybody who would listen some garbled version of her flight from her stepmother's house. Vaguely she began to realise how far it was in his power to injure her; and she knew that, had Lance been in possession of the actual facts, he would have had no power to injure her at all. She had left her lover in the position of being unable to contradict effectively anything that might be said.

The figure she must cut was not a dignified one. If she broke off the engagement, it could but seem that she did so because she was found out, and dreaded further revelations. If she confessed to Lance, he must feel that she did so only because concealment was no longer practicable, to say nothing of the suspicions which she must arouse by the mere fact of not having spoken before. She saw that, whatever she did, she must lower herself, perhaps fatally, in the eyes of her lover. She positively shrank from the abyss before her. She could not see how she could avoid public humiliation, and what was worse, she must sink in the eyes of the Helstons too. They had loved, shielded, trusted her. She had wilfully gone her own way, keeping from them all that most nearly concerned her, locking her heart, hiding it away from them....

It was human nature that, at the moment, Lance's regard should seem to her more precious than ever before. No woman is ready to resign her lover because she has ceased to be pleasing in his sight.

She stood by his side, watching, with eyes that swam in tears, the great raw-boned Dalesmen slouching round the sloping, bumpy course with limbs all abroad, yet keeping up a pace that was undeniable, as they completed lap after lap of the walking race, which was the great event of the day, a professional champion from another county being entered for it.

Outwardly she maintained her pride and spirit. She smiled and chatted to Lance so naturally that he began to forget his uneasiness.

"Curious," he observed to her presently, "that I never heard of your father's children."

"Vrouw Lutwyche cast me off," said Millie. "She repudiated me. I never expected to hear of her again. They are well-to-do; there seemed no reason why they should trouble themselves; they only wanted to be rid of me."

"Still, they are your father's children."

"Oh," she said, in her hardest voice, "I suppose so; but nobody could think it. They are all Boer, through and through. I could not love them. I am a cold person, as you know. I should have told you of them, if I had not made quite sure you knew."

He did not reply for a moment; when he did, what he said startled her.

"It at least shows how far we have been from perfect confidence."

She looked at him astonished, taken aback. He was studying the race card.

The invitations to the wedding were actually written. It seemed to Melicent that her marriage was as final a thing as the fact that autumn follows summer. She was frightened, shaken.

"Surely," she faltered, "perfect confidence is a thing that comes by degrees?"

"I think it ought to come before marriage, don't you?" said Lance.

She felt as if he had opened an oubliette at her feet. How could she tell him what ought to be told? But evidently she must either do that or lose him. She firmly believed that, in his wholesome, out-of-doors life, were no dark corners concealed from her.

However far she was from passion, she liked Lance dearly. The idea of his contempt was extremely painful.

All her life she had prided herself upon her honesty!

And her attempt to assert her independence of spirit had led her into this *impasse*!

CHAPTER XXXIV
THE DISCOMFITURE OF OTIS

> "We build with strength the deep tower-wall
>   That shall be shattered thus and thus.
> And fair and great are court and hall;
>   But how fair—this is not for us,
> Who know the lack that lurks in all.
>   "... the years
> Interpret everything aright,
>   And crown with weeds our pride of towers,
> And warm our marble through with sun,
>   And break our pavements through with flowers,
> With an Amen when all is done."
>
> —MRS. MEYNELL.

Sybil Ayres, who was animated by a very lively desire to pay out Lancelot for being about to marry someone else, manœuvred repeatedly to approach the Burmester party, and fling her fire-brand into their midst. But in some unaccountable way they seemed to elude her. After a time she appealed to Captain Brooke, who happened to be passing by.

"Captain Brooke, do persuade Miss Lutwyche to come this way! Her brother is here, and wants to see her."

"What, one of the Boer boys? He had better go and call upon her to-morrow at Glen Royd, I should think. This is a public sort of meeting-place; and as you see, she is leaving the ground now with Lady Burmester's party."

"It looks just as if Miss Lutwyche was avoiding him," tittered Miss Ayres.

"It is Major Otis whom they are all avoiding, by my advice," said the Captain gravely.

"Because he knows all about Miss Lutwyche's African life? That looks as if there were something to be ashamed of, doesn't it?" said the girl impertinently.

"Not on that account, but because—you will pardon my speaking so of the General's guest—with my consent, no woman of my acquaintance should speak to such a man."

"Captain Brooke!"

"I will say the same to Otis himself, if you wish. He has no business in any gentleman's house, and he knows it. Whatever he told me, I should be sure was a lie, merely because Otis said it."

"But—but—" stammered Sybil, crimson, "the vicar says that all Major Otis tells him is borne out by his own knowledge, only the real facts were kept from him by Mr. Mayne. The Major says he is prepared to swear before any magistrate that all he says is true."

"Then he has actually presumed to make charges against Miss Lutwyche?" asked the Captain, his eyes like blue fire. "You can tell him from me that wilful perjury's a serious matter in England."

"Oh, Captain Brooke, do you really think that what he says about Miss Lutwyche is untrue? Because the vicar is gone to lay the matter before Sir Joseph. He felt it his duty. Major Otis says Miss Lutwyche, if asked, can't, and won't deny it."

"Deny what?" asked Brooke, in a tone that, as Sybil afterwards declared, sent cold shivers down her back.

"If—if it's true, Miss Lutwyche ought not— But I couldn't possibly tell you!"

"Yet you could listen," he broke in. "You could stand by while that coward dared to mishandle the name of a girl you have known for years! You could believe his vile accusations! Well, now, he has chosen to do this thing in public, and I'll make him regret it to the last day he lives. I'll just trouble Major Otis to repeat his lies to me! Excuse plain speaking. But I know this man, and you don't."

The Burmester party, including the vicar and the Helstons, were just driving away as he strode with his long, firm stride, across the field to where the Major stood, a cluster of eager listeners around him. His hand rested on the shoulder of a big, slouching boy, swarthy, with high cheekbones and little black eyes, who seemed about as unlike what one would imagine Melicent's brother as anything could be.

"This boy can tell you it's all true," he was saying, "and so could Mestaer, if he hadn't got shot as a spy later on, in the campaign."

"I knew Mestaer," said the Captain, in a carrying voice. "Perhaps the fact may serve as an introduction between us, Major. Now you tell me, straight out, the truth about him and Miss Lutwyche, just as you have been telling these friends of ours, will you?"

Eager faces, wearing expressions of various kinds, pressed nearer as Otis, wholly unsuspicious, repeated his version of Millie's flight from her father's house.

Alfred Dow was close to Bert; Mrs. Cooper and her daughters not far off.

The Captain listened with perfect calmness. When it was done, he said quietly: "That all?"

"That's all; and if I were Burmester, I'd think it enough," he said, laughing brutally.

"Well," said Bert, "then my turn comes. You have had no scruple in saying this abominable thing out before ladies, which alone might have opened their eyes as to the kind of refuse you are; so I have no scruple in telling you, before ladies, that you lie. You lie, sir, as a Boer traitor might be expected to do. Yes, grin! Show them all the false teeth you wear in place of those Mestaer knocked down your throat on the day you laid your plans against Miss Lutwyche! Hold your tongue! You've had your innings this afternoon; now I'm going to have mine! You lied again when you said Mestaer was shot. He is alive, as you probably know. What you don't know is that he is in England. The Bishop of Pretoria is in England too. Both these witnesses can prove the untruth of your story, as you know; and I both can and will produce them—not here, but in open court, unless you confess yourself a malicious liar, and offer a public apology. If you don't withdraw every word you have said against Miss Lutwyche this afternoon, you shall pay such swingeing damages as shall exhaust the last of the loot you stole when you were in the Boer Irish Brigade, before the taking of Kroonstadt. Ha, you see, I know!"

He had spoken without a pause. The white intensity of his rage had carried him along, and the silent sympathy of the excited audience seemed to make itself felt. Amurrica had several times tried to break in, but in vain. But now he uttered a howl of rage, and fuming, turned to those about him.

"He thinks to frighten me! He thinks he can— By the—— Who are you, sir? Who are you to take up the cudgels for this young lady?"

"I have the privilege to be a friend of Miss Lutwyche," said Hubert, raising his hat as he spoke with a quiet grace which gave the effect of saluting her name. "I also know the Orange Colony like the palm of my hand. There's not a man in that colony that would believe you on your oath. If I allowed this gathering to disperse without knowing you for the scoundrel you are, I should be failing in my duty to this country. Ladies and gentlemen, you have heard the slander uttered by this renegade. I shall now tell you the truth, in as few words as possible. Miss Lutwyche was left an orphan at the age of sixteen, in a Boer village which a year or two before had got filled with sweepings from other parts of Africa, come there in search of diamonds. This man, who had long cast eyes on her, paid her stepmother a sum of money to hand her over to him on her father's death. But Mr. Mayne, the chaplain, had been left her guardian, which interfered with their design. Mayne had to go away on urgent business connected with the will. In his absence it was plotted that Otis should go through a form of marriage with the girl at the hands of the Boer Predikant. But, as they knew the indomitable spirit of Miss Lutwyche, the Boer woman thrashed her within an inch of her life to reduce her to a proper state of submission. In escaping from her torturers, she fell down a ladder, and dislocated her arm. That seems to have frightened them somewhat, for they let her creep away to her garret to die. Mestaer, who had been asked by Mayne to keep watch, went to the house, found her lying in a pool of blood, and carried her to his home. Where else could he have taken her? He put her in charge of his housekeeper, fetched a doctor at once, and mounted guard until Mayne's return, when he went off to the war. Now, you ask that boy there, whether this is true or no. Here, boy! did your mother sjambok your sister?"

All eyes were turned upon the uncouth lad. He lifted his eyes to his questioner with a very curious look; he did not seem to notice Otis, who still kept a heavy hand on his shoulder.

"Yes, she did," he replied sulkily.

"Was it done at Otis's suggestion?"

Here the boy shook off the Major's touch, and stood up.

"Yes; to make her go quiet; only mother was drunk, and she done too much."

There was a kind of growl all round among the listening Dalesmen. Otis grew green, and clenched his fist.

"You shall pay for this!" he muttered to the boy.

"Had Otis paid your mother to arrange the matter?" went on Bert relentlessly.

"Yes."

"And this is the cur," said Hubert, between his teeth, "who has dared to slander a young innocent girl before you all this day."

The Man Who Won

Otis was literally foaming at the mouth. His mortification was choking him.

"I said what was true!" he screamed. "Mestaer did carry her off! I said no more! She was in his house! That's all I said."

"Yes, and that's what you'll go to hell for saying!" shouted Dow, cracking a formidable whip he held, and stamping with excitement. "It isn't a sjambok, Captain, but let me lay it round him once or twice! Let me just give him the feel of it! Do now!"

Bert waved him back.

"If it wasn't for his health," he said, "I would be inclined to let you do as you liked with him. But he's ill, Dow, and he mustn't be touched. But if there's a soul present will let him inside his doors after this, I shall be surprised. You're a discredited traitor," he said fiercely to the livid Otis. "How you got your commission is one of the many mysteries of the late campaign. Having come through so far, you might have had the common decency to lie low and keep your poisonous tongue quiet!"

Otis appealed, gasping in his rage, to General Ayres; but the General turned his back upon him.

"We took our convalescents on trust," he said coldly. "That trust the War Office has betrayed. I will send your luggage to any address you like to give me."

"But look here—is this justice, bare justice? His word against mine, that's all you've got, except for this lying little Boer—"

"We all know and respect Captain Brooke," said the General, bowing to Hubert. "I may add, we all know and admire Miss Lutwyche." He raised his hat, as Hubert had done. "Gentlemen, may I venture to suggest—three cheers for Miss Lutwyche?"

The field rang again. The hurrahs rolled away across the Dale, and Brenda remarked, as they drove silently.

"That must have been a close race! Hark, how they are cheering the winner!"

"You rat—you little viper!" hissed Amurrica, as he hastened, with Arnie at his side, to get the dog-cart from the farm where it was put up, and drive away from the scene of his disgrace, "why in thunder did you give me away like that?"

It was a long time before the sullen answer came:

"Always was afraid of him."

"Afraid of me?"

"No fear," said Arnie, with a laugh. "Not much. But I always have been feared of Bert Mestaer."

"What?" Otis gave a kind of jump into the air. "Mestaer? That? Mestaer coming the county gentleman? And I never knew it! You little devil, why didn't you tell me?"

"Thought you'd know him."

Otis stood still in the dusty lane. He went from red to pale, and almost to purple again.

"If he thinks he's done with me, he makes a mistake, that's all," he growled; and he snarled like a wild beast.

CHAPTER XXXV
CONFESSION

"Well, I have played and lost. But that is best.
   Where was my right to win and keep such glory?
Now I will let the book of living rest.
   Closed is my story."

—ALICE HERBERT.

Hubert's motor traversed the distance from the sports to Ilbersdale at a rate so far beyond the police limit as to make limits seem ridiculous.

On his way he encountered Mr. Cooper, pushing his bicycle up hill. The seething excitement which had gripped him that afternoon had not yet expended itself; and he pulled up.

"Good evening, Vicar. Just a word! I hope you have not been to the Burmesters with any of those awful lies about your niece that Otis was getting off his chest in that field?"

The vicar assumed his most stony aspect. His cold eye said eloquently, "Beware!" Aloud his reply was: "I fear I do not understand you, Captain Brooke."

"Sorry; it's my slang makes me difficult to follow. I drop into it when I'm excited. You see, I happen to know all about Otis, and I've just been enlightening the bystanders a bit. There isn't enough of him left to make a War Office clerk! They've hissed him off the ground, General Ayres has washed his hands of him, and I've given him twelve hours to choose between a libel action and a written apology."

"It is a—surely—a somewhat extraordinary proceeding on your part to talk of libel actions on behalf of a young lady who has her own relatives to protect her," said the vicar, fastening, in the whirl of his mind, upon a breach of conventionalities which he might legitimately resent.

"Her own relatives didn't seem to me to be doing much protecting this afternoon," observed Bert drily. "However, Mrs. Cooper and your daughters will be able to tell you all about it. They saw the brute knocked out of time."

The vicar began to be anxious to get home.

"I fancy you are under a misapprehension," he said. "I have just been to Ilbersdale to correct a misunderstanding. I own I was disturbed this afternoon to find that Mr. and Mrs. Helston had allowed the engagement between Mr. Burmester and my niece to take place, without informing the bridegroom's relatives of the serious family disabilities of the bride. I was anxious to assure Lady Burmester that, had the affair rested with me, I should have been quite frank; but that I naturally imagined that Miss Lutwyche's adopted parents had supplied all the facts."

"That was very thoughtful of you. But if you were, as you say, in possession of the facts, how is it that you did not contradict the horrible misstatements made by Otis up at the field?"

The vicar grew still more stony.

"I have never been made acquainted with the exact truth concerning my niece's injuries at the time of her father's death."

"Injuries?" echoed Bert. "Injuries, indeed! But I've seen her righted. She was the darling of the Dale before; she'll be its idol now! Did you hear them cheering her?"

The vicar stood amazed. "Cheering my niece?"

Hubert laughed mischievously.

"And who may you be, to have the intimate knowledge which I lack concerning this young lady?" inquired the vicar.

"Hubert Brooke, late Captain in Lacy's Brigade," laughed Bert, as he drove away.

Mr. Cooper pursued his road, in much wrath and discomfiture. His reception at Ilbersdale had affronted him, his encounter with Bert bewildered him. He remounted the bicycle which he was pushing at the time of his meeting, and rode home with what speed he might.

By the Vicarage gate two men were awaiting him—Otis and the unattractive Boer boy. Evidently they meant to speak with him.

Otis approached with the easy confidence and winning smile that he could assume at will. He begged pardon for troubling, but he had unthinkingly mixed himself up in what looked to him like a local scandal of formidable dimensions, and he had come to the vicar for advice. Mr. Cooper's anger was not altogether proof against the insidious appeal. He was used to being ignored and left out of things, and, to one whose own idea of his own importance, both socially and parochially, was enormous, the way this man approached him was a salve to a wound always more or less smarting.

After a short parley, understanding that Otis had material facts to communicate, he invited him in.

Mrs. Cooper and her daughters were at tea; and there was a flutter of consternation among them for they had seen the exit of Otis from the Fransdale sports. Mrs. Cooper became unspeakably coy, blushing like a girl, and dismissing her brood, with their tea half done, on the flimsiest of pretexts.

"This is not surprisin', Mrs. Cooper," said Otis sadly. "I was a stranger up there, and nobody knew me. It was my word against that of a bad and dangerous man, who is sailin' among you all under false colours. These young ladies heard him givin' me the lie up there. In justice, I should like to have them hear what I want to tell you now. You may have heard Mr. Mayne or Miss Lutwyche talk of the man Mestaer?"

"Yes, yes," gasped Madeline, at the door. "She had one letter from him after she got here—you remember, mother, the letter she would not show you. She said he wanted to marry her!"

"She wouldn't show you his letter?" slowly said Otis, standing by the table, and turning his hat round in his hand as if on the point of taking leave. "Has she ever told you that he goes now under the name of Brooke?"

"What's that you say?" sharply asked the vicar.

"He's well disguised," replied Otis. "He bluffed me, I own it. But Arnie here, he knew him from the first; didn't you, boy?"

Arnold looked at the three tall, full-blown girls, blushed admiringly and assented.

Surprise deprived them all of speech.

"Now, I'm told," said Otis, "that this fine Captain Brooke is buildin' himself a house, and that Miss Lutwyche is his—architect." He gave a little chuckle, "Excuse me: I really got to laff," he drawled humorously. "The idea of him an' his architect is a bit too thick—eh?"

"Miss Lutwyche is duly qualified," began the vicar, in his stateliest manner.

"Do I doubt it? No, sir! But I hear she has been stayin' down in the shires with him pretty near all summer, gettin' this house ready while her lover's in Russia. Now, I couldn't help just wonderin'—we really couldn't help it, Arnie and me—whether young Burmester knows that Brooke's her old lover."

"Why, do you think *she* knows?" cried Theo excitedly.

Otis bent on her the sliest, most waggish look, and slowly closed one eye.

"Dear young ladies, you live in Arcadia," he said. "You remind me of three hedge-roses; an' you're doubtless as simple as you're sweet. But your cousin, Miss Lutwyche, she wasn't born yesterday, you know. She knows a thing or two, you may take my word for that."

The vicar was silent, struggling with mortification. That day he had broken through his lifelong rule to do nothing hurriedly. He had gone straight from hearing Otis's revelations to be first with Lady Burmester. He felt sure that what was said must ultimately come to her ears. He thought his duty was plain.

But if he had only waited! If he had only gone to Millie, armed with this fact! If he could have charged her with knowing who Bert was, and concealing her knowledge, how differently things might have gone!

He looked at his wife, who seemed to be still blushing. She rose from table.

"As you say, Mr. Otis," said she, with archness which was unutterably comic upon her middle-aged, substantial personality, "my dear girls are very unsophisticated. They have been carefully brought up, as English girls usually are. I will leave you to discuss this serious matter with Mr. Cooper, and take them away. Come, my darlings."

Meanwhile Bert drove straight to the Grange, inquired for Lance, and found him alone in the smoking-room, sunk in profound gloom and a large arm-chair.

"Burmester," he said abruptly, "I've come to talk to you—to tell you something that will perhaps sever our friendship for ever. Confession is good, they say; but I funk mine." He sank down in the opposite chair, drawing out his cigar-case. "I funk it; make it as easy as you can, old man."

Lance was not smoking. He lifted a haggard young face from the depths of his chair.

"Sorry," he said nervously, "but fact is, I'm feeling a bit off—preoccupied. I must own I'm not in a sympathetic mood."

"It's about that—same thing. My confession touches the spot," said Hubert.

"What are you talking about?"

"You are upset because you find scandal busy with the name of ... your ... the girl you love. And because you feel she hasn't been open with you. You don't doubt her, but you feel there are things you should have known, which she has kept back. Is that so?"

"That's precisely it," said Lance hurriedly. "I oughtn't to talk to you about it—about her. But there must be some kind of understanding between me and her if—if things are to go on. I feel a brute, to talk like this, but I am all abroad, so to speak. We have had a very unpleasant scene here. Old Cooper turned up, and said there were wild rumours flying about, on the authority of those who claimed to have known her in Africa, to the effect that she, Melicent, had got out of her bedroom window and gone with a man called Mestaer, and that she had been in his house three or four weeks. He said he came to Melicent for an authoritative contradiction. He wished to be able to refute the story; thought he had a right to ask for the exact facts."

He leaned forward, running his hands up through his hair.

Hubert sat very still. "And what did she say?"

"... Said it was true."

There was a pause. "Not as if she meant it?" asked Hubert tentatively.

"She was very angry. She looked splendid. She said that it was at her uncle's own request that she had kept silence—that when she first came to England she was anxious to tell him everything, but was forbidden to mention the subject. If we wanted to know the truth we could write to the Bishop: he knew. Then she got up and took her leave, and went off with the Helstons. Of course I know this is a cock-and-bull story; but I feel ... I ought to have been told."

"Yes," agreed his friend, "you ought to have been told."

"One thing I do wish," said Lance, clenching his fists, "that I had that man Mestaer here to strangle."

"Well, if all our wishes could be as easily granted," said Hubert. "I'm Mestaer."

Lance bounded from his seat, then sank back, as red as fire.

"Is this a time for your rotting?"

"No rotting here. I told you it would mean the breaking of our friendship very likely. I am Hubert Mestaer. I took the name of Brooke because it was English, and my mother's, and I wished to live in England and be English. May I go on, or are you too angry to hear me?"

Lance rose to his feet again. He stared blankly for a minute or two, then his eyes suddenly blazed.

"You're Mestaer! Good God! *Then you're the man that knows!* You can tell me ... what happened that night!"

"Yes; I can tell you: and I will. Mayne knows, she knows, I know. Nobody else."

A shiver ran through Lancelot; he seemed on the brink of a hundred questions; he choked them back.

"Speak, can't you?" he said.

Hubert spoke. He told his story from the beginning, making Melicent's attitude towards himself throughout quite clear. He did not dwell on his own feelings, but made it no secret that he had come to England solely in the hope of being able to obtain her regard.

Lancelot listened to it all, as to information respecting some girl whom he had never known.

"That she should have undergone all this, and never told me a word!"

"I can see where her difficulty came in," said Bert "Before she engaged herself to you, she had guessed who I am. That altered everything. If you can see what I mean, it turned the past into the present. She could not speak to you of Mestaer without adding that he was here, in England, under another name. That would have been giving me away—"

"Why couldn't she warn you that she should speak?"

"She never confessed to me that she knew. She tried to avoid intimacy."

"You ought to have told me yourself!" cried Lance.

"Well, until she engaged herself to you, it was certainly no concern of yours," said Hubert bluntly. "Do you suppose that what you are feeling now is anything like as bad as what I felt about you, when I heard you had carried off the only thing that made life worth living to me?"

Lance paced the room restlessly.

"Is that still the same?" he cried. "Do you still care about her?"

"It's chronic," said Bert calmly. "There's only one woman in my world. She might have Boer relations on every bush for aught I should care. Nothing she could do, nothing anybody could say of her, would make any difference to me."

"But—then—when she's my wife?" stammered Lance.

"When she's—your wife I shall never see her any more," said Bert quietly. "It wouldn't be safe."

"Safe? No! But am I safe now?" cried the young man bitterly. "I don't understand. What is the situation at this moment between you and her?"

Bert folded his arms tight, hunching himself together as if to keep control over his temper.

"That's a question, surely, that you must ask her to answer," he said, in a colourless voice.

Lance uttered an exclamation of rage.

"You ought to know without asking," went on Hubert presently. "Does she love you? Surely you must know that, If she does ... I'm out of it, you see."

Lancelot paused in his pacing. He leaned against the window-frame staring out Hubert had touched the weak spot. He knew that he had persuaded Millie into the engagement, had ever since continued to assure her that she was happy, or that, if not, she certainly would be. He knew that, were he sure of her love, distrust would be impossible to him. He was not sure. He did distrust her. He was madly, wildly jealous of Hubert. Crossing to where he sat, he seized his shoulder, shaking him violently.

"When she promised to marry me, did she know who you are?"

"Yes."

"Then it's all right! It must be! She said she liked me better than anybody else."

"If she said so, it was true."

"She's—she's not like most girls, you see. She's a cold nature—"

"Is she?"

Hubert closed his eyes, thinking of the lips that had clung to his, the eyes that had looked into his, the hands that had trembled beneath his, as they stood together in the chalky pit He got up suddenly: he had had about as much as he could stand.

At the moment a footman entered, with a note on a salver.

"From her," said Lance, very white, as the man left the room.

"Breaking it off," said Hubert, relighting his cold cigar with a shaking hand.

Lance read it

"Just so. She declines to give any kind of explanation of the statements made by Mr. Cooper. She prefers to consider the engagement at an end." He stood silent a moment, the note crumpled in his hand. "I'll go to her," he said unsteadily. "I've simply got to have it out with her! When she hears that I know—that you have told me"—he was half-way to the door. Then he stopped, as if choked. "When I think that I have never known all this! When I think that I have been shut out from her confidence, and that you—you—have known all the time! When I think that I've been away in Russia and you two, with this common memory between you, have been together! Day after day! Over that confounded house-building! I feel that I have good ground to consider myself hardly used."

Hubert turned slowly round. He was so white that Lance considered him attentively.

"Why have you told me now?" he cried. "Why?"

"Only because it couldn't be helped," returned Hubert, in a hard voice.

"And, but for this scoundrel turning up, she would have married me without a word! Brooke, I can't stand it! No man could! She's right, it had better be broken off."

"Steady on!" said Bert, getting out his words with difficulty. "Listen a moment! She may be offering you your freedom because she believes you desire it. She is—very proud. She may think this miserable tittle-tattle has shaken your faith in her, and she offers you your way out. What you have to discover, or so it seems to me, is *the cost to herself*. Does she want to be free?" He took out his handkerchief and wiped his forehead. "Everyone round here will say you have treated her badly if it's broken off now. That doesn't matter if it isn't true. But make sure—make sure, for God's sake!"

Lance stared at him.

"You're a queer chap. You must want the engagement to be off—that would give you your chance. Yet you send me to her!"

Bert shrugged his shoulders.

"Well," he said, with a half laugh, "I've discovered to-day that I've been mistaken all these years. Ever since I was four-and-twenty I have believed that most of everything on this earth I desired—her. Now I find there is something that I desire more—her happiness. If you're the man to make her happy, in God's name go and do it."

CHAPTER XXXVI
WHAT CHANCED UPON THE MOORS

"What can I give thee back, O liberal
And princely giver, who hast brought the gold
And purple of thine heart, unstained, untold,
And laid them on the outside of the wall
For such as I to take or leave withal?"

—SONNETS FROM THE PORTUGUESE.

Lancelot had gone to Glen Royd.

Bert found that he could not stay indoors. He wandered out, through the gardens, into the long carriage drive which ran upon the side of the ravine, among the pines, with a sheer ascent on one hand, and a sheer dip on the other, down to where the trout stream rushed over its noisy bed.

He paced along the road, dark beneath the over-arching trees, till he came to the lodge and gate at the end of the wood. There was no sign of Lance returning, so he walked on, and bending to the left, came, after a climb, out upon the highroad to Fransdale. Nobody was about. He sat down upon a grassy hummock, watching the pretty horned sheep cropping the short grass about him in the fragrant evening. He was so still that the sheep grazed nearer and nearer.

He was thinking that man is strangely in the grip of circumstance.

Since that night of parting at Clunbury, he had been through deep waters. Carol, who had been so long excluded, was summoned at last. The final knock-out had been too serious for the champion to bear alone.

He had laid all the circumstances before the Bishop, and told him that he would follow his advice as to the course now to be pursued—whether he should let things go on, or make one more effort to show Melicent what he believed to be the truth, to induce her to break her engagement.

In the light of what he now heard—namely, that Melicent had almost at once recognised Bert—Mayne had little difficulty in falling in with Bert's opinion as to her reason for engaging herself to Lance. His disapproval of the said proceeding was so grave that he felt, and said, that he really thought it would be better for Bert to have nothing more to do with her.

"Incredible selfishness and duplicity," he mercilessly called it at first, till warned by Bert's rising anger that strictures upon Melicent would merely have the effect of drying up the flow of confidence.

"I began the duplicity," said Bert doggedly. "I don't see what she could do but follow suit."

"Does that excuse your further duplicity," came the answering thrust, "in proceeding to make love to her while Lance was in Russia?"

"I'm hanged if I see what the d—" A sudden pause. "I quite fail to see what other course I could have taken. They were to be married when he came back. I had got to show her before then that the thing couldn't be done. And I succeeded, within a hair's-breadth. If it hadn't been for my d—! Beg pardon! if it hadn't been for my—unfortunate temper, I should have succeeded."

"From what you tell me," the Bishop opined, "it really seems as if she does like you best, but as if her pride would not allow her to give way. The question is—Has your violence destroyed your chance finally? I think you ought to find out."

"You do?—you do? You think I might have another try?"

"Well, are you to be trusted to keep yourself in check? You know of old that when you lose your temper you have no chance at all with Millie, because she never loses hers."

Hubert grinned. "She did the other night, though."

"Do you think she said things that she will be ashamed of when she thinks them over?"

"Yes, I do."

"Then I think that should give you a hold of a new kind over her. If you can only manage to put her in the wrong, old man, and be magnanimous and forgive her—see?"

Bert's admiration was open and glowing.

"You have a genius! You ought to marry, Bishop—you ought really."

"My advice is," finally said the mentor, "that you go at once to Fransdale, and see how the land lies. See what frame of mind Millie is in. If she is scornful and gay, and wrapped up in Lance and her marriage, your course will be more difficult. If she shows you, by word or look, that she thinks she behaved ill, or wounded you, or desires your good opinion, then to my thinking you have a chance that you ought to take. You have now been disciplined by failure; you should have learnt something; and Melicent also must be wiser. For if she has any feeling at all—which, as you know, I always took leave to doubt—she must have suffered keenly during these last few months."

It was with the ring of this advice in his ears that Bert had hurled himself and his motor through England, and arrived at Fransdale, where in his rage he had vowed never to set foot more.

At the first sight of Melicent he believed that he had done right to come.

And behold, an hour later, all things were changed; the chance appearance of Otis had, as it were, altered the entire situation. Bert was no longer suppliant, but defender of Melicent's name against all comers—even against the man she was to marry.

It seemed to him that, whether she ever came to care for himself or no, she must break with Lance; for, knowing her as he did, he was sure that now she must feel that, if the engagement went on, full confession of all that had passed was imperative; and that seemed impossible.

Suspense grew and mounted in him till he felt desperate; yet still he sat there, with a kind of charmed stillness, while the quiet-coloured end of evening slowly merged in twilight.

It was growing dark when at last he saw figures moving along the path that led up on the other side of the ridge from Glen Royd—two figures, indistinct at first in the dusk, then clearer. It was Lancelot and Melicent walking together. Bert felt dizzy.

Then he had lost! They were reconciled! They moved slowly along, and he saw that Lance was pushing her bicycle.

He rose and obliterated himself hastily behind a craggy boulder.

They both turned into the road leading to the carriage drive of the Grange, which was also a short cut to the lower parts of Fransdale. They passed in complete silence, and he watched them along the white track of road until they were lost in the shadows of the wood.

A light glimmered out in the lodge window. It was the only sign of human life within his ken.

Lance must be bringing her back to dine, and intending to cycle home with her afterwards. He lit a match and looked at his watch. A quarter to eight. He could not meet them. He realised that he must have time.

He had done what he believed to be right—told the truth, as far as he thought it permissible, to wipe away from his conscience the stain of his treachery to Lance. And the result was that they were reconciled, and he was left in outer darkness. He knew that he had not expected it.

His misery was too great for him to reflect at present. He could not tell what he should do. He plunged down the hill-side with no thought at first but to walk, to get away, to move fast, to fight down some overwhelming bitterness of darkness which was clutching him.

At the bottom of the valley by the mill he turned and hastened up stream by the fishing-path among the thick trees. Careless of his direction, he walked on until he was at the head of Ilbersdale, and had emerged from the woods upon the open, broken moor that lay at the feet of Fransdale. There he lifted up his eyes, and saw far above him, perched upon the very verge of the precipice, the lights of Ilberston Church and Vicarage.

He thought of Mr. Hall. It occurred to him to wonder whether this man, whose personality had impressed him, as it impressed most people, would have help or counsel for him. Anyhow, to breast that hill was something to attempt—something that chimed in with his mood just then.

It was choir practice night, and the church door being open, the sound of the sweet Cleveshire voices floated out over the uplands, and made articulate the beauty of the night.

Hubert pushed his way hurriedly, yet not fast, because heedlessly, over the broken ground, with which he was not familiar. There were short cuts, but in the dusk he did not find them. Several times he was brought up short by hollow ravines or boggy ground, and it was long before he struck the road that leads up to the steep verge.

He had been walking for nearly two hours when at last he found himself at the top. The full moon was up, and was flooding the moors with silver. The prospect was grand. On the horizon line the Three Howes stood up black against the radiance—the prehistoric burial-place of forgotten chiefs. At his back the white crosses that mark the resting-places of the Dalesmen glimmered among the neatly shorn grass of the churchyard.

He sat upon the low wall, gazing out over the silent waste. The church was in darkness now, and closed; the village beyond showed but few lights. The lamp over the Vicarage door beamed steadily upon the night, and showed a lady's bicycle leaning against the Vicarage garden wall. Surely the little brown basket on the handle-bars was familiar to him? Surely he had seen that same machine leaning against the trees of the plantation at Lone Ash?

He sprang from his seat and went up close. It was Melicent's bicycle. Then she herself was within! She had not gone to dine with the Burmesters; she had come straight up here to Mr. Hall. A wave of excitement passed over Hubert. Should he go in, and let the priest hear both sides of the question? What had happened—what had passed between her and Lance? If he had not played the coward, and run away, he would have known by now. As he hesitated, the Vicarage door opened. He saw Mr. Hall stand in the light, with the girl beside him. For the second time that night he drew back and hid himself.

"Don't ride the steep bit to-night," he heard Mr. Hall say, as he lit her lamp.

"I know every inch of the way; it's really quite safe," was the characteristic response.

"I shall feel more comfortable if you promise me. It is late for you to be returning alone, but I cannot come with you; I must go on to poor old Martha Hirst."

Millie's little laugh sounded sad. "You needn't be nervous about me on these moors at night."

"I don't think I need, or I would not let you go; but the moon is glorious. Good-night, and God bless you!"

She mounted, and rode swiftly away, past the church, along the little level bit of road that came before the steep dip over the mountain-side. The brief dialogue had decided Bert. Mr. Hall was not at leisure, and Millie was riding home late, alone. His place was to follow her. He had ascertained that there was a footpath which was far shorter than the windings she must go down with her cycle. If she were going to walk the steep bit, he thought he could overtake her when she dismounted to walk up the next ascent.

At the lower end of the steep hill, if you followed the road, you came to a stone bridge; and here the Ilba flowed more silently, and deep pools harboured many a fat trout. Trees arched over the road, growing by the water-side; and under them were inky shadows.

Melicent's lamp gleamed brightly, but not bright enough to show the wire fastened across the road. She was riding fast, with the impetus of the long hill just negotiated, and she checked herself with difficulty as the figure of a man detached itself from the shadow, waving his arms and crying, "Stop! Danger! You'll fall!"

"What is the matter?" she cried, putting on her brakes and just managing to alight "You!"—she stopped short, recognising Amurrica.

"We were gettin' ready for someone else," said Amurrica drily. "This is an unexpected pleasure. Are you ridin' alone?"

"You see that I am."

"Our friend's gone home another way then, seemin'ly. But as you're here, let's make the most of it. Give us a kiss, little Millie."

"Don't be a cad, Amurrica!" said Millie, with a most unlooked-for gentleness. "I don't know why you stopped me, but I am glad you did, for there are things I want to say to you. Is my brother here?"

"Yes," said Arnie, slouching out from the gloom.

"Amurrica," said Millie earnestly, "first of everything, I want to beg your pardon. You were very cruel to me in the old days, but I have been shown to-day that it was my fault. I was hard and insolent. If I had been a different kind of girl, perhaps you'd not have wanted to injure me?"

Amurrica stood staring. Was this Millie? "What yer givin' us?" he growled.

"I want to say I am sorry," said the girl steadily. "I was hard and insolent to you again to-day. I provoked you to try and do me harm. But I—didn't know you had Arnie with you. I—I remember Arnie when he was a dear little curly-headed baby. I never was good to him. I was always— disagreeable. Arnie, I—am—so—sorry! I want to say—forgive me!"

Her voice broke. She turned her head away and drew out a handkerchief. Amurrica was stricken dumb. That Millie could humble herself—that Millie could cry—these incidents had seemed to him utterly out of the range of the things that happen. He had nothing to say. Arnie giggled awkwardly.

"Amurrica," said Millie earnestly, laying a hand on his sleeve, "you would have been a better man if you had known better women. I am one that helped to make you worse, because I never appealed to the good in you. There was only one of us who did the right thing all through; and that was Bert. He saved me then, and to-day he has saved me again. He has done more for me this day than I could ever tell anybody. Oh, Amurrica, we ought to be so ashamed of ourselves—you and I!"

Amurrica, during this remarkable interview, had been like one bereft of his usual faculties.

"Well, I'm d—d!" he said at last. "What kind of palaver's this? Mestaer's playin' his own hand, same as I am—him an' his bloomin' millions! Thought I didn't know him! Thought he was safe, did he? Bless his kind heart, he'll find out that I'm goin' to get even with him—if not one way, then another!"

A thought went like lightning through Millie's brain.

"Are you waiting here for him?"

They did not answer.

"What makes you think he will come this way?"

"He went up there," said Arnie.

"Up there? Up that hill? He's not there now; I've just come from there."

"Hist!" said Otis.

They all heard a footstep, clear in the night stillness, swinging down the hill at a steady run.

"If it is he, Amurrica, now is your time to make it up," urged Millie, and her heart began to beat faster, and sweet, wild thoughts surged up within her at the thought that she was hearkening her lover's approaching feet.

"I'll make it up, no fear!" was the muttered reply, as Otis, who was standing behind her, gripped her firmly by both elbows, pinioning her in his strong hold, and backing into the deepest shadow on the farther side of the bridge, under the trees. "Hold her!" he gasped to Arnie; "hold tight, we've only a minute!"

The inky darkness, rendered blacker by contrast with the white wash of moonlight on the road in front, held the struggling group invisible. Had Millie had an inkling of her captor's plan she would have screamed, but intent upon her peace-making desires, she still wished to try gentle methods. Before she realised his intentions, Otis had rammed a handkerchief forcibly against her mouth, and swiftly wound the feather boa she wore round and round her head, forming a most excellent impromptu gag. He was reckless now, and cared only for his revenge, consequences had faded out of sight. Millie, sensible in a flash of her own helplessness and Bert's danger, fought with all her strength.

The light, firm steps came on fast. They were round the corner. Hubert hastened in the moon's full radiance to the darkness where the trap lay for him. Just before he reached the fatal spot, a sound came to the trained ear of the scout—a muffled, indeterminate sound, which was not running water, nor the sound of feet upon a hard road.

Full in the light he stood, a brave target for a bullet; and even as he paused, before he had drawn a breath, there was the report of a revolver, a cry of some kind, a sound of scuffling, a splashing as of someone wading in water; and silence.

He stood bewildered. The idea that somebody had tried to shoot him never suggested itself. He thought it must be poachers, though the report did not sound like a rifle shot, and there were no woods quite near. He at once started to run on and see what had happened; and at once tripped and fell, caught by the unseen wire.

Having fallen with some impetus, he came to the ground heavily; and regained his feet with quite a new impression of some danger imminent, though still he never dreamed that the entanglement had been set for him. His heart flew to Melicent. What of her? She must but a moment ago have passed the spot. His first action was to pull out matches and strike a light. Holding the wax vesta low, he moved slowly forward; and there, on the right hand, in the deep shadow, a motionless form lay upon the ground. A little farther on, a bicycle stood against the wall. Stooping over the girl he saw that his fears were true. It was Melicent who lay there; and beside her, among the grass, he stumbled upon a hard object, which proved to be a revolver. He pocketed this, and stretching out his arms to her—"Millie!" he cried despairingly. He thought at first that she was lying on her face; and experienced a shock of a quite peculiar kind of horror, on finding her head wrapped about with choking feathers. He snatched her into his arms, raising her from the ground; as he did so, a second revolver slipped from her left hand, where she had grasped it, apparently by the muzzle. In the dark he could see nothing; and there overswept him that maddening sense of helplessness which is the worst thing a man can feel. He bore her out from the fatal shadow into the moonlight, laid her upon the thymy turf, and with trembling fingers cut away the brutal gag from her drawn face. Then he saw wet blood upon his sleeve, glistening in the light.

Was she dead? That was the one question. He satisfied himself that she breathed, that her heart beat. Whether the shot had entered her head or her body, he could not say. She was very still; was she dying there, under his eyes, passive, unconscious of his presence—of all the things there were to say, which must for ever rest unsaid? ... His head was whirling. Millie gagged! Millie shot! By whom, and for what conceivable reason?

The bleeding came from the left arm, which was cruelly mangled, the flesh below the elbow being actually singed by the shot. The pistol must have gone off while actually in her hand. Mechanically he began to slit away the white silk sleeve with his pocket-knife, while he wondered dully what he should do, how best help her. If she were going to die, there were just two things for him; to kill the man that killed her, and then to blow out his own brains. He thought she was growing cold....

What could he do? To leave her was impossible; and they were far from help. To carry her to Ilbersdale Grange, or to carry her back up the hill to the Vicarage, seemed equally impracticable. As he turned the question over in his mind, he heard a sound—a rustling, quite near. Turning his head, he looked straight into the eyes of Arnie Lutwyche, who, dripping, had emerged from the river under the bridge, and was creeping towards him on hands and knees.

Quick as thought, Bert pulled out a revolver and covered him. The boy at once knelt up, raising his hands. His face wore a look of terror.

"Is she dead?" he whispered.

"So," said Bert, through his teeth; "what do you know of this butchery?"

"It was Otis. He was out after you. She fought with him, and got hold of the pistol," panted Arnie, in his unaccustomed English.

"I don't believe a word you say. If Otis meant murder he wouldn't have brought a witness along."

"There were two pistols," said Arnie, gulping down a sob. "Did you find the one I threw down?"

"Yes—what of it?"

"There were to be two shots. I was to swear you fired first, and he only in self-defence. Let me get you some water, and tell me where to run for a doctor."

There was sense in this proposition, and after a moment's rapid thought, Bert availed himself of it. There was practically no doubt that Otis was off; he wasted no time in questioning or upbraiding the boy. Tearing a leaf from his pocket-book, he scrawled a note to Helston, telling him what had happened, and asking him to bring a conveyance of some kind at once, and to send Arnie on for the doctor. Meanwhile Arnie had brought his straw hat full of water, and the moment he received his instructions, set off running fast along the road.

Bert was alone again with the girl.

There was a huge lump rising upon one side of her forehead—he guessed it to be the result of a silencing blow from a brutal fist. Possibly it was merely the effect of her fall to the ground. This it was, he hoped, which was rendering her unconscious. He felt about carefully among the long hair, and could find no trace that a bullet had struck her head, nor was there any mark upon the white silk blouse she wore. He bathed her forehead with her own little handkerchief; he knew where to look for it, in her sleeve; he knew every little habit which was hers. For so long he had been garnering up his deep knowledge of her—for this? It was all to be in vain? The thing was so preposterous that he laughed.

This white brow, over which he passed the cold water, was his treasure-house. That it could be empty was a thing manifestly impossible.

Everything was quiet about them in the glorious night A little wind shivered among the trees that overhung the bridge. He pulled off his coat, tucking it carefully about her. As he did so, she opened her eyes, looking fully at him.

Almost immediately she took in the whole situation, and spoke.

"You're safe," she said contentedly.

She was always wonderful; but this was the crowning point of all the sensations she had ever given him. Through the wild exultation that filled him, he, as usual, thought first of her. For her sake he must be very calm.

"Oh, I'm all right," he said, in scorn of any idea of danger to himself. "But what about you?"

She smiled, a smile that lit up all her face and danced in her eyes. Directly he saw it, he knew she could have no vital hurt. The imp of mischief was in it.

"Bert, I've done it," she said.

"Done what?" he asked uncertainly.

"Moved the mountain."

He began to think she was wandering.

"Have you really?" he asked, absorbed in the play of her dimples in the moonlight, and realising that there were possibilities in her smile that he had by no means fully appreciated hitherto, connoisseur though he believed himself to be.

"I think I know what happened," she said. "I wrestled for the revolver, and it went off. I believe it shot me! I saw you come running, and stop short in the road, and I couldn't scream because he had gagged me.... Is that what happened?"

"Yes—exactly."

"Well, then," in tones of exultation—"well, then, Captain Mestaer Brooke, I have saved your life!"

"At what cost, Millie? At what cost?"

"Did you think about the cost when you saved mine?"

"Ah, that was such a different thing!"

"Why was it a different thing?"

"You know! Because I loved you."

She closed the eyes into which he would persistently gaze.

"Well," she said, "now that we are quits, now that you too have a burden of gratitude to carry about, I feel ever so much happier, or at least I should, only—Hubert, you don't know how fearfully my arm hurts!"

"I know it must! I can do so little for it until help comes! I daren't leave you here alone—"

"Oh, no; don't!"

"What is the very nearest house?"

"A mile away at least. Don't go! I'll lie here till someone finds us."

"You need not do that. Arnie has taken a note to Glen Royd."

"Arnie? Oh, I am glad of that." She closed her eyes and panted.

"Will you let me try carrying you a little way? Every step would bring us nearer to relief. If it shakes you, I could put you down. May I try?"

"I am heavier than I was in Africa."

"I am stronger than I was in Africa—tough as leather."

"Oh, you always were strong! But never mind. We're quits now! You can't stand there any more, saying: 'Just look how you treat the man that saved your life!'"

"Millie! When have I ever said so?"

"You did—you did—you did! You have never left off saying it for one single minute for the last five years."

He broke into a laugh that was a little tremulous. "Millie, what do you mean?"

"Oh, you know what I mean. That has always been the trouble, hasn't it? You have always known what I meant. You knew, that day the water spouted out. I didn't. It seemed so impertinent of you to know more about me than I knew myself. But now ... I think it may be rather restful ... to think you know the worst of me! You know it all, you see ... even about the scars on my back."

He made some kind of incoherent exclamation. He had always meant to succeed; but now that this amazing success was his, he could not believe in it. A wild idea came to him that his bliss, like the dread sword of Damocles, was poised above his head by a hair; that in an instant it might fall, and irretrievable ruin would result. He was too exalted to try to think out how it had come about that this girl was his at last. She was injured—he could not say how deeply; she was in pain, and he was distracted with anxiety. He was unable to grasp the idea of happiness. Afterwards, when he looked back upon it, he believed that the underlying idea of his mood was that of greatness. All triviality seemed to be washed away from life, and he trod the paths of a vast experience as the Greeks trod the tragic stage, raised up on cothurns. It was best, he saw, that joy should come thus sublimated by grief. If it was to be transient, he should still have had it. He had lived indeed; he had seen the Vision of the Grail. Life was a sacrament henceforward.

"Oh, I am so thirsty!" gasped Melicent

He suddenly remembered that he carried in his pocket the flask that he used when travelling. There was still a little wine and water left in it, and he poured it out. Seating himself beside her, he carefully drew her up, propping her weight against him, and held the cup to her lips.

When she had drunk, they sat on so, in silence.

"Mr. Hall has been telling me how it has all been my fault," she said, after a pause. "He has told me how vain and selfish I am, and how I take all and give nothing. Poor Lance! I never gave him anything, Bert—not even a kiss. I did give you one, didn't I?"

"Yes, thank God!"

To his amazement, she begun to bubble and murmur with laughter.

"But Mr. Hall didn't know I was going to meet my chance! Oh, Bert, it's so wonderful! I don't think you quite realise that Otis meant to kill you! He did, really! Don't you want to thank me for saving your life so nicely? Do thank me, just to make it seem real!"

The chest that pillowed her head heaved mightily. He forced an answer, but the effort broke him down.

"How could I thank you for saving mine ... if it was at the expense of yours?" He bent down his cheek upon her hair, and sobbed helplessly.

"I'm not dead, Bert, dear," she whispered.

"No; but you're in awful pain. Do you think I don't know? I can see you are chatting on like this, just to make me think you're not suffering! I can't bear it, Millie—I can't indeed! I am going to carry you a little way. Put your other arm round my neck; I'll raise you as slowly as I can. There! Did that shake you? I'll walk a few steps, and if the discomfort's too great, you must tell me."

It seemed to him that, as he moved along, his soul ran the gamut of all human emotion. Death and Life brushed sable and silver wings over him as he trod, and the glowing rose of Love warmed and lighted all things like the white heat of a furnace. Clear before him lay the picture of the former time when this very thing had happened. His memory of his feelings on that occasion was tinged with pity and contempt. What had he then known, or understood, of Love or Life?

Now at last he knew the value of both. The rapture and the insecurity swayed him to and fro like the motion of a pendulum. He had the gravest apprehensions about Melicent's injuries. The shattered arm was the same that had been dislocated five years before. He feared serious complications.

"Millie, Millie," he murmured, "is it very bad?"

Her face was pressed against his neck; he could hear her gasping breath. She gave a little moan, as if to intimate that she heard, but could not answer. After a minute, she began to whisper, as though to herself:

"Though I walk through the valley of the shadow, I will fear no evil.... I will fear no evil, for thou art with me.... Bert! ... Is the fish-pond full?"

He followed the rapid transition of her mind.

"Quite full, and the water as clear as glass. The lilies are planted already."

He had kept on a steady, slow pace for some time, and was feeling rather done, when she whispered, begging him to stop a little. He chose a lump of heathery turf, and sat down with her upon his knees, cradling her as comfortably as he could. So he had sat in Africa!

"Oh, that is good! That is rest!" she sighed; and after a pause—"Bert, you know I love you, don't you?"

Her eyes were wide open, searching his face. For a moment he forgot his devouring anxieties, and was sensible only of the rapture.

"Yes, I know," he answered solemnly, returning her deep gaze.

"I loved you that day, of course; but truly, Bert, I didn't know it. I thought I did right to send you away. Oh, what a beast I was to you that night! I thought if I stood firm that once, it would be over, and you would let me go. But you never did. Bert, if I am going to die—"

He clashed in harshly, in furious repudiation of the idea. "To die, you little fool? You're not going to die!"

She laughed weakly. "Oh, Bert! You'll never improve, will you?"

"I can't," he brought out, with anguish. "I can't say pretty names. You're—so much more to me than dear. You're ... life itself!—my life! How can you be going to die?"

"Well, I feel ... most strange: as if I were coming away out of my body. I feel as if I could float. I want—you know—'to swim in lucid shallows, just eluding water-lily leaves.' ... The lilies are planted already. I keep wishing to be there, in the house; don't you?"

He could not follow this. "What house?" he asked her gently.

"Lone Ash. I should like to die there."

"You shall live there, Millie, please God!"

The words were a passionate appeal. Stooping, he gathered her to him, drawing her close, close against his heart, and laid his lips on hers. She answered his kiss, and then he felt her limbs relax. A blessed unconsciousness had come to relieve her pain.

Far along the road he heard the distant beat, beat, of approaching horse's feet.

The serious accident to Miss Lutwyche gave Brenda the best reason in the world for cancelling wedding invitations.

CHAPTER XXXVII
THE HOUSE IS BUILT

> "To which my soul made answer readily:
>   Trust me, in bliss I shall abide
> In this great mansion, that is built for me,
>   So royal-rich and wide.
> "... An English home—grey twilight poured
>   On dewy pastures, dewy trees,
> Softer than sleep—all things in order stored,
>   A haunt of ancient peace."
>
> —TENNYSON.

Gwendolen Cooper sat with her parents in the drawing-room of Fransdale Vicarage on an afternoon in late October. She had come home for a holiday, and also to condole with her parents over the family troubles.

Theo had gone to Australia, as Principal Boy, with a Pantomime company. Barbara, the fourth girl, the quietest and most reserved of the family, had, on her twenty-first birthday, announced her intention of marrying Alfred Dow.

It was this second calamity which the Vicarage found overwhelming. A certain gloss might be artistically cast over the doings of Theo in Australia. Barbara's doings in Fransdale must be proclaimed upon the house-top; and should she persist in her intention, the vicar felt that nothing remained for him but to exchange livings and depart from the scene of his humiliation.

To be openly defied and set at naught by the smallest and most silent of his daughters, was a blow he had not anticipated; as indeed he had wholly failed to anticipate in the smallest degree any of his children's undutifulness. His jet-black hair was silvering fast, his mien colder and more severe than ever.

Mrs. Cooper was growing very stout, and already somewhat infirm. Recent events had chafed the surface of her smiling cheerfulness a little. Her company smile was now wont to come off at times. But her own belief in her own exemplary rectitude was as unshaken as ever.

"We have nothing to reproach ourselves with, and that is such a comfort," she remarked to her newly arrived daughter. "It was our duty to offer poor dear Melicent a home, and we did so. In the space of three weeks she corrupted the entire family; and we still feel the effects of her deceit. Had it not been for her, Alfred Dow would never have forgotten his place in the way he has persistently done of late years. But really, if one's religious beliefs were not too firm to be shaken, it would put them to the test, to think that, after being publicly exposed in the way she was here, in Fransdale this summer, she is now to marry a millionaire."

"Well," observed Gwendolen drily, "I understand that Captain Brooke knows the worst of her, so I suppose that is all right."

"But think of his past life, my dear—the son of a poor ignorant Boer farmer—another Alfred Dow, only worse! And, with his money, his wife and he will be in the county set, while we, in consequence of Barbara's conduct, will have to hide our heads in disgrace."

"I don't see any disgrace in marrying Alfred Dow," bluntly observed Madeline, who was also present.

"With our position and family connections—"

"That does seem such tommy-rot, mother. We couldn't all five have married Lance Burmester, even if he had wanted to marry one of us, which, of course, he never did. And he's the only man we were allowed to think about as a *parti*. Except for Gwendolen's affair with Freshfield—"

"Oblige me by not slandering your sister," cut in the vicar.

"Tommy-rot again, father," calmly said Gwendolen, who laughed. "You know, mother knows, I know, how near we were then to a scandal of the most serious kind. I wonder how many girls in the world would have held their tongue about that as Millie has, after the way we girls let her in! What liars she thought us! I say, let Barbara marry a good man if she likes, and live the life she likes. I would have married Alfred Dow like a shot if he had asked me. Far better than slaving away as I do, teaching other people's children."

The vicar, in wrath, said something about the dignity of teaching.

"Yes; if you have brains or education," retorted Gwendolen coolly. "I have neither. I am only fit to be a farmer's wife."

"Your mother had no more," began the vicar, in his most weighty tones.

"Please let's leave mother out of the discussion," hastily said Gwendolen, rising and going to the window. "I might say something I should be sorry for. Here comes Bee."

Beatrice came in hastily.

"I met Sybil Ayres," said she, "and heard quite a lot of things. Sybil and the General went to London last week, and they called on the Helstons, and got all the news. First of all, Melicent is to be married in London, next week, very, very quietly. The Bishop of Pretoria is staying in England just to perform the ceremony, and sails the next day. They are going for a few weeks' honeymoon, and then into rooms at Clunbury, to superintend the finishing of their house. Melicent is not strong yet. They are quite sure now that the arm need not be amputated, but she will never have quite the proper use of it. No bridesmaids or anything at the wedding, because of Lance Burmester's feelings."

"Well," said Madeline, "I'm hanged if I'd marry a millionaire and have no bridesmaids!"

"And what do you think? They've had a letter from Major Otis, from the United States, saying he's sorry."

"What!" cried the vicar.

"Yes; Mr. Helston told the General more about it all than has ever been allowed to leak out. The General has had such an enthusiastic admiration for Captain Brooke, ever since the Fransdale sports, so I suppose they knew he would be interested.... It appears that, after what happened that day at the sports, Melicent thought it right to break her engagement. They say she had known in her heart for a long time that it was a mistake, but did not like to say so, but I suppose after what had been said about her family, and so on, she thought if she did not break it off, the Burmesters would, so she wrote to Lance, and then, feeling very low in her mind, she went off to confess her sins to Mr. Hall."

Madeline giggled.

"Fancy confessing one's sins to you, father!" she said. "Our only idea in old days used to be to hide ours, wasn't it?"

Her father ignored the impertinence. "Proceed, Beatrice," he said.

"Well, Major Otis and the boy were lying in wait for Captain Brooke by the Ilba Bridge; and Millie saw them, and as far as I could gather, she spoke to Otis, and asked him to reform; and then she suddenly got to know that they were waiting for the Captain, and they gagged her to prevent her crying out, and she fought like a demon, and the pistol went off and shot her right along the arm, from below the elbow right up to the shoulder—she had hold of the muzzle, you see—and then Otis was scared and bolted. But Arnie Lutwyche went and got help. And they wouldn't have Otis searched for.... They let him go, and as you know, tried to say it was a poaching affair, only everybody knew better. And now he has written this letter, saying that ever since, the things Millie said that night have been ringing in his head, and he's going to have a try to run straight."

"Beatrice, your slang!" said her father hopelessly.

"Well, I'm quoting the dear Major. I did like that man! Just my style, down to the ground! I think I'll go to the States and look him up. Twice as amusing as Captain Brooke! He's a regular stuck-pig! How hard we all tried to fascinate him! You might as well have tried to fascinate one of the Three Howes! He'll bore poor Millie to death, but he seems free with his money. He is doing a lot for that hideous Boer Lutwyche boy."

"How they must all have laughed in their sleeves next morning at you, mother, when you solemnly went up to Glen Royd with your mysterious secret about Captain Brooke!"

Mrs. Cooper grew very pink. The remembrance was among her least happy reminiscences.

"Beatrice darling, ring for tea," she murmured.

"Sybil saw him, when she was up in town," pursued Beatrice, as she obeyed.

"Saw whom?"

"Captain Brooke. She saw him and Melicent together. She said you would hardly have known him, he seemed so gay and lively. She said she had never thought Melicent pretty before."

"Sybil wasn't likely to think so, as long as Melicent was engaged to Lance," remarked Madeline caustically.

The maid brought in tea.

"Ingleby's been down to town and brought up a letter," said she. "Its for Miss Barbie."

"For Barbie?" Gwendolen snatched it. "It's from Millie," she said. "I'll go and call her."

Barbara presently came in. Her eyelids were rimmed with pink, for she had done a good deal of weeping lately. But her aspect was determined. Gwendolen was only just home, and she feared more brow-beating, but was evidently prepared to face it. In expression and colouring, she was not unlike Melicent on a larger scale.

"A letter for you, Babs," said her elder sister kindly.

Barbara looked surprised; she had no correspondents. She opened her letter, and Gwendolen read it aloud over her shoulder.

"MY DEAR BARBARA,—I am writing to tell you that Hubert and I have just heard from Mr. Dow of his engagement to you. He says that Uncle Edmund and Aunt Minna are not pleased, which we are sorry to hear, as we both think Mr. Dow a man in a thousand. We hope that any difficulties may soon be overcome. Mr. Dow has been having long talks with Mr. Hall, and I believe the religious barrier can be removed. He loves you deeply, I feel sure, and that is the great thing. As long as you know he loves you, you can be content to bear things.

"We want you to accept this cheque for £500 as our wedding present, and as soon as Lone Ash is ready, you must both come and stay with us.

"Hubert is as fond of Fransdale as I am, and we shall always be there some part of the year, so we shall see a good deal of each other in the future, I hope.

"Hubert wants Uncle Edmund to know that he wishes to give a sum of £500 to each of you girls on her wedding, as a small acknowledgment of his goodness in offering to take charge of me when I was left alone.—I remain, your affectionate cousin,

"MELICENT LUTWYCHE."

Gwendolen rose from her seat as the letter was concluded.

"Well," she said, "I always knew Millie was worth the lot of us. I shouldn't wonder if she asks you to Lone Ash, girls, and gives you a good time. She doesn't bear malice, as I should in her place. We were brought up on scruples, not principles. We were urged to a certain course of conduct, not because it was right, but because it was the proper thing. Conventions were to us instead of Commandments. Here is Barbara, wanting to do a thing which at worst is only a social blunder, and she is treated as if she wanted her neighbour's husband. I'm on your side, Babs; you may count on me."

The vicar and his wife found themselves, as usual, in a minority of two.

Two or three years after these events, the Bishop of Pretoria told the outlines of the story of Hubert and Melicent to a lady for whom he had a great respect.

When he had finished, she asked, in dissatisfied tones, whether the marriage had turned out a happy one?

He replied that it was completely happy; almost ideally so.

"You ask as though the story had not pleased you," he added, in tones of disappointment.

She shrugged her shoulders.

"To tell you the truth, it does not. I can never give my unqualified approval to any story in which it was the man who won."

"You forget," he corrected her, "or perhaps I should say, you fail to grasp the essential point Hubert could never have won Melicent, had it not been that first of all Melicent won him. Love is like that spiritual life to which it is so closely akin; who conquers there, does so by virtue of being himself defeated."